The Silent Partner

HERB CURTIS

THE SILENT PARTNER

GOOSE LANE

Published by Goose Lane Editions with the assistance of the Canada Council,
the Department of Canadian Heritage and the New Brunswick Department
of Municipalities, 1996.

Edited by Banny Belyea and Laurel Boone.
Cover photography ©Kramer Photography (1996). Reproduced with permission.
Cover design by Julie Scriver.
Book design by Chris Cooke.
Printed in Canada by Imprimerie Gagné.
10 9 8 7 6 5 4 3 2

Canadian Cataloguing in Publication Data

Curtis, Herb, 1949-
   The silent partner
   ISBN 0-86492-214-0

I. Title.

PS8555.U842S45 1996   C813'.54   C96-950149-8
PR9199.3.C826S45 1996

Goose Lane Editions
469 King Street
Frederiction New Brunswick
Canada E3B 1E5

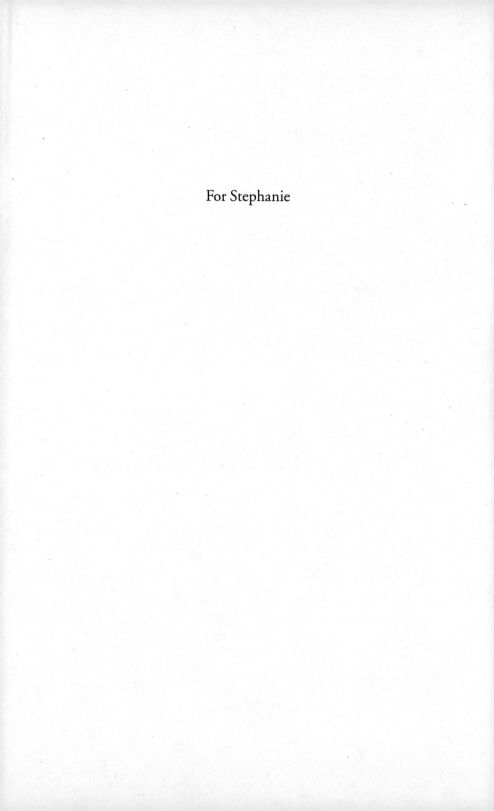

For Stephanie

I could only feel them. The river seemed mapped and peopled with rain, thousands of little blue dancers in the six a.m. light. Eons of erosion had carved this scene, this stage: the massive boulders rising like curtains twenty feet up, the caves that wormed from their twilight mouths to their ebony bowels, the falls that backed off like a reluctant denizen of the Paleocene, gnashing in fear, roaring a bit. I contrasted the grey of it all — waist deep, the water pressing my rubber waders tight to my legs and buttocks, the yellow raincoat — alone, front and centre, I could have been a lone mime at the centre of some gigantic stage. Even had I turned, I would not have seen those big green eyes watching me, unwavering, curious. I could only feel them. Hoping they would come a little closer, I hadn't made a cast or scratched an itch for what seemed like ten, possibly twenty minutes. I had made the mistake of turning to see before and always there was the silent forest and nothing more. Would she approach? Could she identify me, the yellow thing on the water? In raincoat and waders, waist deep in the Dungarvon with the rain dancing on and about me, surely I was odourless. How long would they watch, those eyes? And was that a sound? Did a rock tumble from the falls? Surely she would not be clumsy enough to make a sound. . . . The swish of falling rain . . . the pounding of my heart.

1

Pens and paper are my two best friends in the world. That's how I feel more often than not. As long as pens and paper are at hand, I do not feel inferior, I have a voice.

Kahlil Gibran, in *Tears and Laughter*, wrote, "In the depth of my soul there is a wordless song — a song that lives in the seed of my heart." That's how it is with me. All my songs are wordless, at least until I get my hands on pen and paper. Any paper will do — brown paper, lined white paper, expensive stationery, the flap from a cardboard box, toilet paper, the back of an overdue bill from Lounsbury's. . . . And any writing implement from a wax crayon to my Pilot Hi-Tecpoint to my little old Macintosh Classic that I managed to acquire recently.

This morning I wrote a letter to Princess Anne. I wrote her the words to one of my songs.

Your kindness makes you wealthy
And your wealth makes you kind.

I hope it was not too melancholic for her. Anne does not need sadness . . . Anne may be married again and puts up a good front because she's so strong, but underneath, she's the loneliest of all women.

"For you, my voice is Pavarotti's," I wrote.
Pavarotti.

I used to impersonate Pavarotti occasionally. I got more laughs from that. "Some Enchanted Evening," I'd sing, and the boys and the girls would laugh themselves to tears.

*

My name is Corry Frederick Quinn. I am eighteen years old. I have little formal education, but I love to read and I have aspirations to become a writer. My greatest ambition is to write a novel, even get it published. Someday, perhaps. I'm working on it. But, for now I must content myself with the more important matters at hand: guiding, cooking, cleaning, general maintenance around the house, Izaak Walton's, the sheds and barn, looking after Uncle Kid, making sure he doesn't fall asleep and burn the place down. . . .

I've been living with my Uncle Kid Lauder, with the exception of a month in Toronto, ever since my father went to Ontario. I remember when my father left. Uncle Kid said, "You go, get yourself straightened out, I'll look after the boy. That's the least I can do for poor Mary."

Mary was my mother and Uncle Kid's sister. She died of cancer when I was little.

I like living here by the river with Uncle Kid. It's a good place. It was a great place for a child to grow up. Uncle Kid let me do pretty much everything I wanted — hang around the river, ramble around through the woods, stay up all night. Uncle Kid was and still is a great guy. He's a very insightful, wise and intelligent man. If he needs a bit of watching these days, it's only because his fondness for liquor has been weighing him down a bit. He's been drinking a lot lately, I think because he's so frustrated with his existence. But he's still wise and his mind is as sharp as a whip.

I once wrote him a note asking, "How come you know so much?"

"Ha!" he replied. "I learned on the Microdot Express, the Mushroom Subway, on scotch voyages and marijuana orbits."

His trips are getting to him now, I'm afraid.

Uncle Kid is forty-five years old, has green eyes, is short and thin, has long brown hair streaked with grey. He sometimes wears a cap, other times a headband, but mostly he just ties his hair in a ponytail that dangles down his back all the way to his hinder. He has good teeth and grins and smiles a lot, especially when he's stoned and drinking. He has a strong deep voice and is a pretty good singer. He sings a lot of the old folk songs. He likes Gordon Lightfoot, Peter, Paul and Mary, Leonard Cohen, Bob Dylan and even some of the old Miramichi stuff like "Peelhead," "One Winter on Renous" and "The Scow on Cowdon's Shore." Sometimes at night, he'll bang his guitar and sing "Jumping Jack Flash is a gas . . ." He sings or whistles all the time, under his breath, out loud, sometimes he hums, there's always a little melody coming out of him. He likes to philosophize, too, especially when he gets his hands on some good Mexican or Colombian pot.

Not long ago, he rolled a big joint, lit it up and said, "Ah! Sweet inspiration! You know, Corry, me boy." He stopped, squinted, seemed to listen to the cogs working in his head. "Have you ever stopped to think about how many things that happen back there in the woods that really don't happen at all?"

I shook my head.

"Now, you take a great big old black bear that's eaten maybe a whole bushel of crab apples, pretty green old crab apples. After which he squats and lets a great big loud fart. That old bear is all alone, you see, so nobody really hears it! Ever hear a bear fart, Corry? Ha! That's not to be mistook for a *beer* fart, now!"

I grinned and shook my head. It was funnier for me, knowing that he was really talking about the tree-falling-in-the-forest-does-anybody-hear thing. Uncle Kid is an old hippie and, as far as I can see, all old hippies rant and rave about that kind of thing when they're stoned. Uncle Kid and his cronies do, anyway.

"No, sir," he continued. "Nobody hears it. Has to do with science, philosophy, all that kind of stuff. And the stars. It's the same thing with the stars. If you had real good eyesight, a star might look as big as the moon! Bad eyesight and you see a pinprick. Know what I mean?"

I nodded.

"It's all right up here," he said, tapping his head with his index finger. "It's all in how you perceive it. Pretty profound stuff! You should write that down."

Sometimes I write his theories down and sometimes I don't. I've heard them all a thousand times and more often than not he gets them all wrong or rambles into something incomprehensible. Once, I did write them down, thinking that if they were all together, they might somehow form some kind of a chain and make sense. I called it *The Old Wizard's Book of Records*. While writing it, I learned that not only does Uncle Kid talk in circles, but nine out of ten times, he talks *about* circles. "Lost men walk in circles!" he'll say. "Dogs attract dogs! Live by the sword, die by the sword!" Somebody walks up to him and says, "How are ya, Kid?" Uncle Kid says, "Fair to middlin'! Makin' ends meet! Could be better, could be worse! Havin' me ups and downs! I've seen better days, but there'll be better days ahead!" and "Come see come saw!" whatever *that* means.

You see, I believe that Uncle Kid believes that he's right in the middle of the universe, that everything revolves around him and only him, that he's in the middle of the yardstick of life. He's like an axle or something.

Anyway, he's a good lad. He took me in, knowing that my father would've lost me somewhere in the crowd.

You see, I have this slight handicap. Nothing to lose sleep over, but the Lord knows I *have* lost sleep because of it. You might call it an impediment. I was about eight years old when it happened.

A couple of years after Mom died, Dad sold the trailer and we moved to live here at the old Lauder homestead with Uncle Kid. They weren't brothers and didn't like each other very much, but Dad had no choice — no job, no car, the trailer wasn't paid for, so he didn't clear any money on that deal; he was beside himself with grief, blamed himself and me for Mom's death; he was a mess.

And me?

I was a basket case. I was one of those kids who cries all the time. Point a finger at me and I'd whimper, mention the word ghost and I'd cry, call me by any other name than my own and I'd gasp and turn red in the face and the old tears would begin to flow, leave me alone for five minutes and I'd scream my head off. I was a bed wetter, too. I don't know why I was that way. Some psychological problem, I guess. Who knows? I've seen other kids like that, though. They're weak or overly sensitive, I guess. Some kids just need more attention than others. No wonder Dad didn't take me to Ontario with him. Can you imagine trying to go to work and leaving a kid like me with a stranger? I'd have been in the laughing academy within a week.

You know what I think? I think I was eating too much sugar. Dad and Kid used to feed me cake and cookies and candy and pop all the time to keep me happy. Funny, eh? What they gave me to keep my mouth shut was the very thing that kept my mouth open.

I opened my mouth once too often, as it turned out.

The Lauder homestead is a hundred-and-thirty-acre farm and wood lot on the bank of the Miramichi River. It's pastoral, scenic, or wild, depending on where you are. Besides the Miramichi River, a smaller stream, Dolan Brook, winds through the property, which means that there's never a shortage of fish — salmon, shad, gaspereaux, eels and smelts in the river and trout in the brook. The Hemlock Road and the railroad also cross the farm.

On the Lauder farm, when I was a boy, there was a shed for everything. Drive up the Hemlock Road past our farm and you'd see a house, a garage, a barn, a calf pen, a pigsty, a chicken coop, the binder shed, the junk shed, the wood shed, the outhouse, the summer kitchen, the greenhouse, the boathouse, the old doghouse, three birdhouses designed to attract purple martins, and Izaak Walton's. Izaak Walton's was and still is the building closest to the road and it's where half the men in the settlement hang out at one time or another. It's where Uncle Kid sells his rods and reels, flies, waders, vests, lines, leaders, etc., but I see it as being more of a place for drinking rum and smoking dope. At least, it used to be.

With all those buildings, the Lauder farm was a pretty good place for an imaginative child to grow up, even if he did sulk and sob about every little thing. I had a lot of good times here, playing cowboys and Indians in the woods or the hay loft. Hide and go seek was great fun, and all the kids in the area used to come here to play and hunt or fish. I had this friend, Kent Holmes, who used to spend half his time here. All the men would gather at Izaak Walton's, and while they stood around talking, laughing, making fun, drinking and smoking, their children would play with me, around and about the farm, in the barn and the sheds. If you had all the children gathered in one spot, you'd have a total of seven girls and five boys — the Hemlock Road wasn't very populated.

Just about always, when the kids gathered at our place to play, I'd end up sobbing and screaming about something or other. After a while, they started avoiding me, ignoring me, and that made me worse. And it snowballed! The more they ignored me, the more of a brat I became, and the more of a brat I became, the more they ignored me. I was a hellion and the kids began to hate me, to play tricks on me, to point and hiss at me. And I spent half my time running to Dad or Uncle Kid for a piece of chocolate or the candy which they gave to me to keep my mouth shut.

Kent Holmes was the one that put me in my place. He didn't mean any harm. I know now that he was only trying to help me, to be kind to me. But as fate would have it, I was put in my place. My mouth was shut, in a matter of speaking, for good.

It was an extremely cold day in January.

Kent and I were about the same age chronologically, but physically and mentally I think Kent was quite a bit older. When I was a very young eight, he could have been ten or twelve. He was taller, more informed; he was bolder and braver, more athletic, probably a lot smarter and never a wimp. He had curly auburn hair and eyes as bright and blue as sapphires; his teeth were white and straight and his shoulders were straight and square; he had nice clothes and money.

I was small and thin and weak, my hair was the colour of sand and as straight as cat whiskers; my eyes were neither green nor brown but somewhere in between, and my teeth had spaces between them. The only things Kent and I had in common were our freckles and the fact that we were in the same grade. Of course, he was at the top of the class with As all over the place, and I, at the bottom, never saw anything higher than a B until I was in high school. He intimidated the hell out of me.

God, it was cold that day!

It had been relatively warm and had rained enough the day before to make good skating on the pond in the swamp. Then the snow froze as hard as boards as the Arctic demons strayed south. Thirty below zero, fifty below with the winds. Everybody had to play hard just to keep warm. Being intimidated not only by Kent but by everybody else on the ice as well, I played extra hard and had actually worked up a sweat.

The game was hockey, four on the ice and a goalie. You could get very cold guarding two boots, the goal posts, in the middle of a pond in January, so we took turns being the goalie. When you scored five goals, you got to go to the net. When you scored fifteen goals, you won the game. There were no offsides, no icings, no rules at all, really. It was every man for himself. This made for the strangest of games because no matter who had the puck, he was immediately attacked by four other guys all looking for possession. It's a wonder we didn't kill each other.

If I had had my way, we would have played two on two with one in the net. At least with two on two, you get to pass the puck around a bit and I wouldn't have been at such a great disadvantage. It was Kent who demanded that we play every man for himself, which was great for him — he was bigger than everyone else. Not only that, but he had a real hockey stick and skates, a tremendous advantage considering the rest of us were playing in our rubber boots and using crooked alders for sticks. And the other guys went along with Kent, I suppose because no one wanted to be teamed up with me. I was a disadvantage no matter how the coin was tossed.

There was Kent Holmes, Lorne Myers, Paul Quinn (Aunt Linda's illegitimate son), Bubby Sonier and me. Lorne Myers had just scored his fifth goal and was in the net or, more precisely, between the boots. The goalie, in a way, was also the referee, for it was he who threw in the puck. Four men face off in the middle of the pond, the goalie throws in the puck and all hell lets loose.

Being in the net also meant that you had a chance to rest up a bit. I hadn't been in the net all day and was so tired that my legs were trembling and I was perspiring like the proverbial racehorse. Nevertheless, I was optimistic. I had scored four goals in a row, all in the past few minutes, and things were looking up. With some more hard work and a little luck, I'd soon be getting my rest.

Kent, Bubby, Paul and I formed a circle in the middle of the pond, Lorne threw in the puck and the scramble was on. Kent, of course, with his superior stick, came up with it. He found a clearing and, skating backwards, retreated to the far end of the pond. I figured it was his intention to draw us all back so that he could quickly outmanoeuvre us, break away and get a shot at the net. I was determined not to let that happen. Kent had something like twelve or thirteen goals already. He was getting close to victory. Not having at least one turn at being the goalie was like getting skunked. I had to score one more goal before he won the game.

But his plan was working. Paul and Bubby, so naive, so stupid, were following him back. Why couldn't they see what he was up to? He was actually grinning at their gullibility.

When they were almost to him, he side-stepped and within two strides had nothing between himself and the goal but me. Little old sulky me, the one and only defenceman.

Some defenceman! I was the smallest man on the ice.

I positioned myself and watched him gliding swiftly toward me. On his skates, with that extra two or three inches, he appeared even more intimidating than usual.

I knew there wasn't much I could do — he was faster and bigger. If I were to get in front of him or try to check him, he would either go through me or swerve and pass me by as simply as he did Bubby and Paul. The only thing I could hope for was to somehow get my stick on his, to try and knock the puck away, kill time until Bubby and Paul could slide into a defensive position.

But then, unexpectedly, he stopped, turned in a little circle and began to stickhandle the puck.

"Oops," I heard him say, and the next thing I knew, the puck was coming toward me. It seemed he had lost control at the perfect moment for me to gain possession.

I did not waste any time. I was but a few yards in front of the net, I took possession of the puck, turned and shot. It was a weak shot, even for me, and Lorne shouldn't have had any trouble making the save. It was so slow and smooth that all he had to do was put his foot in front of it or grab it. But, to my surprise, as if in a trance or something, he made no attempt whatsoever to stop it. With barely enough momentum to get there, the puck slid between the boots. I had scored the big number five.

Now, you would think that any kid in his right mind would be happy about that. I had scored a goal! It was goal number five! I was tired and needed my turn at being the goalie and this was it, fate had given it to me.

Well, perhaps I was not in my right mind; perhaps I just had too much sugar in my blood, or perhaps I was just too cold and tired and cranky because of it.

"Hey! You scored!" yelled Kent, and he might as well have thrown turpentine in the wound.

You see, I suddenly realized what was going on. Fate, as I knew it at the time, had nothing to do with my scoring the goal. Kent had intentionally given me the puck. Yet fate was there and playing a bigger role in my life than anyone, let alone a boy of eight, could possibly imagine. That moment, there on the ice, triggered a series of emotions and events that would change my life forever.

At that moment, I saw myself through the sapphire eyes of Kent. He saw my intimidation, self-pity and sugar-induced hyperactivity, saw how small and thin I was. He saw my poverty, my threads woven for a milder day. He saw an orphan, a little boy that needed a rest, a little boy who could not score his own goal.

"You beat me clean! What a shot!" shouted Lorne, rushing from the net, and I felt the mockery, heard the lie, saw the conspiracy there.

"Hey, Corry! You scored a goal!" yelled Bubby. More turpentine.

The whole play had been a set-up. All of them, even my cousin

Paul, had felt sorry for me and now looked pleased and smug, not about my success in scoring the goal but about their own success in allowing me to do it. An act of friendship, maybe, but I saw it as something quite different. I saw it as a ruse, an act based on pity, a ploy to help me, the wimp, feel better about being small, stupid, inferior; a kid incapable of scoring his own goal. All of my goals had been a set-up. Cascades of adrenaline and tears overwhelmed me.

"MOM!" I screamed. "MOM!"

To call out for my mother like that came as a surprise, even to me. I hadn't called for her in a long time; she'd been dead for more than three years. And the boys were surprised, too, perhaps even shocked. I could see it in their expressions. One moment they'd been wearing the mask of good will, a mask moulded from pity and concern for me, and the next moment they were staring in awe, wearing the mask of failure and disappointment.

"Oh, Mom!" I screamed and ran from the pond.

I ran through the swamp and crossed the Hemlock Road, slid into the frozen ditch, climbed out and entered the forest that lay between the road and the railroad. I did not follow any path, I had no destination in mind. I only wanted to get away from Paul, Kent, Lorne and Bubby. I felt that they had made a fool of me and that I had done nothing to prevent it. I felt that I *was* a fool, that I did not deserve friendship, the five goals, and especially their pity. I was feeling that the worst thing that could possibly happen to me at that time was for them to follow me, find me and try to soothe me. I did not want their soothing. I did not want their pity. I hated them all. I hated myself. I threw reason to the Arctic wind.

I don't remember what I did next. Cried and screamed and hollered, I guess, for that's the way I was in those days. But I do remember coming out on the railroad and feeling very cold. All that hockey and subsequent plodding through the bush had me sweating, a good candidate for hypothermia, pneumonia.

No doubt I was in the mood for self-destruction, had a loose grip on life, but somehow, somewhere within me, there was the will to survive. I harnessed my tears, picked up my pace and headed for home.

And then I did something very, very stupid, and I can't for the life of me remember or comprehend why. I reached down and picked up a thirty-below-zero railroad spike, eyed it curiously, as if it were a candy or some such thing, licked it. My tongue stuck to it like steak to a red-hot pan.

So *that's* why Dad told me never to touch cold steel with my bare hands. Why hadn't he mentioned my tongue? I don't know if that's what I thought or not, but someone *had* told me that if you stick yourself to something cold like an axe or a railroad spike, you shouldn't pull yourself off right away, you should keep still until your skin warms the steel and lets go. And that's what I did. I held the spike there and cried. I was a little boy with a railroad spike frozen to his tongue, assuming his number one role as the village idiot.

The spike did not warm up. It wasn't until my tongue froze that it let go. Actually, it didn't just let go. I helped it a little, you know, when the initial fear subsided and the freezing made it feel OK. I sort of pulled it off.

The sight of a bit of my tongue on the spike brought the fear back soon enough, however.

And then there was the pain of thawing.

By the time I got home I was close to insanity. I screamed and hollered and ran about the house in such a frenzy that my father and Uncle Kid hadn't a clue what to do. They didn't even know what was wrong with me. I wouldn't tell them. I was ashamed. Surely no one but an idiot would lick a cold railroad spike. I could only cry. I remember my father yelling at me to shut up, and when I didn't, he threatened to hit me. I didn't care, perhaps even invited him to do it. It would have been just wonderful had he hit me. It might have brought me around. But the day was not a good one, nothing was as it should have been, everything was going all wrong. Instead of hitting me, my poor, confused, distraught father slumped down in a chair and began to cry.

The sight of my father, a full-grown man, crying, broke my heart.

It seemed extremely mean of him to try and upstage me. Who did he think he was? This was *my* scene, *my* tantrum! I was the one who had just fallen into the pit of humility and physical pain. What right had he first to throw heartbreak at me, then upstage me with his own tears? Not just any tears, either. No, he had the audacity to come up with nothing less than dramatic full-grown-man tears!

"What will I do, now?" I asked myself. "How can a kid whose tears flow as easily as water through an onion sack compete against the tears of an adult?"

Then I thought of the answer. I'd had it for quite some time. It had been with me during the scene on the pond. It was dramatic and powerful, the perfect solution. Every selfish, nasty, hyperactive kid who has been bribed and wired with sugar should have such a weapon.

And boy, did I wield it!

I drove it as deeply as I could into my father's heart.

"I waw my mitha!" I screamed. "I waw my moyer . . . my momma . . ."

The effects were wonderful! My father's mouth fell open as if I had stabbed him. Think of it. Not only did I have the power of a little boy screaming for his dead mother, but I had a speech impediment as well. Throw in a little blood trickling over the lips and you have the makings of a star. I was once again front and centre.

But justice was handed down. Not by my father, though. My father was too grief-stricken to punish anyone. By mentioning my mother, I had infected a very sensitive wound. I was a part of my mother and he could see her in me. At that moment, he couldn't have beaten me anymore than he could have disappeared, which is what he probably wanted to do, and eventually did. But the punishment came long before he left. It came almost immediately, handed down, no doubt, by God. I had picked and infected the scab of my father's sorrow.

God did not like that.

"What was that adage?" He asked Himself. "Eye for an eye? Tooth for a tooth? Infection for an infection? Tongue for a tongue?"

You know, every kid in Canada learns about cold steel the hard way, but I'll wager that I'm the only person that lost an inch or more of his tongue because of it. Most kids would lose a little bit of skin on the axe, the shovel, the wheel wrench, the railroad spike, whatever, the tongue would be sore for a day or two, heal, and that would be the end of it. But in my case, I had left it on the spike too long and it was extremely cold. Old Jack Frost had entered a bit deeper, would have crawled right down my throat had he been given the chance. There had been a blister the size of a marble, and blood. By the next morning, my tongue was as big as a hockey puck. I walked around for about three days looking as if I had a slab of baloney sticking out of my mouth.

Uncle Kid and my Dad were never ones to hastily run off to a doctor. I doubt if they ever would have taken me had I not been starving.

"You know, Jerry, I had lover's nuts once," said Uncle Kid. "Wasn't about to go to a doctor with that, the doctor being a woman!"

"So, what did you do?" asked my father.

"Healed it up myself."

By the time I ended up in the Miramichi Hospital, infection had my tongue looking like a dill pickle. Doctor Ruben had no alternative but to amputate.

"I've no alternative and the quicker the better," he said.

I really didn't know what was happening, and I was in so much pain that I didn't care. I think if he had suggested removing my head I would have nodded and welcomed the axe.

There was no waiting around. I was rushed to the operating room.

2

I woke up in a bed by a window. I was alone in the room and it was night-time; the lights from the town below lay on the ceiling. I could hear sounds, the moaning of a woman in pain, a child crying, a peculiar thumping or banging that came from the walls or the ceiling. It was snowing outside. Big feathery flakes. I remember thinking, "It must have warmed up. Big flake mean a small storm," and that seemed very important to me. Big flakes, small storm, a bit of comfort perhaps.

A nurse came in after a bit and she was the most beautiful woman I had ever seen. She put her hand on my brow and smiled. It was only when I smiled back that the reality of my condition flowed over me. It hurt like hell to smile.

I started to cry. Crying hurt, too.

"It's all right," she whispered. "You're going to be just fine."

My mouth was full of foul tasting gauze or something. There was a needle in my arm, a tube running from it.

The nurse dabbed my tears with a tissue.

"Don't cry," she said.

Her voice was very warm. Everything was very warm. Even the snowflakes outside the window seemed warm.

I wanted to tell her that big flakes mean a small storm.

"You have freckles," she said. "I like boys with freckles."

I whimpered and grasped her hand as if I were falling and she was all there was to hold.

For the next month I dealt with the physical pain. I was not a good patient. I hated the hospital. I hated the nurses, the doctors, the preachers and the other patients. I hated the food and the eating of it. The taste was one thing, the consumption of it with only half a tongue was another matter.

I had an emergency buzzer and I kept it red hot from pushing it. I pushed for every little thing — I need a painkiller, close the bathroom door, turn on the light, get me a drink. What kept you so long? Where were you? Fix my pillow. Every time I pushed the buzzer a nurse would rush into my room and for the next five or ten minutes of her time, I tried to make her understand what I needed.

"The pillow? Is it the pillow you want fixed? No? A drink? You're too warm? Then why don't you just remove the top blanket? It's not the blanket? You'll have to write down what you want. I can't give you more drugs. You'll have to wait another hour and a half."

When they refused to give me what I wanted, I cried. When I cried, it often hurt my tongue and that was an excuse to throw a tantrum. I'd turn red, sweat, get angry and cry and scream.

It embarrasses me now to think about it.

Not having a whole tongue presented me with a great many difficulties, not just physically but psychologically as well. Physically, it was hard to keep even half a tongue still and I kept opening up the wound. Eating was virtually impossible for the first few weeks, and although I was being nourished intravenously, I was losing weight to such an extent that the doctors grew concerned for my life.

Psychologically, I didn't want to see anybody other than the doctors and nurses. When Dad and Uncle Kid came to visit, I spent most of the time crying, hating the questions they asked me because I couldn't answer. When they finally realized my problem, they sat for long periods of time and just looked at me, saying nothing. When that happened, all three of us grew uncomfortable. They kept coming every day or every other day, but the visits grew shorter and shorter.

"Well, Corry, my boy, we better get back to the farm. The fires will get low. It'll get dark soon and the lights are bad on the old truck. Gotta get to Stothart's and get a new pair of gumshoes before they close. I know you can't eat the chocolates, but I'll leave them here with you. Cheer up. You be a good boy."

It was even harder when my friends came to visit me. With them, I didn't want to cry. With them, I didn't want to feel inferior.

When Kent Holmes came to visit me, he made a joke. "Don't worry, Corry. Losing a bit of your tongue won't slow ya down. Us lads never have much to say anyway."

Kent didn't stay long. I think seeing me so pale and thin and unable to communicate scared him. Either that or he felt sorry for me.

Whatever sorrow he felt for me was minimal in comparison to the sorrow I felt for myself. I thought that not being able to talk was the worst of all afflictions. It suddenly seemed that my whole life, my whole future had depended upon my ability to speak. Now, without that ability, everything had come to an end, life was not worth living. I forget my reasoning, but at one point I decided that if I could not speak, then listening was an equally futile exercise. I stopped responding to people, started playing the role of the zombie. For days and days I did not utter a sound and pretended I did not hear a word anyone spoke. No matter what anyone said to me, I did not respond. I even tried not to blink an eye.

This attitude, of course, was a role and nothing more. It was something I could hang onto, something for me to do, a game to play; it was a way of getting people to feel sorry for me, of offering me more attention. I practised it and became good at it. Where before I'd had the nurses hopping by ringing the buzzer, the frequency of which had slowed their pace, now they were on the hop again because I wasn't ringing it. I was in power again and knew that if I were to pick up the buzzer and give it a go, the nurses would come running like cougars.

One nurse thought she could bring me around, decided she knew what was best for me. Tender loving care.

She was short and plump, about forty-five years of age, had short, dark hair and dark-rimmed glasses. Her name was Stella Brown. Pleasant, matronly. Although I tried hard not to show it, I liked her and looked forward to her visits.

"You're such a good-looking boy," she would say to me. "The girls will be lined up at your door."

It's hard for a boy to admit, even to himself, that he likes girls. Other than in the playground and in my classroom, I had never associated with girls. To me, girls were petulant little beasts who ran crying to a parent or a teacher even if you missed them with your snowball. But in the hospital, the mention of them gave me something to ponder other than my own sorry state. I suppose I was thinking that not being able to talk would make me unpopular with the boys and that out of desperation I might have to seek friendship elsewhere, with the girls.

Even though I kept ignoring Stella Brown, kept staring at whatever object happened to be in front of me, she kept coming and kept talking. When she asked me something and I refused to respond, she'd respond for me. "How are you today?" she'd ask. When I didn't blink or smile or shrug, she'd say, "Oh, you're better, I can tell. You're getting your colour back and your eyes look bright and clear. You're going to be just fine. You'll be out of here in no time. Did you have a good night's sleep? It rained all night. Took most of the snow. You must have heard it on the window. I like the rain. When it turns cold and freezes, there'll be great skating. We'll have to get you back in shape so that you can get out there on the ice. You like to skate, don't you? I used to love to skate. We used to skate on the river. We'd skate for miles and miles."

One day she said, "Have I ever told you about my Molly? You'd love Molly. She's pretty and blond. She's got the most beautiful eyes. . . . She loves boys, loves to play . . . I'd love for you to meet her. She'd be particularly fond of a nice boy like you. Maybe I could arrange for you two to meet sometime. I know you two would hit it off really well.

25

"You know what I'll do? I have some pictures of her. I'll bring them in tomorrow. She's about nine, I think. How old are you? Nine? You look to be about nine. I'll bring the pictures the first thing in the morning."

I can't remember just how I felt about this newest development. A bit perplexed, I guess. It was only after she showed up the next day all apologetic about forgetting the pictures that I started to consider the matter.

"I'm so sorry, I'm so sorry! I promised I'd show you Molly's pictures and I walked right out of the house and left them lying there on the kitchen table. I'm so stupid! I promise I will bring them tomorrow. You'll fall right in love with her, I know you will."

I was staring blankly at the closet door, pretending I was the zombie. Stella Brown wanted to show me pictures of her daughter. Why? Did she think that would make me feel better? Could a little girl be that beautiful? Did she think that a little boy would suddenly feel better about himself just because he gazed upon the photograph of a little girl?

"You know, last night I was thinking that when I take my vacation . . . did I tell you I was planning to go to Holland next summer? I can't take Molly with me, you see. And anyway, I was thinking that, well, that is if your father wouldn't mind, that maybe Molly could stay with you guys. How would you like that, Corry? Would you like for Molly to come and stay with you while I'm in Holland? Of course you would."

Stella was all bubbly and happy with this new idea while I couldn't believe my ears. "How could this woman consider leaving her beautiful little daughter with two strange men and a boy from twenty miles up the river?" I asked myself. "Is she insane? How would I like it if I was dumped into the lap of strangers like that?"

I was too contrary to respond, but I sure as hell wanted to. I just sat there staring at the closet door feeling very, very weird.

Stella left and moved on to her other patients, and during the day I gave the concept much thought.

What did I know about life, about the world, about strangers? Up until this little trip to the hospital, the Hemlock Road had been my world and I had rarely ventured beyond the village of Silver Rapids. "Maybe it was not so unusual for a mother to leave her eight year-old daughter with strangers. Maybe people do that type of thing all the time. She sees me every day. She probably met Dad and Uncle Kid in the corridor and maybe she needs a baby-sitter. But what about Molly? Would she be happy with us? It would be strange to have a little girl in the house. A pretty little blond girl."

By the time the next morning rolled around, I had justified everything and was beginning to feel excited about the prospect, beginning to like the idea of having a little girl as a friend. I was thinking all sorts of things — how she and I could play games together, go on picnics, go swimming in the river. "There's lots of things that a boy and a girl can do together," I thought. "We'll make up games. She will be my friend and if she really likes me she won't laugh at the fact that I can't talk."

The possibility of having little Molly as a friend was beginning to sound so favourable that I was considering responding to whatever Stella Brown might say to me. I was even beginning to consider how I would gradually come out of my trance.

"First I'll blink an eye, maybe glance quickly at the picture of Molly," I thought. "Then, I'll look at Stella. Later, when she asks me something I'll nod or shake my head ever so slightly, show a little comprehension. I'll act my way through it. If I can act being in a trance, I can act the cure."

I was thinking along these terms when Stella walked into my room with the pictures.

"Here we are," she said cheerfully. "How is Corry today?"

I wanted to respond but managed not to. I stared at a place at the foot of the bed instead.

"Now! I have a treat for you! You're going to love her!" And without further ado, she went "TA-DA!" and the picture of Molly was there before my eyes.

So much for acting.

Even though my glance had been brief, when my eyes took in the photograph of Molly and it hit me that she was not a little girl but a big fat golden Labrador retriever, all my bratty contrariness and stubbornness slipped from my reservoir of self-control like, as Uncle Kid would say and for lack of a better simile, a needle through the eye of a camel.

I broke down and sobbed.

Poor Stella didn't know whether I was in a state of joy or sorrow.

"What's wrong?" she asked. "Don't you like my Molly?"

At that moment, I loathed Molly.

She tried to show me another picture. "Look. . . . This is when she was just a puppy."

I grabbed the picture, crumpled it in my hand and threw it on the floor.

"Now, why did you do that? What's wrong with you?"

"I . . . I . . . I . . . ahhhhh! Wah, wah, wah, wah!"

It was about then that I realized that I had revealed my act, and I felt even more stupid. I felt I was good for nothing, that I couldn't even play a zombie well, and the embarrassment of being caught for the fraud I was was enough to throw me into a tantrum that reached the ears of half the hospital.

Another nurse came running in.

"What's wrong with him?" she asked. "What have you done to that boy?"

"Nothing! I just showed him a picture of my dog!"

Embarrassed, hurt, broken-hearted, filled with fear, pain and self-pity, I crawled under the bedcovers and hid myself from the cruel world for hours and hours.

When I finally emerged, I had a new act.

This one was much the same as the old one in that I feigned a trance-like state, but this time I added a facial twitch.

My father and Uncle Kid came to visit me that afternoon. They had been called, I suppose. My father looked tired, pale, lonesome. Uncle Kid seemed restless and frustrated, paced from my room door to the window, time and time again.

"Corry, you must try to be a good boy," said my father. "It's not the end of the world. Now, stop that twitching! I'm sorry. I . . . oh, here, your Aunt Linda sent you some oranges. Yeah, well, I thought they might be a little acidy on the tongue, but she meant well."

Uncle Kid tossed a book on my bed: *The Hobbit*, by J.R.R. Tolkien.

I ignored it, twitched.

"That rain took pretty near all the snow," said Uncle Kid. "The river's like a bottle. You could skate for miles on it. I was thinking, soon as you're back on your feet, I'd maybe get you a pair of skates."

There was a long silence, during which my father sighed several times.

"You and me are gonna have to do something," he said in a moment. "I've got no work. How would you like to move to Ontario, Toronto or somewhere? There are good schools up there. You know, for si . . . learning to, ah, communicate . . ."

"Looks like he's about had it," said Uncle Kid. "When ya get that twitch? It'll take a strong man to overcome that twitch. Poor old Bub Doyle twitched so bad that he couldn't keep a cigarette in his mouth. Every time he put a spoon to his mouth, he'd twitch and tomato soup would rain all over his clothes. Would've starved to death if he hadn't learned to suck the soup from his shirt."

When Uncle Kid said that, it took every bit of strength I could gather not to grin.

The next day Stella came to see me as usual. At first she was apologetic. "I'm sorry. I didn't know you disliked dogs. If I had known you'd been attacked by a dog, I wouldn't have shown you Molly. You poor little boy."

Attacked by a dog? Where the hell did she get that idea? I liked dogs. I could only suppose that it was my father or Uncle Kid who told her that I'd been attacked by a dog. That would be their way of apologizing for my temperament, of justifying my childish behaviour, of switching the blame from themselves to a dog for the fact that I was a brat.

"I think you're bored," said Stella. "Let's walk down to the TV lounge. You can watch the afternoon movie. Now, get out of that bed."

She lifted me to the floor. I pretended I could not stand, slumped to the floor on rag-like legs.

"Heavens!" she said. "It's your tongue that's damaged, not your spine. Stand up!"

I refused to stand and stuck to my act to the point where she had to carry me into the hall and plop me into a wheelchair. She then wheeled me to the other end of the hospital and into the TV lounge.

"I've got other things to attend to, but I'll come back and get you in a little while," she said and was gone.

There were three other males in the TV lounge, a wheezing old man, a very thin younger man and a boy about my own age. The men smoked, the older one coughing painfully with every puff he took.

The boy eyed me.

"What's wrong with you?" he asked.

I said nothing, of course.

"What's yer name?"

I ignored him, looked away.

"You just get here? You ain't in the ward with the rest of us."

I wanted to tell him to shut up.

"I've had an operation," he said proudly. "I had my appendix removed."

So what, I wanted to say.

"What's wrong with you?" he persisted. "What's the matter? Cat got yer tongue?" That was the first of about a million times I'd get that line thrown at me. I've since learned to shrug it off, but that day, under the circumstances, it was like a dagger thrust into my heart. How fragile I must have been! It brought tears to my eyes.

The boy stared at me with disbelief.

"What's the matter?" he asked, this time concerned. "Are you in pain?"

Out of rivalry, I fought back my tears and opened my mouth to reveal what was left of my tongue. When he saw it, his expression took on such a look of horror that it scared me. How awful it must have appeared to him; how awful he must have felt.

He gathered himself. "I'm . . . I'm sorry," he said.

The look that had crossed his face and the pity in his voice took the proverbial wind out of my sails. I could not tolerate him another moment. I stepped out of my wheelchair and ran as fast as I could to my room. I jumped in bed, covered up my head and wept.

That's the way it was with me. I think that's the way it would have remained if I hadn't met up with a man that I now call God.

I was getting better in spite of myself. My tongue was healing and I was beginning to eat a little more every day. I started to put on a bit of weight and my energy was returning. With the energy came the need for recreation. Having the imagination and curiosity of a boy, I started wandering the halls of the hospital, peeking into rooms and wards. I even started going to the lounge to watch TV. I was still depressed and as much of a brat as ever, I was still refusing to communicate with anyone and still playing with the twitch, but at least I was up and about. It was in the lounge on one of my last days in the hospital that I met the man. I was watching TV when he hobbled in.

It's difficult to describe him after so many years, but I do remember that one of his legs was about six inches shorter than the other and that he made up for it by wearing one very thick-soled boot. His body was bent at the waist so that his left arm dangled from his shoulder to nearly touch the floor. It's hard to know which is imagination and which is reality, but I recall that he wore bib overalls with the leg on the short side rolled up in a wide cuff to reveal the thick-soled boot. Because I was so small, it seemed that he was quite big. And he seemed to be quite old.

That's what I remember about the man from the neck down. His face was a different matter. His face I remember with crystal clarity.

It was not a handsome face. Comparatively speaking, it was quite ugly — pale skin, big nose. His teeth were gapped and crooked, and, except for a few strands of white hair behind his tiny ears, his head was bald.

He seemed to put a great deal of effort into every step he took, as if it caused him much pain, but it did not weaken his determination or cloud his smile.

I was rude, I think, for I stared at him for what seemed like a long time. I watched him enter the room, cross the floor, step after painful step. I wanted to root for him, to call out, "You can make it! Keep going! You can do it!"

Finally he reached his destination, a chair. It was only after he had eased himself into it that he acknowledged me. As if reaching that chair and sitting in it had been a great accomplishment for him, a feat that he was tremendously proud of, he looked at me and smiled that wonderful smile.

If a sculptor could capture that smile, if a mime could play that role, it would be a masterpiece. I was changed forever. I would not feel sorry for myself ever again.

For months after that, I dealt with all the other pains, fear, embarrassment. When my tongue healed completely, I tried to talk, but it came out gibberish. I decided that the best thing for me was to not talk at all. When I ate, I slurped and drooled. I learned to control the drool, but I still sound like a piglet when I eat.

Feeling inferior caused me pain. I'm still dealing with that. Perhaps I will always feel inferior. Perhaps I *am* inferior. But I think the greatest pain I had to deal with was loneliness.

Kent, Paul, Lorne, Bubby, just about every one of my friends came to visit me when I got home from the hospital, and it wasn't long before I realized that they suddenly became more tongue-tied than I. They'd ask me a question and I'd shake my head or nod or write down what they wanted to know. Pretty soon there was no communication at all and we just sat there in the awkward silence. Soon, of course, they quit coming.

There's one thing I can say about that time in my life, I learned to shrug remarkably well and I learned to enjoy books. My father allowed me to stay home from school for the rest of that term, I suppose because he saw the need for me to get used to the idea of not being able to talk. Not having much of anything to do, I turned to books. I started with *The Hobbit*, no easy read for an eight-year-old. It took a great deal of perseverance to get through it, but that was spurred by the fact that it was such a wonderful story *about* perseverance. I became friends with Bilbo and Gandalf, the

Elves and Dwarves, even Gollum. When I saw that I was nearing the end, I slowed my reading. When Uncle Kid came into the house one afternoon with the trilogy, *The Lord of the Rings*, I couldn't believe it. I think it was the best gift I was ever given. Like the deformed man I had encountered in the hospital, it gave me the strength and courage to continue.

Except for Uncle Kid, everybody speaks louder than necessary to me. Everybody thinks I'm deaf. It's one of those assumptions that people make — if you can't talk, you must be deaf; dumb is the companion word of deaf, you can't have one without the other.

Once when I felt it was necessary and not too outspoken of me, I wrote, "Why are you talking like that? I'm not deaf!"

Uncle Kid read it and smiled.

"I know you're not deaf, Corry," he said. "It's just that . . ." He sat at the table across from me and I could see he was trying to reason it out, put it all into some sort of perspective. Uncle Kid had a way of not just trying to make me feel better about my affliction, but of often moving things beyond that; he thought I should actually feel superior because of it. The trouble with Uncle Kid is that he pretty much always comes up with metaphors and parables that have so little to do with the topic at hand that he totally confuses the issue. I sometimes wonder if he has drawn a parallel reasonable even for himself.

He put his index finger to his temple and thought for a minute or so. He had that luxury with me. He could think for as long as he wanted and I could never really interrupt, or more precisely, verbally intrude on the conversation. The finger-on-the-temple pose usually meant that he was seeking some profound explanation, a cue for me to get ready to record his thoughts on paper. It was also an indication that he was stoned.

After what seemed like a great struggle between the negative and positive forces of his mind, he came out with his totally irrelevant hypothesis.

"Way back before the aliens landed on Earth and planted their seeds into the most susceptible animal . . . er . . . the most fitting and compatible . . . er . . . receptacle . . . er . . . the chimp . . . er . . . the orangutan . . . anthropoid apes, I think they call them . . . primates. . . . Anyway, the females and the young slept up in the trees. The males stayed on guard at the bottom. We, the males, were always talking up, while the females were always talking down. It was a vulnerable situation to be in, I tell ya! Easy to get shit on, eh? Ha! But, you know what I mean. If a female wanted to get rid of you, all she had to do was yap and hoot, coo and screech, lure the tiger.

"Yeah, oh, ah . . . innate's the word. The way I see it, it's all innate. That's why we talk so much and that's why we speak louder to everybody we think is below us. Ever hear anyone reprimanding a dog or a cat? Stop that! Get off that table! Go and lay down! You'd think to hear them that the animal was as deaf as a doornail, when in fact the animal has better hearing than the person yelling.

"Yes, yes. It always comes back to the primate. The monkey is the noisiest animal in the jungle. You've watched Tarzan, haven't ya? Well, all them animals you hear in the background are monkeys. . . maybe the odd bird, but most of them are monkeys. Go to a party where everyone's half cut and you'll hear a whole bunch of monkeys; everyone talking at the same time, tryin' to speak louder than the other lad. The drunker they get, the more primitive, the more monkey-like they become. Get more booze into them and they're all trying to screw each other. They lose their inhibitions, their self-esteem, their humility and their humanity. Corry, me boy, it's a jungle out there! Corry, me boy, not being able to talk puts you a step higher on the evolutionary ladder. I've heard it said that the man who talks all the time ain't learning anything. You'll be a wise man by the time you're forty. You'll learn something every day and . . . and you won't have any woman shittin' on ya. Now, don't get me wrong! Don't get me wrong! You're not a bad lookin' young fella and you might very well end up with a wife. A man that can't

35

talk back is what every woman's lookin' for. But what I'm sayin' is that you have such a great chance to be wise! You got time to think, to learn! Take me, now. I learn something every day. This day, for instance, you taught me that I don't have to talk loud to you just because you can't answer me.

"I know! I know, I know! You can say a few things. . . mom, ma, eh, I, ha, huh, yeah and stuff like that, but, you know what I mean. You'll never be a great orator." He seemed to lose his temper. He slapped the table, raised his voice. "And by God, I don't care what Plato says, beauty and speech has nothin' to do with wisdom!"

I looked at him. "Huh?"

"You see these people all dressed up in pinstripe suits, hummin' and hawin', lookin' for the appropriate words. Makes me sick! Standin' up there behind a podium, talkin' for a whole hour, maybe two. . . . They could say it all in five minutes, if they had half a brain!

"No, Corry, you're just as well off. Talkin' ain't the answer. Thinkin' and listenin' is the answer."

I wrote, "But if nobody talked, what would be the sense of listening?"

"Ha, ha! Boy, you're the right lad, ain't ya! Always keepin' me on my toes! Well, there's lots to listen to."

He stopped talking and listened for a minute or so.

"Hear that fridge?"

I nodded.

"B-flat."

"Huh?"

"B-flat, the key of electricity. Now, if you were outside, you might hear a bird singing or the wind blowing; you might hear a little brook trickling over the gravel, makin' its way to the river. There's lots of stuff to hear, if you're let alone five seconds to hear it. And there ain't nothin' wrong with bein' alone. I let you alone all the time, don't I?"

I nodded.

"And you don't bother me when I need to be alone, do you?"

I shook my head, the slightest little negative.

"And we get along better than any two lads on this here river —

36

no arguments, no fights. Men were wise long before the word society ever crossed their lips. I'm sorry I raised my voice at ya, Corry. There was no need of it! It's just that I . . . I fell into the old innate stuff. Know what I mean?"

I knew what he meant. I think.

*

Some people call Uncle Kid a collector. I think that "collector" is an understatement. Pack rat suits him better.

Some people have a junk drawer in their cupboards. Uncle Kid has a junk shed. It's a big shed, too — twenty feet wide and thirty feet long, grey shingles, one door, a big stained glass window high up on one end. I was never allowed in there when I was a child. Uncle Kid was afraid I'd get hurt. I couldn't imagine how anyone could get hurt by simply entering a shed, but that's not saying I lacked an imagination. I imagined that the contents of that shed consisted of everything from dynamite to set bear traps, from wild animals to treasure. When puberty coursed through my mind and body like a thorny skewer, I even imagined him having pictures of naked women in there. He spent so much time in there that I wouldn't have been surprised had he been harbouring the real thing!

Naked women. One of the great mysteries that plagues every thirteen-year-old boy's mind. With me, it was an obsession bordering on insanity. I'm still not over it.

If there was the minutest possibility that Uncle Kid kept a picture of a naked woman in that shed, I wanted to see it.

"What else would take him out there so often and for such long periods of time?" I asked myself. "Unless. . . . naw. . . . he wouldn't have a *real* woman in there. It's got to be pictures. Pictures would do it for me, anyway."

The shed had a couple of little windows on the south side that wouldn't open and were too dirty and cluttered to see through. The stained glass window was too high, and even if you could get up to it, which I did with a ladder, you could see very little through it.

The door had a padlock the size of an alarm clock on it. There were several places where you could crawl under the shed, but there were no hatches or holes of any kind in the floor. Neither could you enter under the eaves or through the roof.

One day I wrote, "What's in the junk shed?"

"Junk, of course," said Uncle Kid.

"What kind of junk?"

"Junk. All kinds of junk."

"May I go in?"

"Ah . . . no, I don't think you should . . . you might get hurt."

"I'm thirteen years old! I'm as big as you are! How can I get hurt in a junk shed?"

"There's old stuff all over the place, hanging from the beams, stacked on the floor — old scythes, mowing machine blades, barrel hoops, bedsprings, engine parts, grease cans — I can hardly get in there myself."

"I won't touch anything."

"Well, I'll take ya in someday."

"How come you spend so much time in there?"

"Well . . . it's . . . that's where I tie me fly-hooks."

I didn't understand. If the place was so dangerously cluttered with junk, where did he find room to tie flies?

I tried a different approach, wrote, "Why don't we tidy it up?"

Uncle Kid sighed. "I'll tidy it up," he said. "Then I'll take you in."

"Stupid!" I thought. "If he cleans and tidies the place, he'll hide the pictures! I'm not going in there to look at mowing machine blades!"

I quickly wrote "Don't bother. I'll wait."

"Now, what's gettin' into you? First ya want to go into my old shed, then ya don't! Do you want to go in, or don't ya? Make up your mind!"

I didn't know what to say about that. What could I say? I just want to see your pictures of naked women? I decided I needed some time to think. I shrugged, wrote, "It doesn't matter. I was just curious. Want to go fishing?"

"Naw. I'll be goin' guidin' Monday mornin' and I'll be gettin' my fill of the river. You go. Hope you get a keeper."

So I donned my waders and vest, grabbed my fishing rod and headed for the river, hoping that Uncle Kid would not jump right around and tidy up the junk shed. I wanted it to remain untouched, at least until I had a chance to get in there.

I headed for the Thomas Bar. The water was low in the river and the Thomas Bar was, and still is, one of the better low-water pools. There are two ways to get there from Uncle Kid's: take the path to the river and canoe a mile downstream, or go down the Hemlock Road to Roland Dewar's place and head across the field. It takes you the best part of an hour to get there if you go by canoe. If you take the road and cross Roland's field, you can make it in half the time. But Roland has a couple of dogs that would rather howl and bark, fight and bite than anything else, so I usually take the canoe.

It was one of those days when the sun was about to start its journey through autumn; one of those days when the dew hangs around late and the smell of the ripening flora tickles your nose. A younger boy, in anticipation of the approaching school year, the frosts of autumn and the cold, lengthy winter, might have found the season somewhat depressing. But school was still a week away and I, like Uncle Kid, took on life one day at a time. I was young, healthy and free; I was experiencing the metabolic rage of puberty; the future seemed no more distant than the end of my . . . nose. I would not let the approach of autumn depress me on this day, for I was a master angler with a seasonal licence, and the salmon ran bigger, hornier and more abundant in the fall. They take better in the fall, too, for the water is cold, the way they like it best.

Carefully, I paddled down the very shallow river, keeping an eye out for any boulders or gravel bars that might be hidden just beneath the surface. A sharp rock can wreak considerable damage on the bottom of a canvas canoe.

I paddled past the mouth of Gilead Brook, below which lies the Peacock Pool, a pool that is surpassed in productivity by no other on the Miramichi River, perhaps the world. There'd be salmon there, I knew, but not for me. The Peacock Pool was and still is owned by an American fellow called Ken Sherman. Ken Sherman, like many Americans, believes that pools have cream on them.

"Get the hell out of my pool! Do you think I paid the bucks for this pool so the likes of you can sneak in here and remove the cream from it?"

Although nobody was fishing in it so late in the morning, I kept to our side, as close to shore as I could go without scraping the bottom. To not disturb the pool is good public relations. Treat the Americans right and maybe, one day, they'll treat me right. One day I'd like to fish the Peacock Pool.

Just in the few minutes it took me to paddle through, I must have seen five or six salmon roll, jump or move in some fashion or other. It's hard not to be envious of such a store of wealth as the Peacock Pool. Gilead Brook runs in just above it, which keeps it cool even on the hottest weeks of summer. The river narrows there, which means that the salmon are congregated in a smaller area. You don't have to wade so deeply or cast such a long line. The water's about four feet deep, a good depth for salmon, and there's plenty of boulders for the salmon to rest behind. Add the strong current that keeps your line taut and your fly moving, and you have all the necessary ingredients for the ideal salmon pool.

But that day my mind was not on the sleek beauties that swam and played in the river. That day my mind was on the sleek beauties in Uncle Kid's girlie magazines. That says something about me, the frame of mind I was in. There I was thinking about girls, but not the real living and breathing type. In those days, and I'm not too sure about the present, I felt that the real, live, walking and breathing girls existed so far beyond my expectations that I couldn't be bothered even fantasizing about them. What girl in her right mind would go for a guy who couldn't talk? Try walking up to a girl when you haven't got a tongue and ask, "Wah oo heh oo o um eh meh?" and see how she'll react. You might as well be ringing bells at Notre Dame.

I'm still reluctant to approach girls, to deal with their reactions. Everything from horror to silliness, you never quite know what to expect. They giggle and blush, tease and mock, roll their eyes in disgust, twitch, move away, switch chairs — a few even leave the room. A couple have been kind, but I have a tendency to link this kindness with pity and I'd rather they freak out than pity me.

Uncle Kid has more women than you can shake a stick at. He's such a nice guy. Women love him. He's so easy-going, so wise. Women take advantage of him.

An old hippie, Uncle Kid, a flower child, an advocate of peace and the sexual revolution. People tend to underestimate Uncle Kid.

I paddled ashore slightly upstream from the Thomas Bar, pulled the canoe up and picked my way down along the rocky shore. My thoughts were so preoccupied with visions of naked women, it's a wonder I didn't trip, or slip on the rocks, fall and break my neck.

When I got to the pool, there was just one other guy, Cam Berkeley, casting thoughtfully, patiently, chewing on a dead cigar.

I held my arms out as if measuring a fish.

"No," he said. "Seen a few, but they won't take a fly. Sam picked one up earlier, but that's the only action all morning."

"Ha!" I said and waded in above him, a respectable distance away.

"See any action at the Peacock?" asked Cam.

I shook my head.

"If they're not getting them up there, we don't stand much of a chance down here."

I made several casts, and a big salmon surfaced to look at my fly. I had rolled one!

"Ha!" I exclaimed.

"You rolled one? God damn it! I just fished all down through there and didn't see a thing. What've you got on?"

I had on a number ten GP, but I wasn't about to describe it in full detail to Cam.

"Ma woo ma!" I shouted. "Ha!"

Cam said something but I couldn't hear him over the din of the river rushing through and around my legs.

I made another cast and this time the salmon surfaced again, but with much less enthusiasm. I thought about changing flies. It might want something darker, less orange, less brilliant than a General Practitioner. A Silvery Grey, perhaps, or a Green Machine.

41

I wondered what fly Cam had tried. A Butterfly, no doubt. Cam always fishes the Butterfly.

I made three or four more casts.

Nothing.

Salmon are like that in August and early September. They're there, lots of them, but they won't take a fly. Theoretically it's because it's dog days, and I'm not sure if the theory goes beyond that.

"Why won't those fish take a fly?"

"It's dog days."

"Oh. That explains it."

Warm water? A lack of oxygen? Bright sunlight? The decomposition gasses of dead lampreys? Bird shit? Eel grass? Who knows?

I changed flies, tied on a Copper Killer. It was too early in the season for a Copper Killer, but I figured, for that very reason, it might be something new and different. Nobody would be fishing the Copper Killer yet.

I made a few more casts.

Still nothing.

I gave up, moved down a few paces.

"Hear about Bill Hall getting caught by the wardens?" asked Cam, the cigar clenched in his teeth.

"Uh-uh."

"Got nailed last night. Took his net, canoe and seven salmon."

"Ha!"

"He'll do time this time, no doubt. Son of a bitch is always gettin' in trouble! It's only been about six months since he got caught breakin' into Strub's store."

Bill Hall was a poacher and a thief, a handsome fellow who bubbled with imagination, a sense of adventure. He would fish with a net for no reason other than that the risk of getting caught was so great. He would do anything for a laugh. He could drink a quart of scotch and reveal no hint whatsoever that he was the least bit intoxicated. Bill Hall dated other women while his wife was having a baby. He was fast with the hands and as strong as an ox. He could turn handsprings and whoop louder than anybody else. He could steal and connive, cheat, lie and swear to beat Lucifer. He was double-crossing and two-faced. The whole neighbourhood, with the possible exception of Cam Berkeley, loved him.

Bill Hall was probably the type of guy that Cam Berkeley wanted to be but didn't have the guts or the imagination. Give Cam Berkeley half a chance and he'd be dressing, talking, drinking, stealing, swearing and turning handsprings like Bill Hall. Cam is like that. He's never Cam. When Elvis Presley was popular, Cam greased his hair back and walked around for a whole year with a sneer on his upper lip. He once played a little part in a local production of *Meet Uncle Sally*. Afterward, someone complimented him, told him he could act. With this little tonic injected into his ego, he immediately became an actor. That might have been quite all right, but good old Cam did not become just another actor. Good old Cam assumed the stance, facial expressions, voice, accent and any other idiosyncrasy he could of none other than Richard Burton.

That day at the Thomas Bar, Cam Berkeley was not the guy who lived in the village of Silver Rapids on the banks of the Miramichi River, nor was he the guy who drove a skidder for a living and liked to fish salmon occasionally. Once in that pool, he became not just a local boy fishing for supper. At the Thomas Bar, on that day, Cam Berkeley became an American angler visiting the Miramichi. He was decked out in the very best of gear — Hodgeman waders, Orvis rod, a two-hundred-dollar reel, an expensive vest, a Panama hat, the best of line, quality flies organized in quality fly boxes . . . all of which cost three times more than what he could afford. Cam Berkeley had never smoked in his life, but he was chewing on a dead cigar that morning at the Thomas Bar because he'd seen American sports with cigars in their mouths.

Nobody in Silver Rapids liked Cam Berkeley because nobody knew for certain who Cam Berkeley was.

Bill Hall was a hell of a guy and a good friend of Uncle Kid's. Cam knew that. Cam did not like for anyone to be more popular than he was. That's probably why he tried so hard. That morning in the Thomas Pool, Cam tried his best to undermine the friendship between Bill Hall and Uncle Kid. Since Cam had no guts, he worked it all through someone he thought was stupid enough to lap it all up. Me, the dummy.

"Ya can't trust the bastard!" yelled Cam. "Everyone else is doin' their best to conserve the salmon, and then ya get some dink like that goin' out with a net! Can you imagine seven salmon? God knows how many he took on other nights! What would anybody want with seven, or fourteen, or twenty-four salmon? Well, that's just great! I'm glad! I hope they put him away for six months! It's a wonder he didn't drag someone else down with him! That's his way, you know! Bastard would stab ya in the back, give 'im the chance! Good thing Kid wasn't with 'im! Bill would just love havin' someone to take the rap for 'im!"

Talk talk talk talk talk . . .

Cam talks too much. It doesn't matter whether or not he knows what he's talking about. He couldn't care less, never thinks before he speaks anyway. He's only interested in sounding authoritative. It's the old ego crawling up from his inferior genitalia to spew orally. Verbal diarrhea. It's true what Uncle Kid says about the one talking not learning.

I said "Moo ah meh meh ahhh moo moo."

And Cam said "I know what you mean. Throw the book at him, I say! Killin' all those fish, when the rest of us are doing our best to preserve them! It's . . . it's perposterous! They're makin' it too easy, that's all! Blame the gov'ment, I do! Maybe good-livin' people like me and you should start fishin' with a net and breakin' into stores. It would be a great world then, wouldn't it! Think how Kid would feel if someone broke into his shop and stole a bunch of his stuff. It'd be, well, I can't imagine how perposterous, how scrupulous it'd be! Well, he'll get what's comin' to 'im this time, I'll wager. You just roll another one? There's no damn fish, anyway! No sir, the likes o' that Bill Hall should be aborted." Blah blah blah, on and on and on . . .

But he gave me an idea.

I decided to do what any healthy pubescent boy would do.

Uncle Kid didn't like guiding, but every once in a while he'd go for a few days, just to keep in touch. It meant closing up Izaak Walton's, but he felt it was worth it. "When you're in business," he'd say, "it's good to keep on top of things. When I get out there on the river with the boys, I observe, see things. Ya never know what you're gonna come across — new types of waders that I might consider stocking, a new fly pattern, a different type of line, the newest fishing rod. Ya gotta mix with the masses. And besides, I wouldn't see Burpee stuck."

Uncle Kid usually guided the regulars who came back year after year, guys he'd known most of his life. Leonard Hodge would pick up the phone, call Burpee Storey and say that he would not consider booking in if he couldn't have Kid Lauder for a guide. Leonard Hodge was an Albany, New York lawyer who fished a little and drank a lot. He and Uncle Kid had more stories to tell about sprees on the river than most people I know.

"Kid's my guide," Leonard would say. "He guides me to the fridge, the Budweiser, the scotch, and the few fish we manage to catch get bigger every year."

Sports staying at other camps like Pond's, the Old River Lodge, Wilson's, Wade's, or Boyd's, referred to Burpee Storey's camps as the Snooze and Booze Club. It would not surprise me if Uncle Kid and Leonard Hodge were two of the prime influences in establishing that image.

While Uncle Kid did his time and duty on the river, either I stayed with Aunt Linda and my cousin Paul, or they came and stayed with me.

Auntie Linda Quinn, a raving, raging Holy Roller who'd rather screw than fly with angels. Though she was quite beautiful and somewhat intelligent, she never got married. She had Paul when she was about eighteen for a guy she loved very much, René LeBlanc.

"I loved that man," she'd muse. "I could never marry anyone

else. I gave myself to him and it would be a sin, adultery, to marry another."

Perhaps.

"No Paul and no Aunt Linda!" I wrote, for they were not part of my plan.

"But, you know me, Corry, I might not get back home for three days. . . ravin' drunk. . ."

I quickly scribbled, "And fight with Aunt Linda! I can look after myself."

"Ah, we don't fight, Linda and me, we just disagree. Who'd cook for you?"

"I'll make a big stew, like you do sometimes."

"Hmm. A good big stew would keep you goin' for a few days, all right, but what would the neighbours think of me leaving you alone?"

It's very frustrating trying to state a case when you can't talk.

"I'm not a little kid!" I wrote. "Look at me. I'm as tall as you are."

Uncle Kid frowned and thoughtfully brushed his nose with the end of his ponytail. "Wouldn't you get lonely, here by yourself with no one to talk to?"

"Ah oo oo meh auk?"

"Ah, I'm sorry. I know you can't talk. But, you know what I mean. You'll be alone."

"You could try not getting drunk, and coming home at night," I scribbled.

Uncle Kid sighed. He did not want to come home every night. This was his vacation, his opportunity to get away from me for a few days. I saw this in the way he stood, the look on his face, the way he chewed the end of his ponytail.

I wrote, "Being alone will be good for me." I looked at him, pleaded with my eyes.

"A man needs to be alone," he said in that quiet, equable way he has of talking to himself. "There's lots to eat, really. And I'll give you fifty dollars, in case of an emergency. You could keep an eye on Izaak Walton's, even sell some stuff, if ya wanted. You know, if someone came to the door and needed some flies or whatever. But, it would be so simple for Linda to come over and keep you company. You don't like Linda?"

I shrugged.

"She does get on your back by times, I know that. Wants to convert the whole world. It's a wonder young Paul ain't dressed like a monk or something. Well, all right, Corry, my man, the place is yours."

*

Uncle Kid went guiding for Burpee Storey the very next morning.

I got up at six o'clock and saw him off. I stood in the yard and watched him drive out the lane and down the road. When the lights of his Jeep disappeared at the bend, I went back inside.

I sat at the kitchen table and sipped coffee. I needed to think.

While I was on the river fishing with Cam, I had decided to do what Bill Hall would do. Bill Hall, I thought, was the kind of guy that would do one of two things. He'd either find the key and let himself into that junk shed, or he'd get a hammer and a screwdriver, remove the lock and make the place his own. Both plans seemed great to me. The more Cam had degraded Bill Hall, the more I felt that breaking into the shed was the thing to do. I had decided then and there to do it, just as soon as the first opportunity came along.

The opportunity arose the moment that Uncle Kid drove out the lane. I had all day, perhaps several days to find the key, screwdriver, whatever implement I'd need for the break-in, do it, uncover the secrets there, close everything back up the way it was, and settle down contentedly with no harm done.

That's what I figured was the Bill Hall way.

But there in the kitchen a few short moments after Uncle Kid made his departure, another side of the whole scheme popped into my head to stare at me with the sleazy, phoney, hypocritical eyes of Cam Berkeley.

It seemed to me that to break into Uncle Kid's shed might be a cool, Bill-Hall-like thing to do, but to break in with Bill in mind, thinking I was in some way being like Bill, grinning his devil-may-care grin, moving and looking and even thinking like Bill — this would in actuality be assuming the guise of Cam Berkeley. Cam, if he was courageous enough, would do something like break into Uncle Kid's shed, but he wouldn't be portraying himself. He'd be thinking he was somebody else — a cowboy dressed in black, a cat burglar, Doyle's Moriarity, or even Bill Hall. For me to break into Uncle Kid's shed thinking I was being cool like Bill Hall would in fact be assuming the attitude, the personality of Cam Berkeley.

The question I was asking myself there in the kitchen is a question I have asked myself over and over again and will no doubt continue to ask myself for the rest of my life: "What should I do?"

I have aspirations to become an artist, a writer. Take away individuality from the artist and you're copying the craft and plagiarizing the art. All you have left is mediocrity.

So I sat there sipping coffee, not knowing what to do.

I had learned at a very early age that to score a goal assisted by your opponents is worse than not scoring a goal at all.

"I must be an individual. What do I do? What's my purpose? Getting in and seeing what Uncle Kid has in that shed? Supposing he has nothing in there of any interest? What if he was telling me the truth and a big old saw blade or something fell on me? I'd be in a racket then! But there has to be something more important than saw blades for him to keep such a huge lock on the door. And it's always locked. There's got to be something he wants to keep secret, or why else would he be so secretive? He must have pictures of naked women in there. Naked women. *Naked Women.*"

It was the thought of naked women that moved things along. Once the possibility of seeing the picture of a naked woman entered my mind, my better judgements beelined south like autumn geese, down to hotter climates.

I knew that Uncle Kid carried the shed key in his pocket on the same ring as the house and car keys, but I thought there might be a spare somewhere. I went up to Uncle Kid's room, searched the dresser drawers and bedside tables; I searched the closet, the pockets of his pants and coats; I even looked through the several boxes that were there.

"There's some interesting stuff in here," I thought. "I'll have to come back to this some other time. Old letters and stuff. But no key."

I went downstairs and searched all the cupboard drawers and the pantry. The key to Izaak Walton's was hanging on a nail beside the fridge, but that was all. I searched the nooks and crannies in the dining room, the piano bench in the parlour and the bookshelves in the hall. Nothing.

I went back to the kitchen and sat to think. I hoped I would not have to resort to a hammer and screwdriver. It would be hard to tamper with a lock without leaving some indication that you'd been there.

"Maybe he keeps it out in Izaak Walton's. That would make sense, if he has such a thing as a spare key."

When I stepped outside with the key to Izaak Walton's, the moon, a mere sliver low in the east, pierced the vermilion sky. I love the early morning. I must have been feverish with the need to view pictures of naked women to not have gone fishing on such a beautiful morning.

I entered Izaak Walton's and started my search. In the cash drawer, I found a big key for a big padlock. It had to be the key to Uncle Kid's shed. My heart quickened. "Ma eem um ew," I said aloud. My dream come true.

I ran to the junk shed, all the way hoping and praying that the key would fit the lock.

It did.

The door swung open on well-oiled hinges. I gazed into the dim interior.

Uncle Kid hadn't exaggerated. The shed was a mess. In fact, it was so extremely messy that it very well could have been dangerous. But I did not get the smell of must and mildew that you would usually expect from such an environment. Instead, there was a very sweet smell not unlike that of a hayloft, but not hay, more acrid, herbal, a different yet familiar smell. I lit a match, located a switch, turned on the light.

God, what a mess!

Enlightened by the single sixty-watt bulb, I could see such a clutter of odds and ends that any single item was virtually lost. The first thing I had to step over, just to enter the room, was an old hand-operated lawn mower. There were cardboard, wooden, plastic and Styrofoam boxes, stacked to the rafters in some places. There were old coats, boots, waders, scoop nets, fishing vests; an old seeding bag with a crank, a gaspereaux net, bits and pieces of horse harness, ten or twelve garbage bags with dates ranging from 1975 to 1992 marked on them; sewer, water, tail and stove pipes, broken fishing rods, every kind of jug and bottle from molasses to whiskey, antique to modern. There were chains, ropes, string, cords and wires. There were peaveys, pickaxes, diggers, hoes, rakes, pitchforks, dungforks, snowshovels, round-pointed shovels and square-mouthed spades. There was the stump of a tree that looked like a spider, a hornets' nest on the end of an alder branch, a squeeze bottle attached to an orange tube coiled in a bedpan. There were buckets and cans filled with nails, spikes, nuts, bolts, clamps, pins, tacks, toggles and staples. Uncle Kid hadn't lied, for there were scythes, woodcutter blades and other sharp things that could fall and hurt someone. There were old tires, pieces from old bicycles, cars, motorcycles and chainsaws. There was broken furniture, picture frames, electric kettles, frying pans, radios, a television, even a kitchen sink.

"And this is where he ties flies?" I thought. "Where?"

I looked about, amazed. I spied a door at the far end of the shed, a green door with a large brass lion's-head doorknocker on it. "That must be where he works. Only place it could be. That's where he'd keep his girlie books, too."

With some difficulty and great care not to disturb anything, I made my way to the door.

I don't know what I expected to find behind that door — perhaps a table of some sort with a vice attached to it and feathers, animal tails, threads and other paraphernalia for tying fly-hooks; a few girlie magazines, maybe a *Playboy* centrefold on the wall.

If I'd had an inkling of what was behind that door, I would never have opened it.

Uncle Kid's room ran across the whole back end of the shed. The floor was covered with a rich, red carpet. The walls and ceiling were panelled with cedar, stained auburn. There were framed pictures on the walls — a large one of a leaping salmon, another of a wading angler in the morning mist; there was one of Uncle Kid riding a donkey and looking for all the world, with his long hair and beard, like Jesus in bell-bottomed jeans. There was a picture of his mother and father, my grandparents, and one of me as a little boy. I didn't remember ever seeing the picture of me before, or having it taken. There was a large one of a woman I took to be Princess Anne and another of a dark-haired woman I didn't know. On the end of the room to my right were bookshelves with perhaps several hundred books, all hard-cover, some bound with leather.

I needed more light, the stained glass window was not enough. I found a light switch, turned it on. To my left was a big, dark, wooden desk with a Tiffany lamp and stacks of paper on it, a big leather chair behind it. In front of me was a very comfortable-looking sofa, blue and gold. On a lowboy sat several bottles of liquor and a little marble statuette of a woman in a very flowing gown. There was a larger table where, judging by all the stuff that was on it, Uncle Kid tied his flies.

If I had been amazed at the mess upon first entering the front of the shed, I was now equally amazed at the luxury of this room in the back. Uncle Kid must have invested every spare penny he could rake and scrape in it and its contents.

"I didn't know that Uncle Kid ever had any spare money," I thought. "Where did it come from? Did he just collect all this stuff? Or maybe this is not Uncle Kid's room at all. Maybe it belongs to a sport, or some rich old uncle who only comes around every ten, fifteen years. It just don't seem like a room Uncle Kid would have. But it's been used, lived in, I can even smell smoke, pipe tobacco or something. No, no, it's dope I smell, marijuana, sure as hell.

Uncle Kid comes out here to get high. This is his place to be alone, his very own, private place. And I'm here intruding, I've ruined his secret."

Suddenly I felt like a man in a women's washroom, or a thief. That room was Uncle Kid's sanctum, and if he had wanted me to see it, he would have invited me. "Come and see my room in the shed, Corry. Come and share my very own private space."

"I'll never come here again," I said to myself. "But while I'm here . . ." I took a few steps further into the room, turned to look at the wall behind me. There was a fireplace! A beautiful brick fireplace with a wooden mantel. There was a painting of a big, golden dog above it. I remembered the dog. It was Lady, Uncle Kid's old half-shepherd half-Lab. I remembered her as old and lame. In the painting, she looked sleek, alert, proud.

"I ayk a ah a og," I muttered.

I moved over to the book shelf, scanned the titles — *Great Expectations, The Adventures of Huckleberry Finn, The Republic of Plato, The Complete Works of William Shakespeare, For Whom the Bell Tolls, The Coming of Winter, Of Mice and Men, Prince of Foxes, Still Life with Woodpecker, Who Has Seen the Wind, The Holy Bible, Koran.* Books of poetry, history, philosophy, art, science, travel . . . and on the bottom shelf, close to the floor, to the right, was a stack of magazines — *Outdoor Life, Field and Stream, Trout, Playboy, Hustler, Penthouse* . . .

4

I have this thing about England. Jolly old England. I like the English accent. I like English literature — Dryden, Shelley, Keats, Emily Brontë, Dickens, Sir Arthur Conan Doyle. I like Robin Hood, King Arthur and Merlin. I like the moors, Stonehenge, Big Ben, London Bridge, the Tower. And I am a royalist.

I made love to more centrefold beauties than you can shake a stick at. I went out to Uncle Kid's room once, twice, three times a day, sometimes more. For two whole years, every time Uncle Kid went somewhere, I'd dash to Izaak Walton's for the key, run to the junk shed, scramble through the junk to the room, open a *Penthouse* or *Playboy* and transcend to Fantasyville. I liked *Penthouse* the best, it had sexy stories to go with the pictures.

After a while though, the pictures, the centrefolds, the stories, even the fantasies that accompanied them became a bore. The girls in the pictures all looked alike from the neck down, which didn't matter much as I never looked at their faces anyway, and they all had the same personality. Because they were there to fantasize about, they became like slaves to me, or I to them.

That's when I turned my eyes from the centrefold to the picture of Princess Anne.

As Uncle Kid might put it, hello for a royalist from then on.

In that little hat, red coat, breeches and boots, the proud way she holds her head, her silence, her power. "She's like Victoria," I thought. "She even looks like her! She should inherit the throne!"

One day when I was out in Uncle Kid's private room, I pictured myself as a great lord, the lover of the princess. This line of thinking conjured up other fantasies, and I found myself pretending that I, the great lord, was at war, off in some remote colony, fighting for England, the crown, Anne.

I wrote Anne a letter. I tore it up and burned it, but it was an incredibly exciting thing to have done. The next day, I wrote another one.

> Dearest Anne,
> I miss you more than words can say. O! Will this cursed war never end.

I tore that one up, too. But the seed had been planted. I began writing to her every day.

That's how I began composing things other than just notes for the purpose of communication. If Uncle Kid had a private place that he felt only he knew about, I too had a place, a sanctum right here in my head that I could go to any time I felt like it.

Uncle Kid smoked a lot of weed. That herbal smell in the shed? Marijuana. All those garbage bags in the shed? Filled to capacity with home-grown weed. I checked it out, sniffing like a dog. He must have had a hundred pounds of it.

Finding the dope explained everything — why he had the big lock on the door, why he didn't want me out there, how he could run a little shop like Izaak Walton's, hardly ever work, keep us going, drink, drive a Jeep, have his luxurious little retreat. Izaak Walton's wouldn't have brought in enough money to keep him in cigarettes. It took no genius to figure out that Uncle Kid was a dope dealer, that Izaak Walton's was a front.

Uncle Kid had every reason in the world not to allow me in the shed, and once I found the dope, I realized it. What if I was in there one day, reading, writing, fantasizing, whatever, and somebody, a warden, a cop, or even Cam Berkley dropped in for something. Uncle Kid would be out of business for good, no doubt about it, and it would be all my fault.

So, knowing that I had no right to intrude upon his private world, I went to his room one last time, took a long, careful look at Anne, memorized everything about her, left and never went in there without Uncle Kid's permission again.

In Uncle Kid's house, there's a room upstairs over the kitchen. It's my room now. Uncle Kid helped me build bookshelves and move a desk in there. We went to Newcastle and bought a royal blue rug and curtains.

In the mall, I pointed at the book store.

"What do ya want in there?" asked Uncle Kid.

He followed me into the store and we browsed for a while. I found what I was looking for in a sale bin — three large picture books on the Royal Family. One of them had three great pictures of Anne. I framed them and hung them on the wall of my room. I was a little worried at first that Uncle Kid might see them, make the connection, assume it too great a coincidence and know I had been in his junk shed. But I hung them anyway. I knew I could trust Uncle Kid not to enter my space.

It was Aunt Linda who spilled the beans.

She and Paul came to visit one Sunday morning. They always came on Sunday mornings. She was a busybody, came to snoop. She expected to find the place in a mess and Uncle Kid hung over on a Sunday morning.

We were having lunch when all of a sudden she asked: "So, what's with the room over the kitchen?"

Uncle Kid looked at me in that kind way of his. "Corry's room," he said.

"Corry's room! There's no bed in there."

"It's not where he sleeps. It's your office, eh, Corry?"

I nodded.

"Your office!" Linda yelled. She thought I should be deaf, you see. "What d'ya do in there, audit?"

"It's just his place, that's all. We've been needing to fix that room, anyway. Corry tells me he wants to write a book."

"Ha!" laughed Paul. "He can't even talk! How's he gonna write a book?"

"You don't have to be able to talk to be a writer!" snapped Linda. "Helen Keller was, ah, handicapped. You'll be a great writer one day, Corry. You'll have to let me read some of your stuff sometime. Maybe I can help you." Linda's voice echoed off the walls.

"You don't have to yell at him!" said Uncle Kid. "He's not deaf!"

And then, right out of the blue, for no reason at all, Linda asks, "What's with all the pictures of Princess Anne?"

I blushed and sank, waited for Uncle Kid's response.

He looked startled at first. Then he got angry. What surprised me was that his anger did not seem to be directed at me. He just glared at Linda as if he couldn't believe his ears, as if he couldn't believe she had the audacity to, one, enter my room, and two, bring up the fact that I had pictures of Princess Anne on my wall.

I knew, however, that he knew that I'd been in his room.

And then he looked at me with those great eyes of his.

"You don't understand us, Linda," he said softly, as if to himself. "A man needs his private place. I have a room, too. In the back of the shed."

I was having a tough time handling the situation. I felt cheap and slimy and dirty and guilty. I reached for my pad, and while still looking at him with my most desperate expression, I wrote, "I'm sorry!"

"It's all right," said Uncle Kid. "I meant to take you in there anyway. I've been in your room, too."

I swallowed, tried to control my emotions.

Damn tears!

*

At the upper end of the Peacock Pool, across from the mouth of Gilead Brook, there's about a hundred feet of pretty good fishing water that you can fish as long as you don't step over the line onto Ken Sherman's property. Ken, of course, is an American and the owner of the Peacock Lodge. Step one foot into his water and he'll put the run to you. He won't even let you fish in his pool when the place is empty, hires Nubert Minor to police it. Nubert Minor is not a bad guy, but he takes his job seriously. He has a family to keep.

Anyway, you can fish the upper end from the south side, our side, we call it, and if there's any more than one, possibly two fishermen, you have to rotate. Rotate means that you put in at the top of the pool, keep moving, fish down through and take out at the bottom. One guy follows the other. A hundred men could fish all the way down through the whole of the Peacock Pool and everyone would have a crack at it if Ken Sherman would allow you to cross his line. Believe it or not, Ken painted a red line on the rocks. Ken thinks the pool has cream.

Uncle Kid and I usually fish the Thomas Bar when the water's low, and Poop Rock when the water's high. They're open to the public and there's just about always someone to listen to. But one day we went to fish that little stretch at the upper end of the Peacock Pool.

It was a nice sunny day around the end of June and we had heard the run was on. We get our salmon in June, if we can. June salmon are fresh, fat and bright, the best.

Uncle Kid was fishing with a number eight fly hook called Black Ghost and I had on a Butterfly. The Black Ghost has a black body and deer hair wing. The Butterfly is tied with goat hair. They're similar only in the sense that both their wings are white.

Uncle Kid is one of the best fisherman I know. He has a method that I've learned to use myself. What you do is wade into a pool and cast about ten feet of line at a seventy-five-degree angle, downstream and across the current. Let it swing, lengthen a foot and cast again. Let that one swing, lengthen another foot, cast again, and keep doing this until you are casting all the line that you are comfortably capable of throwing. Then, you retrieve back to ten feet, move down eight to ten paces and do it all over again. In this way, you cover every square foot of water.

Uncle Kid and I rarely throw more than sixty to seventy feet of line. Casting a long line looks clumsy and greedy; it takes something away from the art, disturbs the ambience and seldom produces fish. Any fish that you *do* hook on a long line, you're apt to lose. What's important is to cast a comfortable little line and present the fly naturally. A long leader (a rod-length and a half), tapered from somewhere around thirty-, down to six-, even four-pound test, helps the presentation. Uncle Kid and I usually fish with a four because you can't keep a fish that weighs much more than that anyway. On the Miramichi, you have to release anything above twenty-five inches in length, so by fishing with a heavy leader you're only prolonging the battle and unnecessarily weakening and agonizing the salmon. With a four-pound test leader, you can beach the most energetic grilse.

We thoroughly fished our little section of the pool, then took a break, sat side by side on a boulder at the water's edge.

"Not much happening," said Uncle Kid. "I think I only saw the two fish."

I held up three fingers.

"Three? You saw another one?"

I made a gentle wave of my hand.

"You saw one roll, eh? Hmm. Did you try 'im?"

I nodded.

"Wouldn't take, eh. Well, they're in here, at least. They don't move much this time of the year, anyway. Hope we get a run like the one we had last year. Remember? God! You know, back in the sixties . . . yeah, yeah, yeah, I've told that to you before. Anyway, there's more fish these days. You're still fishing the Butterfly. I think I'll try a Green Machine, but then again, I don't like fishing a double hook . . . all I brought with me was one Green Machine and it's a double. I don't think I'll ever tie another double. They hit the water too hard. . . . I haven't caught a fish on a double since the time I hooked the big salmon down there in the rapids. You could fish down there back then. Now, we're crowded up here in the corner. Two lads fishing a hundred feet of water while six hundred yards of prime water lies empty. Money talks, I guess.

"You know, Corry me boy, they claim history repeats itself. If that's the case, we might get to fish that pool again some day." Uncle Kid took out his tobacco pouch, rolled a joint and lit it. He took a huge drag and handed the joint to me. He had never offered me a puff before and I took this as an acceptance thing, a sign that he recognized the fact that I was growing up. I shook my head. He nodded, seemed to approve. He smoked silently for a while, watching the river. I could tell by his little grin that he would soon come out with the old sweet inspiration line.

"Ah! Sweet inspiration! You know, Corry me boy, if history repeats itself, that means that we sat here before, on this very same rock, and carried on this very same conversation. Physically, if everything repeats itself, or goes in circles, this rock will one day become a much bigger rock, the rock it was before it rolled around and got eroded by the river. Follow me?

"Naw! I'm calling the game too small. Ya gotta think in terms of millions, even billions of years. Ya gotta think that the sun will burn out and rise again, form its planets and crumble and spew and spit, a volcano here, a flood there . . . It takes billions and billions of years to do that, to create two lads sitting on this rock in this river. Now, realistically, I can't see any logic in thinking in infinite terms. History as we know it, the mere few thousand years we've called ourselves homo sapiens, has not, cannot and will not repeat itself.

"Like I told you about the hard fishing in the sixties? Well, I told you that before. If I had've told it to you again, it would have been dwelling on the past. To tell a story once is OK. To tell it more than once, unless you're asked to tell it, of course, is dwelling on the past. It makes no sense whatsoever to dwell on the past. Learn from it, but look to the future; remember who you are and where you come from, but never try to recapture yesterday. It can't be done."

Uncle Kid smoked the joint down to where there was hardly anything left. It was amazing how he could still hold onto it without burning his fingers. He called this little butt of the joint the roach. Unlike most of the other guys that he travelled with, Uncle Kid never ate the roach. He threw it into the river. A minnow grabbed it.

"Ha!" he laughed. "Maybe we should tie on a big joint of weed. Bet we'd get a barrel of fish! Ha! Ah, ya hear lads saying things like, Boys, when I was a boy, or, We used to climb trees, or, We never did the like of that, We snowshoed to school — hogwash!

"Take you, now, wanting to be a writer. . . . Write your little bit of history down, you know, so that you know who you are and where you came from, then move along. If you live in the past all the time, then you'll not see what's happening all around you at this very moment. Yesterday *was* my life, today *is* my life. Surely, what *is* is more important than what *was*.

"A middle-aged somebody asked a middle-aged Paul McCartney if he was considering regrouping the Beatles. Paul asked if he would consider going through high school again."

A big salmon surfaced in front of us.

"Want to give 'im a try?"

"Uh-uh," I said and waved my hand to say, Continue your rave, the fish can wait.

"Oh, maybe I don't have a clue what I'm talking about. As a matter of fact, I probably don't, but some people. Some people! Some people live for thirty or forty years and that's it! After that, they just lock themselves inside little rooms and rock and mope and wish they could do it all over again. A terrible thing! God gave them eighty years to live and they only use half of it.

"I've heard older people say that you become less perceptive, less coherent, that things don't tickle you as much when you get old. Well, I don't know. It might be that they just quit wanting to get tickled. Every dying person has regrets, I bet. A few, anyway. The fewer the better, I say. If there's something you want to do and it's righteous and not gonna hurt anyone, then do it. Don't not do it and have regrets. How's the writing going?"

I shrugged.

"Don't worry about it. Write, if you're so inclined. You might change your mind tomorrow or the day after, decide to become a farmer or a doctor. What do you see before you?"

I gazed on the swift water upstream, the hills of black spruce, fir, pine, birch and poplar; I saw the rocks along the water's edge, the raven in the sky. A blue heron was wading knee-deep near the mouth of Gilead Brook across the way. The sun sparkled on the rapids and in the late morning dew. I looked at Uncle Kid, the thin, long-haired man with the searching eyes and wonderful smile.

He, too, scanned the beauty of the river and with a sigh, said, "We're living in a wonderful place, you and me. No wars, no ghettos, no hunger. We have a little loneliness to deal with from time to time, but loneliness comes from looking into the past, I think, wanting something you can't have. You'd be a very lonesome lad if you spent your life wanting your tongue back. I'd be lonesome as hell if I spent my life dwelling on . . . oh, well . . . let's throw a few more lines. I thought I saw that fish roll again."

"He'll tell me one day," I thought as I waded into the river. "He'll tell me who he's lonesome for."

It's funny how things happen. Maybe Uncle Kid's raves about circles have more substance than he realizes.

That was the first time I ever heard him speak of loneliness, and as if the mere mention of the word triggered something, within moments of that conversation, loneliness began its subtle possession of my being. Could it be that to be totally ignorant of loneliness is never to be alone? Loneliness certainly has nothing to do with being alone by yourself; you can be living in a city with ten million people and still be lonely. I don't know what it is, to be truthful. It's like love, I guess. Perhaps loneliness is love's opposite. You've heard how eye contact between a man and a woman can be considered the very beginning of conception? Well, the mere mention of the word loneliness was all it took to start the ball of loneliness rolling.

From eye contact to conception and love can take minutes, or it can take years. It's the same way with loneliness.

It's like the old speak-of-the-devil thing. Within minutes from the time Uncle Kid spoke of loneliness, Nubert Minor and his daughter Milly came out of the Peacock Lodge, boarded a canoe and paddled upstream to just below where we were fishing. Nubert, because he policed the Peacock Pool, could fish there any time he wanted. I was standing a few yards upstream from the red line. Nubert shoved the canoe ashore and waded in a few yards below the line. Milly was not into fishing, so she sat on a rock to watch from the shore.

Nubert did not even bother to speak to me.

"See any fish, Kid?" he yelled.

Uncle Kid was fishing the very upper end of our stretch. "Saw one roll, that's about it! Gettin' any?"

"The party that just left this morning took sixteen away with them, but fishing hasn't been real great, mind you!"

Whenever I heard this kind of talk, I tended to get a bit depressed.

"Sixteen fish!" I thought. If those sports took sixteen fish back to the States with them, that meant that they had kept sixteen grilse. You keep the grilse, release the salmon. How many fish did they hook altogether? Uncle Kid and I would do well to hook sixteen fish in the entire season, and certainly not all keepers.

"Did ya get those Cossebooms tied?" yelled Nubert.

"I just have about ten left to do! I'll get them to you tonight or tomorrow! Any sports over there now?"

"Just Ken! I think there's three or four coming in tomorrow afternoon! Rolled one! Jesus! A big one!"

"Ya did? What on?"

"A Shady Lady! Number eight!"

"A salmon?"

"A big one! There he is! Got 'im! Whoop! Ha, ha! Wow! Look at 'im take off!"

Nubert hooked a fish on what couldn't have been more than his third cast.

I sighed, reeled in, clipped the Butterfly off and tied on a Shady Lady. "At least I'll have the right fly on," I thought. "Even if I am up here where there's fewer fish." I glanced at Uncle Kid. He was changing flies, too.

Nubert backed in to the shore to play his fish. Milly left her rock to stand beside him, to watch the action.

The current was strong down where Nubert was fishing and the salmon was large and in its prime. Nubert had a good fight on his hands. The salmon leaped and ran almost to the other shore, then leaped again.

"He's a busy devil!" yelled Nubert. "Feels like I got a freight train on there!"

"Fifteen, twenty pounds!" estimated Uncle Kid.

While Nubert played his fish, I worked my way down to within inches of the red line. I wondered what he'd say, under the circumstances, with no sports at the lodge, if I were to step over the line and continue on down through the pool. He'd probably say something like, "I'm sorry, Corry. If I owned the pool, I'd let you fish. But you know how it is, I have a job to do, so get your ass back over that line."

I did not put him to the test. I reeled in and waded ashore, sat on the rock where Milly had been sitting.

It was then that I noticed that Milly had stopped watching the action and was curiously eyeing me.

She smiled at me!

A pretty smile! I'd never seen a smile quite like it before. I'd always assumed that a smile stemmed from humour, amusement, happiness. But Milly's smile hadn't come from the fact that she thought I was funny to look at or listen to. Nor was she elated about the fact that her father was landing a large salmon. She was smiling a kind, warm smile! It was obvious that she liked me!

She knew who I was, of course, and I knew her, but that was the first time I ever really noticed how pretty she was. She had inherited her father's curly blond hair, her mother's dark eyes and slimness. She did not bear the slightest resemblance to Princess Anne, and she was in no way centrefold material, but she was not bad at all. She is seventeen, now, so she would have been fifteen, then. I was sixteen — sixteen and experiencing my very first eye contact with a member of the opposite sex.

I'll never forget that moment, how we just stood there looking at each other. Just thinking about it now, my heart quickens in the same way.

To hook and land an Atlantic salmon, especially a large one, is one of the most exciting things that life has to offer; even to be there and witness the event is exciting. Uncle Kid had reeled in and was coming down the shore to watch the fish being beached, and he'd seen it all a thousand times before. And normally I, too, would have been out there ready to assist, or just to see. But, that day, it all happened while I stared at Milly Minor. I missed the whole event. And so did Milly. She had wasted her time looking at me — dropping her eyes, lifting them again, looking away, looking back, smiling . . . had I seen her blush?

The salmon was beached and released before we knew it.

Then she shrugged, turned away and began to walk down along the shore. I watched after her, feeling strangely burdened.

Nubert and Uncle Kid were discussing the battle, laughing, lighting cigarettes. I could hear them talking.

"Boys, she hit some hard!"

"And ya got it on that little Shady Lady, eh?"

"Third cast!"

They were celebrating, but I was not interested. All I could do was watch Milly walking away, a spring in her step, sure-footed, her slim legs in tight blue jeans, her red jacket, her curly blond hair. I followed her with my eyes, my heart, experienced both the pleasure and the pain of loneliness.

"That's one of the biggest salmon I ever landed, I think," said Nubert.

"Twenty pounds, I'd say. They're some pretty this time o' the year, ain't they!"

"Be a lot prettier in my freezer!"

"Ha! Corry."

Milly stopped, looked about, picked up a pebble and threw it in the river. She watched it fall on the water, and, perhaps catching a reflection there, looked up at the sky. I thought maybe she'd seen an eagle or an osprey, but she was eyeing a cloud. It was one of those big, rolling clouds of summer, a distant storm which we were only getting the wind of, the wind that played in her curls.

"Corry."

And then she looked back at me. She was a hundred yards or more away, but I could still see the smile, I'm sure of it.

"Corry!" It was Uncle Kid. He and Nubert were grinning at me as if they knew what had grown in my waders.

Thank God for the waders. Thank God I was not expected to stammer a response.

5

If you meet someone for the first time and have a hankering to meet that someone again, then I suppose, in a way, you've experienced love at first sight.

"Love, like life, is so methodical," Uncle Kid told me. "You can't do one thing without the other thing happening. If you place a ball on a hill, it will roll away. What goes up must come down, conception, death, love, hate. Half dust, half deity, Byron called us. We're a weird bunch, us humans."

We were side by side on our knees, weeding and thinning the beets. There was the hot sun on my bare back, blackflies everywhere, the persistent buzzing of a chainsaw in the distance and Uncle Kid's voice beside me. "It must be written all over my face for him to bring it up so soon," I thought. "Uncle Kid is usually more subtle, more casual than that." The fact that I was walking around sighing every five minutes might have had something to do with it, too.

"You plant a beet seed, you get a beet. Live by the sword, die by the sword. . . . You reach puberty, you get horny. Being horny is to desire. To desire is to be lonely. Ha! A grub! Who knows! Looking up at the stars is like looking down upon a great metropolis; the Earth spins, light is warped, and love is in the old mystery pot, too. You're growing up, getting to be a pretty big guy. Not bad looking. Play your cards right and you'll have women all over the place. You gotta remember that women like to talk and they'll love having all that space for doing it. You'll be a popular lad."

Two weeks had passed since Milly Minor smiled at me, but I could see the smile as clearly as if only seconds had passed. I woke up with it, carried it around all day and went to bed with it. I found myself romping around the Peacock Pool area, hoping she'd show up, maybe smile at me again or even speak to me. When I got tired waiting for her to show at the pool, I walked down the Hemlock Road past Nubert's place. One day I did catch a glimpse of her. She was leaning against the upper end of Nubert's oat shed, smoking a cigarette. I wanted to watch her, but I didn't want her to know, so I moved along. When I returned a few minutes later, she was gone.

One day I sat to write a letter to Princess Anne and found myself staring at a blank page. I had nothing to say. I felt I was flirting, you see. I couldn't very well tell her about it.

In the soil between the drills, I wrote "Milly."

Uncle Kid sighed, nodded.

I sighed a much bigger sigh, looked at the sky.

Uncle Kid laughed and said, "I thought so! Don't blame ya!"

Then there was a moment of listening and thinking. I heard the breeze playing in a nearby grove of birches, a crow caw, the buzzing of a fly, Uncle Kid sigh.

"What will he say? How will he tactfully get me out of this racket?" I asked myself. "Any man as into opposites and circles as he is should be able to come up with a loophole for me."

My own reasoning, even though it was warped with dreams of warm, moonlit rendezvous down Lover's Lane, told me that I'd be wise to tread a bit carefully, that Milly Minor was probably just teasing me, that the smile that day at the Peacock Pool had nothing more in it than youthful freedom. But I was hoping Uncle Kid would give me a reason to be optimistic.

I waited. "The cogs in Uncle Kid's brain are rusty today," I thought. "It's taking longer." I glanced to read his face, saw a frown there. I didn't like it. It displayed truth. I wanted him to be profound, not truthful. You can ponder theories, but you must accept the truth. I did not want my dreams to end so soon.

Moments passed. Uncle Kid weeded thoughtfully, sighed again, chuckled once. A few more moments passed.

"I can't think of his name," said Uncle Kid, finally. "Haliburton, I think. But I don't have a clue who Haliburton is, or was. Anyway, it might not have anything more to it than just a good line. A plumber, a farmer, a used car salesman can come up with a good line. I can't imagine why I remember it. I must've come across it somewhere, and because of you, I must've figured it was worthy of storing here in my head. It's just a line and it might not mean anything. But, by God, the more I think of it, the better I like it. It falls right in with my line of thinking. And I couldn't have chosen a better time to recall it. It's perfect! Sound advice! Corry, I don't know what to tell ya. An understanding of the affairs of the heart has eluded me ever since I was a lad. Who the hell knows what a man should do or not do with his desires? There's only one thing that I can say and it's not really me that's saying it. Haliburton, whoever he was, said it first, I think. Who knows? He might have stolen it from Shakespeare or someone. Although it don't sound like Shakespeare . . . sounds more like Confucius. But anyway, do you know what old Haliburton said? It has nothing to do with women, really, but somehow, like I said, it seems like sound advice."

I sighed, frustrated with all these preliminaries. I wanted to scream, "Get to the point! What did Haliburton say?"

Uncle Kid was no fool. He saw the frustration, heard the sigh.

"Haliburton said, fellows who have no tongues are often all eyes and ears."

"Hmm."

I waited for more. Uncle Kid kept looking down, weeding and thinning.

"Is that all?" I asked myself. "Fellows who have no tongues are often all eyes and ears is all he has to say about love? Usually he raves on and on about things. What does this mean? Could it be that there is nothing more to say about love? Haliburton could have been talking about spying, for Christ sake! What has spying to do with love? Eye contact, maybe. Maybe it means that I'm making too much out of a little eye contact, a smile. But Uncle Kid would not say so little unless he meant so much."

We were thirty feet further down the drill and as much as fifteen minutes had passed before Uncle Kid spoke again. He flipped from his weeding to a sitting position, reached out, gave me a big hug and said, "I don't really know, Corry. I don't really know." And when he pulled away from me, there were tears in his eyes.

I raised an eyebrow at him.

He gave me a tearful glare.

I thought, "Do I see anger there? Why? What have I done?"

"I don't know fuck-all about anything!" he said, got to his feet and walked at a very brisk pace out of the garden and down through the field toward the house.

I was left staring after him, not knowing what to do or think.

The tears hadn't surprised me. I always knew he was capable of crying. He told me about it. "Tears are a powerful thing," was how he put it. "One little tear from the eye can say a hell of a lot more than drool from a wagging tongue will ever say!"

But *those* tears. Those tears were not the tears of poets, the mist between the soul and the moon, or some such thing. There was anger there! Angry tears are the worst.

In my own way, I called out to him, silently. He heard it a hundred yards away, stopped and stood, shoulders drooped. Not knowing what else to do, I walked up to him. Without looking at me, his face hidden behind the long brown hair, he spoke as if to the ground.

"It was foolish," he said. "I should have known better. How could I have thought that I, an irresponsible reprobate with his head in the clouds, could look after you? You, with more brains than I.

"Here you are, a young man, sixteen. We must do something with you, Corry. Sixteen. Damn procrastination! Damn time!"

It was then that I knew that he was angry at himself, not at me.

Looking up at me, he said in a gentle voice, "Corry, we only go

68

through her once and I haven't been to Florence. I haven't walked on a stage any bigger than that of the Public Hall. My whole life has been spent right here. Hell, I'm even here in my dreams at night! One of my dreams, one of my recurring dreams: I'm waist deep in the Miramichi and throwing a line like you wouldn't believe. It esses out two, three hundred feet. I'm trying to reach the brook and I'm across the river, on the other side from the mouth of Cains. When I get up in the morning, I get up to this place. I spend my day in this place and when I go to bed, I go to bed here. It bothers me a bit that I don't have the balls to go, but what bothers me a lot is that I'm afraid you're following suit. Why must we be so simple, so mediocre? I have this friend who's a priest, spends half his time beside the beds of dying people. He says the one thing that all dying people have in common is that they all have regrets, they all wish that they had gone further in school, that they had walked down the streets in Florence flirting with the Gypsies while they were still young and beautiful, that they had given their deepest and sincerest love. I know, I know, you can't do everything, but, hell, if it weren't for my fantasies, I'd have nothing."

"He's switching the whole issue to himself," I thought. "He's discarding my feelings for Milly as something fantastic. And that reference about the stage — he's remembering me doing Pavarotti. He's ashamed of me and he's blaming himself, switching it all to himself. He's feeling sorry for me."

It was my turn to be angry.

"How dare you bring this up out here in the field?" I thought. "How dare you shatter my one moment of love, even if it is nothing more than a misreading of a smile, a fantasy?"

Out there in the field, he had an advantage. How could I argue, defend, agree, attack? How could I do anything without a tongue, without my pen and paper?

I marched to the house, grabbed my pen and paper and sat at the kitchen table. Uncle Kid sat across from me.

I wrote "Pavarotti!!!" so aggressively that I tore the paper.

"Corry, I know they laughed at you when you sang like Pavarotti."

I wrote "It was not the laughter! It was when they *stopped* laughing!"

Uncle Kid sighed, searched for words. "Ah, hell!" was all he could come up with.

My own tears began to flow, and with great difficulty I wrote, "I thought it was funny."

"I know. And it was funny at first. You see, Corry . . . oh, I don't know anything for sure, but, well, you know how it is. They were embarrassed. Corry, there's a thin line between sanity and madness. At first your singing sounded, well, funny. And then it sort of sounded, you know, stupid."

I wrote, "You were the one embarrassed."

"Well, I . . . well, yes I was." He shrugged, not knowing what to say. And then suddenly he began to sing, to mimic me, sang "Some Enchanted Evening" in the same way that I used to — "Um e yaya e aw, oo a eh a aya."

I nearly choked as laughter put the skids to my anguish.

Laughing and crying at the same time, we were like two over-tired kids.

It was an emotional release that lasted for what seemed like a long time. We were perspiring and flushed by the time we stopped for a breather. We sighed simultaneously, in a way that should have indicated, End of topic, drop the issue, get on with life. But, to my chagrin, Uncle Kid had more to say on the matter.

"You know, Corry," he began, "you're what the girls nowadays refer to as a knockout guy. You carry yourself well. But, let me tell ya, I've seen the best-looking men you ever laid your eyes on end up married to sows, living in tarpaper shacks and working in the woods with the snow up to their arses. And for one reason! They didn't get enough schooling, didn't have a diploma. Christ! Even a high school diploma is not worth a pinch of snuff these days.

"Oh, I know, you've probably heard me talking about how a college education is not necessarily a good education and all that, but by God it makes life a whole lot easier."

I held up my hand to interrupt him, then wrote, "You said ambition."

"Well, yes, I said ambition was the key. I said a lot of things. But, well, you can want to walk on the moon, but if you don't know how to fly, you'll never get there. Now, that may not be a great analogy, but . . ."

I interrupted him again, wrote, "I do not have ambitions to go to university."

"I know, I know, you want to be a writer."

I shook my head, wrote, "I want to be a guide!"

Uncle Kid started to say something, but I checked him and continued writing. "I want to be a *real* guide. I want to learn all about it. I want to maybe do some outdoor writing. I think we should expand Izaak Walton's."

Uncle Kid nodded. "Yeah, well. All of that sounds good. All of that seems very well and good, but you have to go to school to learn how to run a business, and you have to be literate to talk to . . . well, I mean, you could write down your suggestions to sports and all of that. How do you know there'll be any future in it? You know what times are like, acid rain, netting, there might not be a salmon to spit at in another ten years. Izaak Walton's would be a hell of a place without salmon, now, wouldn't it?"

I really didn't know whether or not I wanted to guide, write outdoor articles and work at a bigger Izaak Walton's. Those ideas had just entered my head at that moment as if they had always been there, waiting, ready to support me when the time was right.

I thought of something else, wrote "Ambition" like a title on the top of a new page. And underneath I wrote:

1. I learn to be a guide.
2. We expand Izaak Walton's.
3. Clean out the shed.

"Now, what's cleaning out the shed got to do with ambition?"

4. Fix up shed for a sport camp.

"Yeah, sure! There's a bright idea for ya! All we need is three or four old Americans walking around here with nothing on their minds but catchin' fish!"

5. Make a pool.

"Make a pool! Where? All we have out front here is a chub hole! You know that! Do you have any idea how many rocks it would take to make a pool? The river's wide and slow out here. It's ridiculous! Sports, camps, expansion, pools — it's all ridiculous! Who'd pay to stay in a place like this? There's too much competition. You'd know that if you could guide for a day! You need pools, nice camps with comfortable beds, hot and cold water and showers; you need to know how to cook the very best of food; you need canoes. And, and there's no money in it! I know! Believe me, I know!

"Take an old camp, now. Say if we fixed up the shed for a camp. Well, you could do it like I fixed up my room. But have you ever noticed that I don't have any running water out there?"

I nodded.

"Well, there lies the whole kit and caboodle. Water! If you have a sport camp, ya gotta have water; to have water, you gotta run pipes. For three seasons of the year in this country, water freezes, so you're always drainin' pipes, bleeding them, replacing them. Ya gotta either keep your camp heated all winter, which would cost an arm and a leg, or deal with the deterioration the winters cause. I tell ya, outfitting's a pain in the ass. And guiding's not much better. Goin' to work at the crack of dawn, coming home after the sun goes down, putting up with some old American who doesn't know if his arse is bored or punched, wantin' fish when there aren't any fish, complaining about this, pissed off about that. No. Not for me."

With this, he marched out of the kitchen, leaving me not knowing whether I had won or lost.

Outfitting, guiding, expanding Izaak Walton's, renovating the shed, building a salmon pool, I had dwelt on none of those things. But all of a sudden, they seemed very important. Maybe it was just me keeping my mind off Milly, evading the pessimism and the depression that generally accompanied such thoughts. Milly, Princess Anne, a strike against idleness and fantasy, whatever the reason, I found myself rapt with the prospects of becoming a businessman.

*

I spent the next few days pondering and scheming; I sketched camps and redesigned rooms in the house, considered how they might accommodate guests. I even went down to the Peacock Pool and sketched it in the minutest detail — bars, boulders, the points or gravel peninsulas that may or may not affect the current, clumps of eel grass, depth of water in various hot spots, the width of the river; I estimated water speed and temperatures and the various probable influences of Gilead Brook. It was great fun! I was *doing* something! I was in business!

Within a few days I felt I was about ready to start constructing our pool, and I thought I had the ways and means of accomplishing this figured out. Boulders, I concluded, were the main ingredients, and I knew where they were and how to get them.

Sunday evening I turned in early, and, even though my enthusiasm kept sleep at bay, I was up at five Monday morning and on my way to the river. It was one of those warm and humid summer mornings that belongs to the mosquitoes. I boarded my canoe and poled upstream.

About half a mile upstream from our shore is where the old footbridge used to be. It had been abandoned and washed out years before, but the abutments were still there. The abutments had been constructed from cedar timbers and rocks and although the timbers had long ago decayed or had been swept away by floods and ice floes, most of the rocks were still there. Those old abutments, I knew, were built by human hands, which meant that every rock in them was small enough for one or two men to lift. I figured that if those old builders could lift them, so could I. All I had to do was load the canoe with them and drift them downstream to my pool and dump them.

It was hard work, for the rocks were heavy and the days were hot. I got very sunburned that first day out on the water with just a bathing suit on. The next day and all the days after that, I wore a shirt and things improved. It was hard on a canoe, too. Sometimes it was so heavily laden with rocks that all you could see was a couple of inches of the cedar gunwales.

When I got the rocks down to our pool, I piled them one on top of the other until they were close enough to the surface to create a disturbance, a wake on the otherwise smooth surface. Working from early morning to late evening, I was moving ten canoe loads a day. I stayed at it for twenty days and had more than two hundred piles of rocks scattered about. To stand on the shore and look out at my work, at all the ripples and currents the piles of rocks were creating, it appeared to be the very best of a pool, looked as good as some of the better pools on the river. I was optimistic.

Uncle Kid never mentioned my work until one day at the supper table he said, "Corry, my lad, I was fishin' in that pool owned by the Lindsay Club . . . up there below Dan Young's? Well! You know what they've done? You wouldn't believe it! They put car tires in the river! Filled them with rocks and sunk them, if ya know what I mean. Car tires, truck tires, tractor tires. And they hold fish, too! I was thinking there must be fifteen or twenty old tires out in the shed. Might as well add them to your pool for all the good they are. Just taking up room. I'm not doing anything tomorrow. Yeah, I can give you a hand. Kill two birds with the one stone, if ya know what I mean. Clean out the shed and make a pool all in one move."

I nodded, happy that he was finally taking an interest.

Then he said something totally unexpected. He said, "My room can be the living room. There's room in the front there for at least one, maybe two bedrooms and a kitchen. We'll rig up a toilet and shower. That's all we need, maybe a wash basin. There's an old sink out there now. All we need is a few pipes. Don't know what I'll do with all that weed. Most of it's too old to be potent. Give it to the boys, maybe. Sell it for ten dollars a bag, pay for the plumbing."

For a moment, I thought that maybe Uncle Kid was moving a bit too fast for me. Was I hearing things? Had I just heard him say that he wanted to convert his room, his beautiful, rich, private room and clean out the rest of the shed for a sport camp? I had, I had!

To say I was joyously speechless would be a ridiculous understatement. I was dumbfounded! I threw him a kiss, threw up my arms and hollered, "Awooooo!" What else could I say?

"Now, now!" said Kid. "Don't get all excited! It's going to take time, money and hard work. Hard work we can handle, but money's scarce. Those rocks you put in there, you know, of course, that no salmon will lie behind them until they darken up with the water. A rock has got to look natural and it'll take a year, maybe two for that to happen."

"A 'ear!" I screamed.

"Now, now, a year is not such a long time. It'll take that long for us to get rigged up, anyway. At least a year. And it won't matter, anyway. Ya have to book sports on, ya know. We'll have to advertise somewhere. Put a little ad in the New York *Times* or somewhere, the Boston paper maybe. Maybe your father knows someone up in Toronto who might want to go fishing. You don't always have to go to the States. And you know, that office of yours. We could keep a sport there, too, if he didn't mind staying in the house with you and me. Of course, that would mean giving up your office."

Give up my office! I felt like whooping! I would have given up my pecker to be in the outfitting business! My office! What the hell did I need an office for? I could do all the writing I ever wanted to do at the kitchen table, on a tree stump in the woods, sitting on the toilet!

Uncle Kid saw my excitement and grinned. "It'll be good business to have Izaak Walton's, too," he said.

I nodded.

"And one of us will have to learn to cook, or we'll have to hire one. I think I . . . you leave that up to me." With this, he reached out, slapped me on the leg and stood up. "I have plans for you, Corry! Want to get drunk?"

I nodded and grinned. I'd never been drunk before, but I had never felt more like celebrating in all my life. Get drunk! Why not! Celebrate!

Uncle Kid went to the cupboard and took down a bottle of scotch and a couple of glasses. I got some ice from the fridge and the party began.

*

I tossed the first drink back as if it were juice. Uncle Kid cautioned me. "The secret to drinking is to drink slow. Sip your drinks and you can stay with a good party all night. Drink fast and you make an ass of yourself." Then he tossed his drink back, winked and poured us another.

"Drinking has to remain sociable," he said. "A man that can handle his liquor will go a long way."

Uncle Kid had adopted a new habit. He whistled under his breath a lot. The best way I can describe it is that he whisper-whistled. He always lit into the same little tune — "Turkey in the Straw." Sometimes he would tap his foot in time with the tune. After whisper-whistling the complete refrain at our party, he said, "Oh, I don't know, Corry me boy. It's hard to say," then fell back into the whistling again as if I was supposed to know what he was thinking.

Finally he stopped, took another drink and said, "We ain't ever gonna get rich, you know. It's not in us to get rich. It's not in our makeup. Money don't mean a damn thing, anyway. You take a man who has spent all his life in pursuit of money and hoarding every little thing. He'll die just the same as you and me. Christ! I know so many dead people." He whistled some more.

"Have ya seen that girl of Nubert's lately? What's her name? Milly? Ah boys! She'd be great in the sack, eh! A regular pistol-packing little spitfire! Chekhov said that. A regular pistol-packing little spitfire. Well, have ya seen her?"

I shook my head.

"Well, you've been spending too much time down by the river

playing with your rocks. Ha! Get it? Playing with your rocks. Anyway, I saw her yesterday. Saw her the day before yesterday, too, as a matter of fact."

"Huh?"

"She's been walking on the road a lot. She walks up here, stops at our lane, looks in, then walks back home again. What d'ya think she's up to?"

I shook my head.

"Now, from experience, what I figure is she's got the hots for ya."

I shook my head.

"Why not? You're a good-looking young fella! But oh well. A man never knows. Did I ever tell you that to keep a woman, you have to make her laugh? Women love to laugh. They see beauty in laughter, I think. Sulk and be serious all the time and they'll find it elsewhere. Seen it happen a million times. Of course, a man's no different. How'd you like to go way up to Ontario for a little while, Corry? See your father, get a taste of the big city."

I shrugged, downed my drink.

"No, maybe not. I spent some time up there. Hamilton! What a place! You wouldn't believe the bridge! I met a great little darlin' up there, I tell ya! Her name was Sandra Appelon. Quite a lady.

"No. You wouldn't like it up there. No river! Oh, I mean, they have rivers, but not like this one! Course, there's not many like this one, that's for sure.

"Sandra Appelon. All the literature they had in the house was Archie comics! Ha! Oh, well. I get the urge to travel now and again. See the world! We'll start an outfitting business, eh, Corry?"

Uncle Kid tossed back his drink, poured another, a stiff one.

"Ah, but there's no money in it. You'll never get rich in this country. You wanna get rich, go to the States. They don't mind if ya get rich in the States."

Uncle Kid stood with a sigh, went to the window, looked out, sighed again.

"Pour yourself another drink, Corry. You're drinking too slow."

I touched up my drink.

Uncle Kid started whisper-whistling again. "Turkey in the Straw."

He went to the fridge, opened the door, eyed something or other for a moment, closed the door and came back to the table. He sighed for the third time and sat. He downed his drink and poured himself another.

It was plain to see that he was getting restless. I grabbed my pen and paper, wrote, "We'll get up early. Put those tires in the river."

Uncle Kid nodded.

"Yeah."

I wrote, "It's Wednesday night. Not much happening."

"No. A chicken shoot at the Legion, I think. You know, I've been playing darts for years and years and never won a chicken yet. Bill Kerr! Now, there's a dart player! Must've won a hundred chickens in his day. Too bad you're not old enough to get in."

I shrugged, wrote, "Practice. We should have a dart board here."

"By God you're right, you know. A dart board and a pool table. Great fun playin' pool. You'd like it. You've never played pool, have ya?"

I shook my head, suddenly aware that I was feeling a bit drunk.

I figured the best thing I could do was stall him. I knew he liked to talk and drink. We had lots of booze. All I needed to do was keep questioning him, get him thinking and chewing on his long hair, raving.

"Philosophy," I thought. "That could keep him going for hours."

"Tell me mor bout makin women laugh," I wrote.

"I don't know," he said with a shrug. "You don't see *me* married." He whisper-whistled "Turkey in the Straw," drummed the table with his fingers.

"Mabe you weren't funny enough," I wrote.

"Maybe."

"Did yoo make Sanra Aplon laf?" I was speeding a bit, I wasn't writing well.

"Ummm. Sandra? I miss Sandra. I miss Viola and Karen, too. I miss Dianne and Shirley, Dora, Norma. Mary and June . . . I miss them all. Little darlings. Ha! Sandra liked Archie comics and I gave her shit for reading them. I couldn't see what was funny about them. And the stupid things they did. Violent at times. Old man what's-his-name, the father of the rich girl. Threw Archie out on his ass every time the kid visited. And that big goon, the stupid

78

guy. He'd choke Reggie and smash him for making eyes at his ugly girl friend. But Sandra would read that shit and laugh her fool head off. Of course she knew it bothered me and I guess she tried. Ha! She started reading them in the bathroom. I used to hear her in there having a shit and laughing. What an asshole I was!"

He stood and went to the window again, spoke as if to the great outdoors. "When Sandra left, she didn't tell me why. It drove me crazy, not knowing. I beat my head against the wall and cried, laid the old ego trip on her. I was so goddamned hurt. You know, now, looking back on it, I think she left me for Archie comics. Freedom! The all-American dream! The freedom to read Archie comics!"

He went to the fridge again, opened the door, stared at something until the motor started and began to hum in B-flat. He closed the door, came back to the table, sighed and sat, just like he did before; whisper-whistled, drummed his fingers, "Turkey in the Straw."

"Wednesday night," he said. "Friday night, the Boxers are playing at the Legion."

I had no idea what he was talking about.

"The Boxers, two idiots from Black River or somewhere. Chicken shoot tonight."

I took a drink of my scotch and wrote, "B-flat."

"B-flat? What about it?"

"The key of electricity. The fridge."

"Oh! The fridge! You remembered!"

I poured more scotch in his glass, knowing he would not leave a glass until it was empty. The clock over the stove read eight-forty-five, a critical time, my task was not going to be easy.

"Almost nine o'clock," said Uncle Kid. His eyes had followed mine to the clock.

I was searching for a new strategy when he came right out with it. "You wouldn't mind if I took off to the Legion for a couple of hours, would ya, Corry?"

I understand why he wanted to leave. He'd had a few drinks, was feeling restless, wanted to be with people he could really talk to. That's understandable. I had nothing to say and couldn't say anything even if I had. I must have been a complete bore. But at the time, I felt so totally let down. I was lonely and hurt, felt betrayed.

I remember just staring at him for the longest time and him staring back at me with a strange look on his face — a sheepish look, a look of disbelief; I'm not sure what I was seeing, probably confusion, a reflection of the mixed emotions, the incredulity my own countenance portrayed.

I reached for my pen with the intentions of writing down something like, I thought we were celebrating, but instead I scratched the paper back and forth until it was torn to shreds, threw the pen at the cupboards and stormed upstairs to my room. I locked the door and sat alone in the dim light.

Uncle Kid followed me. I heard him try the knob, then knock.

"Corry?"

I did not respond.

"Corry!"

"O a ay! O a ay! O A AY!"

"Ah, Corry? Don't. Please. Look. Corry? All right, all right! What do you want from me, Corry? What is it you want from me? Look here, I'm not your . . . ah, hell, Corry!"

Then he fell silent, waited.

There was a magazine beside my bed. I grabbed it and threw it at the door.

A few seconds later I heard him mumble, "Go to hell." Then he thumped down the stairs and out of the house. The sound of the door slamming behind him was the most lonesome sound I'd ever heard. Night was falling over the land outside and I hadn't turned on the light — I was sitting in darkness. When the door slammed, silence moved into my room to join the darkness.

Before breaking down completely before the torrents of loneliness and self-pity that threatened to wash me away, I listened. I did not hear him start up his Jeep and I did not hear him return. He had either gone to his room in the shed or had gone for a walk, like he often did, down by the river.

6

When I was a little kid, every Easter Aunt Linda gave me an Easter basket. They were pretty little baskets — white, blue and yellow crêpe paper cut to look like ribbons and bows and wrapped around ice cream tubs. Works of art, in a way. They were designed and put together by the members of the AWA, the Anglican Women's Auxiliary. In them, those wonderful ladies put pieces of brown sugar, chocolate and divinity fudge, several Easter eggs, a few jelly beans and a little yellow chicken made of cotton fluff.

It's the chickens I remember most of all. The smell of them.

I've heard that your memory is triggered more vividly by odour than by any of the other senses. I'm not absolutely sure what those little chickens smelled like, patchouli oil or something, but whatever it was, every time I got a whiff of it — until one night years later in Saint John — I thought of Easter baskets made by the AWA. A beeline to Easters past. I wouldn't be surprised if Jesus smelled like patchouli oil when He resurrected from the sepulchre. It's what we'll all smell like on Judgement Day. It's the smell of gay cavaliers and little men in plaid suits and glasses who follow their penises around. Flimflam men and peeping toms gargle it. Grigori Rasputin bathed in it. It works as an aphrodisiac for would-be poets and seedy academics. It's worn by ding-a-lings and French whores. If buxom blond country singers don't wear it, they should.

Both Margery and Letitia smelled like patchouli oil.

*

It was one of those nights that seemed to last about thirty-six hours. I cried in the dark for a while, then decided that was stupid, turned on the lights and wrote a letter to Princess Anne.

> I'm so alone. Uncle Kid couldn't care less about me! All he wants to do is smoke dope and play darts at the Legion with his cronies! And he never does anything! All that talk about fixing up the shed for a sports camp? That's all it was, talk!
>
> You know, sometimes when I look at your picture, I think I see you smile, ever so slightly, but a smile nevertheless. It warms me.

I must've written twelve pages to her, spilled my heart and bared my soul.

After writing the letter, I turned off the light and crawled into bed where I lay listening until the wee hours. The house was quiet and spooky. At the first grey of dawn, I contemplated going fishing but had not the heart for it. "Let the salmon go free," I thought. "Free like Uncle Kid. It's all right if *he* runs the roads! Don't worry about Corry, all alone in that big old house! Go ahead and smoke your dope and drink with your friends! I'll be all right!"

I cried until my throat got sore, and, finally exhausted, went to sleep.

I awoke at noon feeling a bit weird. Downstairs, I found Uncle Kid washing his hands and face at the kitchen sink. He looked dirty and bedraggled. His hair was stringy, held out of his eyes by a headband.

"Good afternoon, Corry," he said, glumly. "It's a nice day. You should have been up and at it."

"Hmm."

"Want some bacon and toast?" he asked, towelling himself dry.

"Hmm."

He went to the fridge, got the bacon, took it to the stove and added four strips to his own sizzling lot. The grease popped and spat at him, burned his cheek. He spewed a string of oaths wicked enough to stain the enamel on the stove. It was plain he was not in one of his more congenial moods. I didn't like it. It was not like him to swear like that.

I plugged in the kettle, watched it come to a boil and made us some coffee. Then I made toast and Uncle Kid sliced a couple of tomatoes.

We sat to eat.

The *Daily Gleaner* was on the table, folded down to the only thing either of us ever looked at, the crossword puzzle. Uncle Kid picked up my pen and began the puzzle.

"Late bloomer," he mumbled. "Five letters."

I wanted to tell him "aster," but he had my pen.

It angered me that he had my pen. "How dare you take my voice!" I thought.

I began to eat and was halfway into my sandwich when he gave me such a black look that I stopped chewing and attempted to stare him down.

"Do you have to slurp your food like a goddamned pig?" he asked.

"Cut half your tongue off and see how quietly you'll eat!" I wanted to retort.

Back to his crossword puzzle, he said, "Who in hell knows who the Ohio senator was in 1959!" Totally frustrated with the puzzle, he threw the paper on the floor and tossed the pen at me. It landed in my coffee mug, splashing the front of my shirt.

With this, he swore a little and stormed out of the house.

After changing my shirt, I went, somewhat reluctantly, to look for him.

I found him in the shed, sitting on a garbage bag of pot, smoking a large pipe.

"Good," I thought. "He's getting stoned. He'll be in a better state of mind."

After a while, he said, "Trouble with cleaning out a junk shed is there's so much stuff to look at, to investigate. This old pipe. This old pipe has seen more parties than old Caligula! See that old spool basket? My grandmother made that."

"Hmm."

"You know, if I could get all this weed to Toronto or someplace, I could sell it for thousands of dollars. We could hire someone to do all this work. A lot of this stuff is antique."

I was poking around looking at stuff. I spotted a 1924 licence plate.

"Ha! Now, look at that would ya! Still in good shape. You know, I've seen bars with them things on the wall. We can use a lot of this stuff for decorations. That old pitchfork there, I have an idea for that. Take the handle out of it, make a candelabra. What do ya think?"

I nodded, wondering if it was his idea.

"Recycle," he said. "Put the tires in our salmon pool, make a candelabra out of a pitchfork . . . *pigliare due piccioni con una fava.*"

"Huh?"

"To catch two pigeons with one bean. Italian. Italy. Now there's a country. Rome! Florence! Venice! Rome Florence Venice Verona Milan, it's like poetry just saying the names. The names around here? Montreal, Quebec, Saskatoon, Sudbury . . . somehow it's not quite the same. Ha! Saskatoon . . . I wonder if there's a place called Phlegm, Saskatchewan."

I picked up an old hair dryer, looked it over and threw it down.

"That old hair dryer. Used to keep my seedlings warm with that years ago before it gave up the ghost. Well, well, well, you know, God! Wonderful how things work! You know, a man should never allow himself to get angry and frustrated and screwed up! Every time you get down, all you have to do is look around. There's answers everywhere you look.

"You and I've been having a spat, eh, Corry? I'm sorry I've been such an ass. It's just that, I don't know, we need to do something. We need, we need, we need . . . that hair dryer. Pass that here, will ya?"

I picked up the hair dryer and gave it to him.

"The answer," he said.

And then he sang a few bars of an old Johnny Cash song.

My mother's words echoed again,
Don't take your guns to town, son,
Leave your guns at home, Bill,
Don't take your guns to town.

He shook the hair dryer, turned its off/on button, peered down the tube, sniffed the hood.

"You can almost smell the perms," he said. "God! Mother, Mother, Mother! You wise and wonderful lady! Sit down here beside me, Corry."

I sat beside him on a bag of dope marked 1979.

"My mother used to do everybody's hair," he said. "All the old ladies in the area used to come here for their perms and stuff. They used to come and pay her, whether they needed it or not, some of them. The poor old souls. Mom made a pretty good living at it. Made more money than she bargained for, really. You know why?"

"Uh-uh."

"Well, I'll tell ya. All the old ladies . . . old Mrs. Clark, old Gwen McLaggan, Caroline Bean, Nancy and Sheena Waters, Laura Carter. Old blue-haired ladies. All older than the hills, all living alone. Lonely old ladies. They'd come here and Mom would pretty them all up. Now the curious thing about that was, they weren't going anywhere and they weren't expecting any company. But they always wanted their hair done. Old Caroline Bean would drop in sometimes twice a week. Just wash it, dear, she'd say. Snip a bit here, curl something there. Come to think of it, old Caroline didn't have much hair for Mom to work with at all, but she kept coming. You know why, Corry?"

I shook my head.

"Well, I'll tell ya! No! No, I won't tell ya! I'll tell ya later! Let's lock up this old shed! There's no hurry to clean it up. We got all fall and all winter."

"Ahhh?"

He slapped his thighs and stood. "C'mon, let's get out of here!"

I grabbed my pen, found a place to write on the top of a box.

"Why did the old ladies come?"

"All right, all right, I'll tell ya. But it might spoil what I have in mind for you. Then again, it might not. It might prepare you."

I stomped my foot. I was going nowhere until he finished his story.

He sighed. "The poor old darlings just wanted to get touched. My mother doing their hair was the only time anyone ever touched them. Now, you and me are going on a little trip, and when we get to Saint John . . . never mind. Let's shower, get into some good clothes, pack a few things and get out of here. We'll take a bit of weed with us."

Two hours later, we were heading south on route eight. We had a bit of weed, about fifteen pounds, in the back of the Jeep, and Uncle Kid was whistling "Turkey in the Straw."

I wondered if we were going to Saint John to get our hair permed.

*

A port nestled in the hills and rocks of the Bay of Fundy, Saint John is New Brunswick's largest and Canada's oldest city. It's the home of the world's highest tides, the Reversing Falls, morning fogs and the Marco Polo sailing ship. Wallace Turnbull invented the variable-pitch propeller there. New Brunswick's only Acropolis is there, on a hill, disguised to look like a windowless hospital. "On a Clear Day" is not a popular choice of Saint John radio stations.

There was a time in Saint John, way back, when you could smell the sea breeze in the mornings. Then someone came up with the bright idea of building a pulp mill smack in the middle of town.

I like it, though. Most people do. It's friendly and unpretentious. It has more of a city feeling to it than other New Brunswick cities and the coastal climate actually has its positive side — it's cooler in the summer and warmer in the winter.

We landed in town about five o'clock in the afternoon.

Saint John is about a three-hour drive from our place on the Miramichi and we were little more than halfway there, at Fredericton, when we drove beneath a canopy of clouds. By the time we pulled to a stop in Saint John, the sky had darkened so that the street lights were coming on and a hard rain was falling.

"You wait here," said Uncle Kid, turning off the engine and jumping out. "I'll just be a minute."

He ran across the street and entered what I assumed was a tavern. A sign over the door read "The Hornpiper."

"Great!" I thought. "Just great! I've come all the way to Saint John to wait in a Jeep while he gets drunk in a tavern!"

I turned on the radio to CFBC and made myself comfortable, preparing myself the best I could for a wait that could extend well into the evening.

Uncle Kid surprised me, though, and returned in no more than five minutes. He drove a few blocks and pulled up in front of another tavern — Jeff's Jig and Jive. It had a neon triple-J in the window.

This time he was gone a little longer, about ten minutes or so. When he returned, he had a little man with him.

"Jesus it's raining!" said the little man as I let him into the back seat.

"Al, this is Corry," said Uncle Kid.

I nodded.

"Corry! Corry! Corry! How ya doin'? How ya doin'? Quite a rain, eh? How ya doin'? How ya doin'?" He had a high-pitched voice and talked fast.

"Corry, ah, can't speak, Al," said Uncle Kid.

"Ah, too bad, too bad! Quite a rain, though. Weather man said we're getting more tomorrow, too. How ya doin'? How ya doin'? How ya like Saint John? Good? Good town, Saint John? Eh, Kid? How ya doin'? How ya doin'? Corry, is it? How ya been, Kid? How ya doin', anyway? Haven't seen ya in a dog's age. How ya been, anyway?"

"Just hanging out on the Miramichi," said Uncle Kid. "Same as always."

"You know where Foxy's is, eh, Kid? Take a left at the corner, then turn right at the lights. Jesus it's rainin'! Rain again tomorrow, too, no doubt. You got it, turn left, and right at the lights. Josh should be there, now. I don't know. Hangs out there a lot. Good lad, Josh. Wouldn't wanna cross 'im, though. You know Josh pretty well, eh, Kid? Good lad, Josh. Yes, sir. Turn right, right here, yeah. You got it, you got it."

We pulled up in front of Foxy's.

With a name like Foxy's, I expected a sleazy bar. I was wrong. Foxy's was a licensed restaurant — a sleazy one.

Al went into the restaurant ahead of us, leading the way back through the room, as if he were a popular campaigning politician — nodding, waving, smiling, winking, patting shoulders, shaking hands. "How ya doin'? How ya doin'? See Josh? Is Josh around? How ya doin', anyway? How ya been? See Josh? Josh around? Good to see ya, good to see ya. How ya been? Josh around?"

A seedy-looking drunk pointed Josh out to us. He was seated at a table at the back of the room. He was big, bald and ugly. He was bearded and gaudily dressed, wore a gold chain around his sweating neck. He had a very expensive-looking watch on his left wrist and a large chain bracelet on his right. He had rings on every finger. He was chewing on a cigar that didn't seem to be lit and had a pitcher and a half of draught on the table in front of him.

"Josh! Joshua! How ya doin'? How ya been? Good to see ya! Remember Kid? You know Kid! Kid's here, Josh! Remember Kid?"

Ignoring Al, Josh looked at Uncle Kid and smiled a yellow, gummy smile. I noticed he had a couple of broken teeth. "Kid! Well, for Jesus sake, Kid!"

"Joshua. How've you been?"

Josh waved his gaudy hand. "Shit! Cops on my back, the old lady ran off with the kids and a stash of hash. Shit! Too many cigars." he patted his gigantic belly. "Too much booze and food! Life's never been better! Sit down, sit down!" he half-voiced, half-whispered.

We all sat.

"Who's this?"

"Corry. My . . . son."

"Corry! Your son? You got a boy this big? Yeah, yeah, he looks like you! Which old lady?"

"Ah, you wouldn't know her. Jane from Richibucto."

"How'd ya end up with 'im?"

"Long story. Corry's lost a bit of his tongue. Can't talk."

"Ha! Cat got yer tongue? Ha, ha, ha, ha! Cat got yer tongue! Ha, ha, ha."

Everyone joined Joshua in laughing at this great joke.

"So! What can I do for ya, Kid? Waiter! Bill! Bring these guys some beer! Yeah, what can I do for ya? Got some of that Miramichi gold?"

"As a matter of fact . . ."

"Can't handle it."

"I . . ."

"Nobody buys that shit anymore! Do well to get thirty dollars an ounce."

"Too bad."

"How much ya got?"

"Oh, not much. Ten, fifteen pounds."

Joshua puffed on his cigar. It glowed and smoked.

"It's not worth much, Kid."

"Don't want much. Corry and me, we're sort of on a tear."

"Bill! Where's that beer? Homegrown's hard to get rid of, Kid. Do well to get thirty dollars an ounce for it."

"Freddy's gettin' thirty-five," put in Al.

"Shut up, Al! Stick to your cab-drivin'! I'll make the deals!"

"Sure, Josh, sure, sure! No trouble. Thirty, maybe, I don't know, I forget."

The waiter sat a pitcher of beer and a glass in front of each of us. I shook my head and pushed mine over to Uncle Kid.

"No, Corry, you have it. The man bought you a beer."

I shook my head again. I didn't care much for beer and Uncle Kid knew it.

"What's wrong with this kid?" asked Joshua. "I thought you said he was your son!"

"Drink it, Corry," said Uncle Kid.

"Yeah! Drink the fuckin' beer! When I buy a man a beer, I expect him to be man enough to drink it!"

I drank straight from the pitcher, a quaff large enough to distort Joshua's jowls into a smile. Suddenly, I did not like Joshua very much at all.

"I couldn't give you a penny more than, oh, let's say . . . three hundred," said Joshua. "It's not worth it. Too much bulk, too much traffic."

Uncle Kid sighed. "Too bad. It's good stuff. I sprayed it with maple sugar and rum . . . I was hoping five hundred. What about Freddy?"

"Freddy! Stay away from that jerk! That jerk's got one foot in the harbour, as far as I'm concerned! And if I get handy to 'im, I'll give 'im a push! You know what he's like! You know better than to deal with him!"

"Well . . ."

"Three hundred's the best you're gonna do in this town, Kid. If you were a regular supplier, I might be able to do a little better. But you haven't exactly been frequenting the place, now, have you! Three hundred! Take it or leave it!"

"Sorry," said Uncle Kid and started to stand.

"Now, just a minute!" snapped Joshua. "I'm not finished with you yet! Drink your beer! What are you gonna do with it?"

"Well, it's worth more than three hundred to me. Freddy's not so bad. Is he in town?"

"Freddy's a jeezless jerk. He'd be crazy to pay more than three-fifty for homegrown!"

"Five hundred."

"He's lucky he's not in the harbour!"

"Maybe I'll just sell it by the ounce, make the profit same as you, same as Freddy."

"I'll give you three-fifty for it! Not a penny more!"

"Four-fifty."

"Three-fifty!"

"Well . . . Maybe I'll get back to ya. Freddy lives in Hampton, doesn't he?"

"You're an asshole, Kid! Four hundred!"

Uncle Kid smiled, offered Joshua his hand.

"Deliver it tomorrow," said Josh. "Al, here, knows where I live."

"I'd sort of like to celebrate," said Kid. "I need five hundred dollars up front."

"Jesus!" Joshua removed his wallet from his jacket, fingered out five hundred dollars and threw it on the table. "Some tear! See you tomorrow! Noon!"

I was calculating: four hundred dollars a pound, fifteen pounds . . . six thousand dollars.

I was very glad to get out of there — I did not want so much beer, I didn't like the place, and I did not like Joshua. Al ushered us out in the same way as he led us in.

"How ya doin'? See ya. Take it easy, now! How ya doin'? How ya doin'? Good to see ya," to everyone and anyone he walked past.

There were all kinds of things going on in my head. Designs, carpets, windows and doors, plumbing, pine walls, furniture. With six thousand dollars, we could turn the shed into a sport's camp fit for any old American millionaire that happened along.

Outside, we found the rain had slackened, downgraded from torrential to something less, pluvial perhaps. This time, I jumped in the back and let Al ride up front with Uncle Kid. We drove back to Jeff's Jig and Jive.

"You wait here," said Uncle Kid. "I gotta talk to Al for a minute."

They entered the tavern. "What are they up to now?" I wondered. "We're going to get in trouble down here, sure as hell!"

Uncle Kid returned in a few minutes, jumped in behind the wheel, started the engine and pulled out, the windshield wipers flapping.

"Joshua's an ass! So is Freddy! Al's a pimp, a gofer and a good friend of Freddy's, if you can call the cut-throat relationship they have a friendship. Joshua hates Freddy, and the feeling is entirely mutual. They've been feuding for years. That's why I went to Al and told him that I wanted to talk to Joshua. Joshua would do anything to get ahead of Freddy, even pay more money. Get my drift?

"Now, Al will run to Freddy and tell him that Joshua's buying a bunch of homegrown from me, and the two of them will plot and scheme more evils than two religious fanatics. A couple or three of them will get together and come looking for me. Freddy will have no intention of buying anything from me at a better price — he'll be coming with thieving in mind, wanting to break into the old

Jeep. Al knows the dope's in the Jeep. Stupid fools! The price ya gotta pay and the risk ya take to get your worth for the goods. All they have to do is work together and they'd both get better deals. In a way, I suppose, it's guys like me that keeps them pissed off at each other.

"Ya gotta keep one step ahead of them all the time. I just told Al that you and I were staying at Keddy's and that we needed a couple of girls and some champagne sent over at about eleven to-night. I did that so they'd know exactly where we are and what we're doing. No sense getting them all frustrated with the search, and we'll be sure to get two of their better girls. They'll want to keep us distracted."

I wondered if he planned to stash the weed in our room and how we'd go about carrying the sacks of marijuana through a hotel lobby.

Then Uncle Kid said, "There's some people I want you to meet. I called them from the Triple-J while Al was busy greeting everyone. Good people. You know who they are, sort of. Know of them, any-way. Mark and Denise Masters."

"Ha!" I said.

Mark and Denise Masters! Denise Bertrand Masters! The au-thor of *Jewels and Other Ancient Things*, *Webs* and *The Lilies Took Over*. Denise Bertrand Masters, the great Canadian writer! And her husband Mark, the biologist with more books than you can shake a stick at!

"Ha!" I exclaimed.

"I thought that would bring you up a notch," said Uncle Kid. "They're home and in a mood for company. "C'mon over," they said. "We'll throw in a few more mussels!"

Uncle Kid seemed very pleased with himself, whisper-whistled "Turkey in the Straw."

Somewhere between the Triple-J and the Masters', Uncle Kid said, "Hope you don't mind me makin' that dope deal. It was just old homegrown. I don't like havin' it around much anymore. Of-ten thought I should give it away, burn it, take it to the dump or something. But then I got to thinking about this outfitters business of yours and that we'd need some cash to get it going. I used to deal quite a bit. Grow it, come down here and sell it. It was a great supplement. But then Freddy, Joshua and the others got too serious, forgot who they were, got into other things, looting, thieving, hard stuff, stupid stuff! I quit when the RCMP searched the farm. You remember that?"

I shook my head.

"They came and searched every square inch of the place with dogs. Joshua gave them the tip. He was pissed off at the fact that I had sold my crop to Freddy. Anyway, they didn't find a thing. I didn't have anything. A week earlier, they'd have found more than twenty pounds of the stuff. Anyway, it got too close to home. You know what it's like on the Miramichi, rural, everybody knows everybody, talk would get around. Here we are! Now, try not to cluck and slurp too much when we're eating. They'll understand, but you know what I mean."

We pulled into a driveway beside a big square brick house. It was a plain house, a couple of chimneys, lots of windows, some vines covering much of one end, nothing fancy.

Mark Masters was a tall, grey-haired man of about sixty. At first sight you would not take him for a genius, an accomplished professor, a man of papers and adventure. He was dressed in an old grey shirt with a button missing and worn threadbare at the elbows. Where the button was missing, you could see the white hair on his belly. He wore very thick dark-rimmed glasses, needed a shave. His green pants were baggy at the knees, and he had on an old pair of fabric slippers.

Denise Bertrand Masters was short, plump, matronly. She had short, straight blond hair, a pug nose and a big smile highlighted with yellow smoker's teeth and pink lipstick. She had on a blue sweater, a white flowered blouse, green polyester slacks and sandals.

They took turns hugging and kissing Uncle Kid. They even gave *me* a big hug.

"Come in! Sit down! Drink?"

"Yeah, sure! Pour one for Corry, too! Scotch! How've you two been? It must be ten years! How's Nick? What's Zelda doing?"

"Ah, Kid, you haven't changed a bit! We're doing just fine. Denise is halfway into a hot new novel, Zelda's at Ryerson and Nick's a mechanic in Hampton, got his own place. Me? I'm still crazier than the proverbial loon. If I can't make my class laugh and make fun of me, I feel I'm failing. As a matter of fact, if the class doesn't laugh and make fun of me, I fail the whole lot!"

"Any signs of your cat?"

"Ha! What cat?" said Denise with sarcasm.

"I'll find that cat, supposing I have to turn every leaf and rock on the North Pole Stream!" said Mark, handing us our drinks, then sitting in a worn, comfortable-looking chair.

We were in the den — big old furniture, a fireplace, several paintings of cougars on the wall, books stacked everywhere. Denise was still standing. Uncle Kid and I sat on the sofa.

Mark looked me over.

"And this is the nephew you wrote me about? How are ya, Corry?"

I nodded, shrugged, blushed. I was very nervous and intimidated in the presence of Denise Bertrand Masters.

"Corry's grown up!" said Uncle Kid. "I took 'im on for a month. He's been with me for, I don't know, eight years? Good lad, most of the time. I wanted to show 'im off to ya. I told ya I could do it. He's coming right along! Writes better than old Keats!"

"Ah! Another writer!" Denise seemed delighted. "So, what do you write?" she asked.

I blushed and shrugged, embarrassed as hell. Me a writer? This woman with a half-dozen thousand-page novels, the winner of all kinds of awards, was asking me what I wrote? I felt like crawling under the sofa.

What substance is this
That falls from the clouds
And places its gentle kiss on Earth —
The very nucleus of life,
It drums its ancient music,
Seducing and impregnating the gardens
As with magic.

Uncle Kid had just recited something I had written! Damn! I'd left that on the kitchen table a while back! It was terrible stuff. A poem! I couldn't write poetry! Damn!

"A poet!" exclaimed Mark. "A chip off the old block, if you were the old block!"

"Isn't that wonderful! A poet!" Denise smiled, raised her glass to me, sipped.

"Writes prose, mostly," put in Uncle Kid. "Pretty good stuff, eh, Corry? Throws in verse here and there, though."

I was so angry at Uncle Kid for shooting his mouth off about my writing that I was about ready to strangle him. I was half expecting he'd read one of my letters to Princess Anne next.

But he didn't. He changed the subject.

"What's your new book about, Denise?" he asked.

"Damn! It's all so complicated. I'm afraid I'm lost half the time."

"She's being philosophical again," said Mark.

"Metaphysical's a better word for it. I'm being, I don't know, metaphysical about being philosophical or some damn thing! That's my problem. I should know better! I've written five hundred pages trying to say what Voltaire said in a sentence — When he that speaks, and he to whom he speaks, neither of them understand what is meant, that is metaphysics."

"Sounds like you've been getting into some good weed," said Uncle Kid.

Everyone laughed — except for me, of course. In those days, I hadn't given much thought to the ultimate anything. Ultimate existence to me was somewhere between something Milly Miner had to offer and a forty-pound salmon. I didn't even know the meaning of the word "metaphysics." And for that matter, who does?

"The last time I got metaphysical, the reviewers tore me to shreds," said Denise. "That was the best-selling book of all, though."

"Well, money's the name of the game," said Uncle Kid.

"Ha! There's more money in sweeping streets!"

"It seems to me," put in Mark, "that to be an author, one must be a *bit* metaphysical, or else you're writing about nothing creative at all. To sit and write about what *is* and what *was* is to border on plagiarism. It's already been said, the reader already knows about it. A creative writer must create."

"There's room for a little of both," said Uncle Kid, and I wondered if he knew what they were talking about.

"Metaphysicians can create a universe. . . how does it go? . . . but they can't pick the petals from a daisy, or something like that. I'm awful without my books!"

"I believe it was tear down a hovel," said Mark.

Denise started, clasped her fingers. "Well! Whatever! I'm off to the kitchen! Mussels, then steaks! No vegetarians, I hope."

I shook my head.

"Ace," said Uncle Kid, toasting her and blowing her a kiss.

"We were going to barbecue, but the damned rain!" said Mark. Denise exited.

For the next while, there was a conspicuous lack of conversation. Both Mark and Uncle Kid seemed engrossed in thought. Uncle Kid played with his hair and whisper-whistled "Turkey in the Straw," and I noticed that Mark Masters had a particularly peculiar idiosyncrasy. Every few seconds, he hummed. It was not the whisper-whistling of a little tune or anything like that, but more of the B-flat hum or drone of a refrigerator. Except I don't think it was in B-flat. It was a C-major hum, I think, reminiscent of Johnny Cash warming up for "I Walk the Line."

The silence lasted so long that I was beginning to feel uneasy, wished I could say something, anything. I scratched my chin instead and immediately regretted the imposition. Both Uncle Kid and Mark looked at me as if I had startled them or something. I shrugged, "Sorry."

They both smiled slightly, but still, nothing was said.

"Hum . . ."

"Turkey in the haymow, Turkey in the straw, Turkey in the haymow, Turkey in the straw . . ."

"Hum . . ."

"Turkey in the haymow, Turkey in the straw . . ."

I figured a fart at that juncture would have shattered the silence like an atomic explosion.

When conversation finally resumed, it was as if they had been telepathically communicating with each other all during the silence, for they seemed to begin halfway into it.

"Yes, sir," said Uncle Kid.

"Hum . . . She's been good to me," said Mark.

"One of the Masters," said Uncle Kid.

"Old joke," said Mark.

"Turkey in the haymow, Turkey in the straw . . ."

"Hum . . ."

"It used to be 'Barney Google,'" said Mark.

"Ha! I guess you're right. I never thought of it. I guess I've changed."

"We've all changed."

"Change is the way to perfection."

"Now *you're* being metaphysical. Only the gods are perfect. It was perfect for Pan to stink and Medusa to be ugly."

"Change never used to scare me," said Uncle Kid and looked at me.

Mark eyed me, too, and went, "Hum."

"Turkey in the haymow, Turkey in the straw . . ."

"Hum . . ."

At this point, I wasn't sure whether to be amused or baffled. I began to wonder whether or not there might be something wrong. I checked my fly to see if it was down. Everything OK there. I checked my shoes, thinking perhaps I had lugged in some dog droppings. My shoes were OK, too. "Maybe there's egg on my face," I thought. "But I haven't eaten eggs . . . tomato soup? No tomato soup . . ."

"Hum . . ."

"Turkey in the haymow, turkey in the straw . . ."

"Too bad it's raining," said Mark. "I could show you the garden."

"Still gardening, huh?"

"It's a hobby. Hard work at times. Work is good. I've never hated work, I've only hated jobs. I like what I do now, and I don't mind working hard at it."

Uncle Kid drew a deep breath and stood. "Finally! Something's happening," I thought. It's funny how a single sigh can sometimes put the skids to awkward moments.

"We're doing all right," said Uncle Kid, going to the window. He tossed the last of his drink back.

"Here, let me get you another," said Mark, rising. "Another drink, Corry?"

I hadn't been paying much attention to my drink. I shook my head.

"Thanks," said Uncle Kid, giving Mark his glass.

Mark went to the bar, clinked some ice into their glasses, poured scotch. Now they were at opposite ends of the room, one facing the bar, the other watching something, the rain perhaps, through the window.

"I was thinking," said Uncle Kid. "Hell, I don't know, Mark. There's a life over there, a future, I think. Corry and me, we're thinking about getting into outfitting, build a sports camp or two, keep a few sports. Corry here has been rigging up a pool."

Mark turned from the bar and handed Uncle Kid his drink.

"I might've got the glasses mixed up," he said.

"No matter. Thanks. Cheers. What do you think?"

"Outfitting? Might be lucrative. Salmon stocks are declining."

"Salmon stocks are always declining. Everything's declining."

"Well, there lies the crux of the matter, everything's changing so fast. Denise is onto the computer, now. You have to keep up, or you'll be left eating dust."

"Yeah . . . I know."

"I mean, it's all right for you and me." Mark glanced at me again.

"Yeah . . . I know."

"I wouldn't worry about it, though, Kid. Who the hell knows what the future has in store?"

"Yeah. It's just that, well, you know what I mean. We gotta do *something*. I mean, like you say, it's all right for me and all that, but, you know, insurance . . ."

"You're not that old, Kid. Security, insurance. Who the hell ever has that?"

"Yeah. It's just that, like you say, ya gotta keep up."

"Then buy a computer!"

"Yeah."

Right about here in their conversation I realized what was happening. It was not tomato soup on my face or an open fly that had put them ill at ease, but it definitely had to do with me. They needed to discuss me and I was in the same room. That was their problem.

"It's a very complex society out there," said Mark. "Not many nice guys anymore. The days of the backyard mechanics are about over. Everything is becoming more and more electronic, specialized. These days, city kids are learning about computers in grade four."

"Yeah, I know . . ."

"There are good ones, you know."

"Yeah, I know. . ."

"You know." Mark glanced at me. "Like" — he couldn't say "sign language" in front of me, of course, so he wiggled his fingers at Uncle Kid.

I felt the hair standing up on the back of my neck. How could he reason that Uncle Kid would catch onto the finger wiggling and not me? Did he believe I was stupid?

"Yeah. In Fredericton, Saint John, Newcastle, maybe."

"Well?"

"It's all very complicated."

"Complicated! Existence in this automated world is what's complicated! Especially for those who don't know what they're doing!"

"Yeah."

I suddenly felt sick — sick of the drink, sick of the conversation, sick of the rain, sick of Saint John, the dope deal, the Masters, Uncle Kid!

They had been figuring out a way of talking about me subliminally, allegorically. "Why couldn't they just come right out and say it?" I asked myself. "Say, 'Corry's growing up! Corry's in need of higher education, a university diploma, a future, a trip to suburbia, an enlightening tour of Europe! Corry's in the way!' Where the hell is my pen? I'll break the ice for the stupid fools!"

I pulled my pen and paper from my shirt pocket and wrote, "I can work, see, read, do all the mathematics I'll ever need . . . I CAN LISTEN!!"

I tore the note from the pad, took it to Uncle Kid and slapped it into his hand. Then I went back to my chair, sat and pounded the arm of the chair a couple of times with my fist.

Uncle Kid read the note, sighed and handed it to Mark.

They looked at each other and then at me. The bastards were blushing like two kids caught masturbating.

"That's good, Corry," tried Mark. "I . . ."

"Don't patronize me!" I wrote, ripped it out and handed it to him.

"Hell, Corry, we're not . . ."

Uncle Kid read it.

"See my problem?" he said to Mark. Now, he was calling me a *problem*! "Now, do you see my problem?"

I was hungry, I'd had a beer at the tavern and a bit of scotch, I'd lost my reserve. I hit the arm of the chair once again.

"See the perception?"

I was trembling with hurt, with rage. "Stop talking about me as if I'm not here!" I wanted to scream.

"See how goddamned smart he is?" Uncle Kid was saying.

Seeing my face, distorted as it must have been, Mark thought it wise not to reply.

"Corry, Corry, Corry! I don't patronize you! It's not that at all! It's you being who and what you are! You deserve so much. You could be a doctor, a lawyer, well, maybe not a lawyer, but you can be just about anything you want to be! Look at you! You're handsome, smart as a whip, young. You intimidate me! I've chosen my life! I love what I do, sort of. I could've done more, I know that. But, hell! Time flies!"

Here he turned from me, went to the window and stood looking out, slumped.

"Goddamn it!" he whispered. "I keep hurting you. What are we gonna do, Corry?"

"Igh!" I said. Guide!

"I couldn't handle it here," he said softly. "I couldn't handle it in Toronto, Vancouver. . . . A long time ago, I went home and hand-cuffed myself to Izaak Walton's. Ha! Izaak Walton's! The yoke, the chain that linked me to reality, sanity, security. The umbilical cord, I thought. Then you came along, a little boy with big blue eyes and blond hair and your father all broken with grief, all screwed up."

Here, Uncle Kid swung and pointed his finger at me.

"Izaak Walton's was a joke, Corry! *You* became my umbilical cord, my lifeline! I needed you more than you can imagine! Jerry was all screwed up! I couldn't let him take you. He couldn't hardly look after himself, let alone a small boy! Yes, and I might have ma-nipulated him a little bit. You needed me, I thought! The truth of the matter, Corry, is that I needed you!"

I looked to Mark to catch his reaction to this scene, but he was gone. I could hear the rain on the window behind Uncle Kid, some clanging in the kitchen. I sat staring at the floor, not know-ing how to react.

"We haven't been pulling too well, you and I," said Uncle Kid. "You've been out on that river from daylight to dark. I didn't help ya, because I knew you needed to be alone, to get away from me. And I've been running from reality, too. I told Joshua that you were my son. I wish! You saved me, Corry. Only for you, I'd be pimping around like Al or dealing like Joshua and Freddy. You helped me, so is it so wrong to want to help you?

"You saved my life, Corry! And how did I repay you? I kept you down, kept you home, kept you from achieving goals, reaching your potential! Not being able to speak is not the problem here! The problem with you is that I've buried you, tied you down!"

We were alone. I could do what I felt like doing. First, I began to cry; then, I ran and embraced Uncle Kid.

He held me for a moment, then gathered himself with a sigh.

"Great guests, eh?" he said.

I nodded.

"I'm sorry," he said.

"E be aw igh," I said.

"Yeah, I know. We'll be all right. And there's lots of time to do whatever we want, eh? Dry your tears."

We didn't realize it, but Uncle Kid and I had been living under a cloud for quite some time. It was a slate-grey cloud that just sat there doing nothing except blocking the sun — no dark threatening eye, no silver lining; a stress cloud, a boredom cloud, a cloud of uncertainty. The scene in Mark and Denise Masters's den had somehow stirred those clouds. We were in Saint John in the middle of a downpour, rain and tears. Old Saint John, with all its history, fogs and rains was where our cloud dissipated, was where we found the sun.

"Mark!" yelled Uncle Kid. "Mark! Come back in here!"

Mark returned immediately.

"You guys all right?" he asked as cheerfully as he dared.

"All right? Of course we're all right! We just needed a bit of a chat, that's all. You must never underestimate the power of the mind and the body! They are constantly in the process of healing themselves. A miracle has occurred in this room today, Mark. Two cadavers entered it and two healthy, living men will walk out, or my name is not Kid Lauder!"

"Praise the Lord!"

"I'm sorry, Mark."

"Don't be. I have a confession, Kid . . . Corry. I've been harbouring a great many uncertainties about you two. I doubted you, Kid, stupid asshole that I am! I should have known that Corry would grow up to be nothing but the tops."

"Ha!"

"Dinner's about ready. Now, I want you to at least pretend that you like it."

"Ha! Denise is the best cook in the world and we haven't eaten all day! That's half our problem! Hunger can get you down."

"Then let's get at it!"

Dinner was served — mussels, steak and mushrooms, a salad, bread. Wine, wine, wine. Uncle Kid hadn't exaggerated. Denise was a very, very good cook.

"The best meal I've had in years!" Uncle Kid announced.

"Cheers!"

"Salute!"

"Here's lookin' at ya."

Clink, clink, clink . . .

"Coffee and a little Courvoisier?" offered Denise when everyone was finished.

"Never turn down a good cognac," said Uncle Kid.

The conversation during the meal centred pretty much around food.

"These are PEI mussels. They're better than New Brunswick's for some reason. Less sandy or something."

"Great steaks."

"Imported from Boston. Aged to perfection. It's so hard to buy good steaks in New Brunswick."

"You pick these mushrooms?"

"Certainly. I haven't bought a mushroom in years."

However, with the serving of the Courvoisier, the conversation turned to different things.

Mark and Uncle Kid started talking about the elusive eastern cougar. Mark left the room at one point and came back with a folder in which were several photographs he had taken of the animals' tracks.

"I took those up on the Little Sou'west Miramichi, the North Pole Stream area," he said.

"They certainly look like cougar tracks," said Uncle Kid.

"Of course they're cougar tracks! And not just one, but two! See? These are bigger, the tracks of a male. I tell ya, Kid, I could almost smell the devil! Next year I'm going on sabbatical, spending half the summer up there. I'm proving once and for all that the damn things exist!"

"They're pretty timid. You'll have to bait them or something."

"I've set out baits a hundred times! They know what they've killed and what they haven't!"

"If you could find some droppings . . ."

"Yeah, if! It's an obsession, you know, Kid. I know they're there, I've come close so many times. But never a turd, never a hair."

"But you've got pictures of their tracks. That's proof, isn't it?"

"It's proof for me, but as far as anyone else is concerned, I could have photographed these tracks in Montana or Alberta. The whole damned world is so sceptical! It seems it's much easier for them to consider me a nut. They've been extinct for a hundred years, they say. You're ghost hunting, they say! I've got to come up with absolute proof!"

"So you're planning on spending the summer on the North Pole Stream."

"We're both going," put in Denise. "I just might come out of this slump with a little adventure like that. However, I'll be visiting, more or less. Someone has to look after things here."

"Where? Where will you stay?"

"In the warden's camp, of course," said Denise.

"I rub shoulders with Natural Resources people every day," added Mark. "The warden's camp will be our base, but as far as I can figure, we'll be tenting a great deal of the time."

"Doesn't the warden stay there during the summer?"

"Yes, and there's the problem. We'll be staying with a warden and that could be bad news — depending, of course, on who he is."

"Why don't you apply for the job, Kid?" suggested Denise.

"Me? A warden? Ha!"

"That's a wonderful idea! Why didn't I think of that before?" Mark slapped the table with enthusiasm. "You could be the warden! Think of it, Kid! It would be great! We could find that cat, Kid. And you'd be government-paid for the whole season! God! I'm glad I thought of it!"

"I couldn't close up the house and Izaak Walton's! Who'd look after the gardens?"

They all looked at me.

"I wouldn't mind," I thought, so, "Sure," I shrugged.

"No way!" said Denise. "Corry will go, too. He can be my assistant. He can help me with the cooking, the packing, he can help me gather mushrooms, all kinds of stuff! And I can help him with his writing. If, of course, he needs it."

"Now, there, Kid! Here's the answer to everything. Say yes!"

"Well, maybe. I'd have to land the warden's job."

"Do you think anybody else wants to be up there in the woods all alone for the whole summer? The job is yours for the asking."

"Well, maybe. Maybe Linda could look after things."

"Good! It's settled."

"Well, we got most of a year to think about it. But you know what I've been thinking, Mark? When I think of you pursuing that cougar, I can't help but think that you're searching in the wrong place. I've told you about the Dungarvon Whooper, haven't I?"

"Yes, you told me. But if I followed that path, nobody would *ever* take me seriously."

"Yeah, well . . ."

Denise turned to me and said, "I'd love to read your work sometime, Corry. Maybe I could get you read by a publisher."

I had nothing that I wanted a publisher to read, but I was ecstatic. Denise Bertrand Masters was interested in reading my work, would even show it to a publisher!

"Yes! Yes!" I nodded.

She smiled warmly.

At about ten o'clock, we stashed the dope, with Mark's permission, in the garage, said our goodbyes and headed back to town. We still had a long night ahead of us, but it was already the most wonderfully exciting night of my life.

Denise Masters! Sheesh!

*

Patchouli oil.

If I had been eight years old and thoroughly naive, instead of sixteen years old and just, shall we say, green, I certainly would have searched Margery's purse for an Easter basket.

Times have changed.

Now when I smell patchouli oil, I think of Margery — long, raven hair; full, sensuous lips as red as chilli peppers; black leather pants, so tight they could have been sprayed on her shapely legs

105

and buttocks; red blouse. She was young, attractive, gentle, kind, understanding and horny, everything this sixteen-year-old boy had ever fantasized about.

I wanted to take her home with me. A ridiculous idea for a lad of my pecuniary means, considering she would have cost me a hundred dollars or more a night.

But, oh, oh, oh!

To this very day, whenever I smell patchouli oil, I . . . well, never mind. Margery must have bathed in it, I think.

In the adjoining room, Uncle Kid spent the night in similar luxury with Letitia.

Al had arranged it all for us — the girls, rooms, champagne. All Uncle Kid had to do was dish out the cash. I've often wondered how much it cost him. A great deal, I suspect.

I also suspect that it would have cost a whole lot more if Al and Freddy had known they'd find nothing at all in the Jeep.

Uncle Kid didn't seem to care about the money — come easy, go easy. It was Mission Accomplished and well worth it, as far as he was concerned.

As for me?

I was touched.

7

There were ten or twelve old tires in our shed and we gathered up fifteen or twenty more from our neighbours. I rolled ours to the river, two at a time. Uncle Kid delivered the rest with the Jeep. Working in bathing suits and sneakers, we sank the whole lot with rocks, out in the channel where the water was deeper.

It was enjoyable work, really, and every tire rewarded us with a gentle, rolling little swell on the surface. The pool was beginning to look up. Even the current seemed to have quickened.

When the last tire was firmly in place, we sat on rocks on the shore and admired our work. The weakening sun of late August warmed us, but a cool breeze ran goose flesh across our skin. The same breeze chopped the water a bit, gave our pool even more of a turbulent appearance.

With a stick, I wrote "The Quinn Pool? The Lauder Pool?" in some sand at our feet.

Uncle Kid smiled, thought for a moment.

"How about . . . let's call it the Firestone Pool. What do you think?"

Firestone! "Ha!"

We shook hands on it.

Uncle Kid stood and began throwing rocks, skipping them across the surface of the water. There's nothing like the river to bring the boy out in the man.

I remained seated, watched him find and skip flat rock after flat rock. Every now and again, he'd pick up a bigger one, one the size of a saucer. These bigger ones would usually only skip once or twice, sometimes not at all.

Kerplunk!

"Ha!"

Uncle Kid was muscular and tanned. His long, brown hair hung loose — no ponytail today. The breeze played in it, must have felt good to him, perhaps tickled his shoulders. He was over forty, but he was as lean and trim as a twenty-five-year-old.

How long he intended to play I didn't know and didn't care. It was just good to be there in the sun by the river.

Suddenly, I got an idea. His shirt and pants were hanging on a wild rose bush by the riverbank. I went to it and removed his pouch, papers and lighter from his pockets.

Back on the rock, I rolled him a big, fat joint and lit it. He was so intent on rock-skipping that he didn't see me doing it, but he smelled the weed as soon as it was lit.

"Is this you intending to get high?" he asked.

I shook my head, offered the joint to him. I didn't need to smoke dope on such a day. I was high already. I had rolled it and lit it for him and him alone. I wanted to hear him talk, philosophize, rave.

He accepted the joint, sat beside me and smoked, deeply inhaling the hot narcotic. I could tell it was good weed, for he relaxed immediately and got a far-off look in his eyes.

"The cogs are turning," I thought. "He'll be raving in no time."

In a few seconds, he looked at me, grinned and said, "Ha!"

I grinned. When Uncle Kid was stoned, he was very, very pleasant to look at.

"You've rewarded me for my work," he said.

I nodded.

"Hungry? Want to go home and eat?"

I shook my head.

"No, me neither. I could stay here all day. Great place to be, eh?"

I grinned, winked.

"You know, one time I was sitting at the bar in the Beaverbrook Hotel in Fredericton and a young lady came in and sat beside me. She was a pretty good looker, so I tried to pick her up. You have to be cool to pick up women, but on that particular night I'd had a few too many and was not cool at all. I got off on the wrong foot right from the start.

"I said something stupid like, I don't know, do you want to go halves on a baby, or something. Turned her off.

"Where you from, she asked. Ha! I'm from the Miramichi, I said. There's nothing worse than a Miramichier abroad. We're all the same. We say, we're from the Miramichi! We're from the Miramichi! So goddamned proud, you'd think we were from some tropical island, paradise or somewhere!

"Anyway, this nice lady looks me up and down and says, you should stay there! Ha! All of a sudden, maybe it was the way she said it or something, but I thought I'd just told her I was from the Ozarks or some ghetto. You should stay there, she said! Ha! God! I can never understand women. They'd love to take over. They won't be happy until they rule the world. One day they will, too. They'll have the parliaments and the White House; they'll have the power to start wars and end them; they'll operate all the big machines, take all the toys away from the boys. And then they'll get into a big spat about what they should do with us men. Half the women will want to wipe the male population out, just keep a few of us good ones for breeding purposes. The other half will want to keep the lot of us, but for their pleasure, for doing the dirty work, as slaves.

"Women want a lot of things. Mankind in general wants a lot of things. But it seems that women are more ambitious, they want more. And . . . I think they'd be perfectly happy to live in Lesbos!

"And ya know, you can't blame them, really. Men are a pretty vile lot! Fighting and raping and murdering; whips and chains, slavery, apartheid, yokes on our women for centuries. Men fear women, feel threatened by them. Maybe they tried to wipe us out before, prehistorically! Who knows?

"But God! I can't understand them! You know what I said to that lady at the bar when she said I should stay on the Miramichi?"

I didn't know.

"I said . . . I wish."

"Ha!"

"It's the best, Corry! The very best! Ha! That lady, Paula was her name, I think. Anyway, for some mysterious reason, like I say, I don't understand women, but for some reason, she liked that, liked my pride or something. She lit right up as soon as I said it! Asked me my name, started up a big chat. Next thing you know, I was buying her dinner!

"Anyway, we have a pool here, Corry . . . sort of. The Firestone Pool! Salmon might stop here. Worth a try, anyway. If anyone asks, we'll tell them it's a high water pool. Most people won't know the difference. A high water pool is not worth a pinch of snuff for two thirds of the year, but if you're ignorant, an American or somebody, what's the difference?

"I can just picture those old Americans wading to the tops of their waders, trying to reach our car tires with their five-hundred-dollar graphites. Ha!"

A salmon jumped right in front of us, not more than fifty feet from shore, right in our own pool!

"Aha!" I exclaimed.

"Yeah. Going right through, unfortunately," said Uncle Kid. We've stirred the bottom up pretty good, moving rocks, splashing around, sinking all those tires. There's new little currents moving gravel in a way that it's never been moved before. No salmon will stick around for long this year. But next year, maybe, or the year after.

"You know, I've been thinking. Up in front of Karl Woods's place, there used to be a footbridge. A cable bridge, you know? The Swinging Bridge, they called it. There were a number of them on the river, but I'm talking about the one that used to be right up there. Know the one?"

I nodded. I knew what he was talking about. The abutments were still there. That's where I got the rocks for our pool.

"Well, they called it the Swinging Bridge because it must have been two hundred yards long, just hanging there on four cables, two on the top and two on the bottom. When the wind came up, it would sway like a bastard. Not a good outfit to try and walk on when you'd had a few too many. Drink a couple of bottles of cheap sherry and walk on a cable bridge sometime, if you wanna know the meaning of the word sick!

"It hung so low that in the spring, the water would rise, and if it came up a little bit farther than usual, it would run right through it. Sometimes the ice would come down and snap the cables, take the bridge out completely. Snap them cables just as if they were twine.

"Anyway, way back, it was a major crossing place in this area — people crossing it all the time, kids going to school, people going to work, visiting their neighbours, going to the store, coming over to catch the train, coming over to Mom's to get their haircuts and perms. And about every third year, the ice would take out the bridge and those people over there would be left stranded. It was too dangerous for women and kids to cross the river in canoes in the spring, anyway. The high water, heavy crosscurrents, upriver ice coming down . . .

"So a bunch of the boys, my father and Uncle Peter, Old Dave Larkin, Elec Parks, a bunch of them, decided to build an abutment in the middle of the river, one high enough to hold the cables out of the water, no matter how high it got.

"Now, I've been thinking about that abutment. I've been thinking about it for two reasons. One, when they built the abutment, they did it in the middle of the winter. They needed thousands of rocks and the best way to transport them out to the abutment was with teams of horses, on the ice. And when they finally got it built, and now I'm coming around to the other thought I'm thinking about — they had this huge abutment, twenty feet high, fifteen feet in diameter, smack in the middle of the river.

"Well, before that, there had been nothing but a big, flat, slow moving river up there, same as it is right here. But when the current came down and hit that abutment, it rolled and swirled, eddied here, rushed there. Pretty soon the bottom of the river began to move around. First thing ya know, a big gravel bar began to build up about a hundred yards below the bridge. Within five or six years, there were half a dozen bars of various sizes in various places below that abutment — channels and currents rushing every which way.

"Well, sir, people started to fish there. Not only that, but it turned out to be the very best of a pool. You know the pool! The Yankovitch Pool! Salmon all over the place!"

"Ha!"

"Karl Woods owned it back then and Karl was kind of poor. Jesus! It was like finding a gold mine! He up and sold it to old Leo Yankovitch from New Jersey, got something like thirty thousand dollars for it! Thirty thousand was a lot of money back then.

"Anyway, I was thinking, if we had a big pile of rocks right up there in the middle of the river, say about up there, out from the quicksand, the same thing could happen here. And we could do it in the same way. We'll hire a truck to deliver us five or six loads of big boulders, and this winter, when the ice is good and thick, we'll either borrow a horse and sled or haul them out there with the Jeep, dump them in a big pile, and in the spring, the rocks will warm up and melt through the ice, and bingo! We'll have our abutment, our current-changer! What do you think?"

I was thinking that old Leo Yankovitch might not be a very happy man when he returned that fall to find a big part of his abutment missing. I knew there was a pool below the old abutment, but I hadn't known that the abutment was why it was there.

With my stick, I wrote, "A good idea!" in the sand.

"So, then, that's what we're going to do," said Uncle Kid. "Put a pile of rocks up there and let the river do the rest. No sense fooling around!"

*

A few days later, on the first of September, Uncle Kid went to work guiding for Burpee Storey. This time there was no discussion of whether I'd get to stay home alone or not. Uncle Kid simply announced that Burpee needed a guide, jumped in his Jeep and went, leaving me to share the house with the silence.

September.

Fewer birds and insects, no mating calls to speak of, no peepers in the swamp — it's quiet in September. The sun has lost much of its radiance, allowing the haze to creep a bit closer; trees paint their nails and apply their rouge; geese finger their dog-eared tour guides; the salmon are on the move and have come-on twinkles in their eyes. In paradise, it's September all year round.

One morning I was sitting in the kitchen, drinking coffee, watching two house flies fornicating on the table and listening to the radio, a talk show out of CBC Fredericton. The host was interviewing two dancers, a man and a woman from the Royal Winnipeg Ballet.

"I can't tell you how much I enjoyed the performance last night," said the host in that smooth, articulate CBC voice.

There had not been a grain of sarcasm in the way he said it, but I chose, perhaps out of boredom, to exaggerate that mere figure of speech into literal meaning. I was like an incompetent, hungry news reporter sensationalizing some politician's slip of the tongue.

My thoughts toyed with: "Who *is* this guy? Why doesn't he think before he speaks? Here's a guy who makes a very comfortable living with his voice and his ability to properly announce and pronounce, and he's saying, I can't *tell* you!"

And then the announcer said, "Now, here's a segment from last night's show, Stravinsky's *Le Sacre du Printemps*," and my indignation flew from me like a trailing goose amid a flock of "Ha, ha, ha!"s. There I was in my bathrobe, sitting in my kitchen on the Miramichi, a guy who literally couldn't put two words together, *listening* to a ballet, a dance!

I realized my cynicism — of course the announcer was introducing the wonderful music. But I was waltzing with the devil, felt like picking the scab, tearing everything apart.

I thought, "The next thing ya know, he'll be introducing a magician! Keep your ear close to the radio and don't touch that dial! I'm going to make the Saint John River disappear! Presto! Wasn't that wonderful, ladies and gentlemen? Wish you were here to see it. You don't believe me? Well, I guess you're just going to have to take my word for it. Believe me, the Saint John River is no more!

"Next, for all you listeners at home and in your cars, on the beach, or wherever you may be, coming to you live and in white-face all the way from France, Monsieur Marcel Marceau!

"Monsieur Marceau, of course, will perform his famous character, Bip, for you. And, without further ado, let the show begin. Now, listen carefully. Bip is now sitting on a park bench. peeling a banana. I think what he's doing now is eating it. Wow! For all you folks out there listening, I must tell you, there's no park bench and, believe it or not, there's no banana. But, boy!"

The irony was too much for me. I laughed until I was gasping for breath, red in the face and teary-eyed. The tears dropped from my face and into my coffee, fertilizing it, impregnating it. When I drank it, I consumed my destiny. It entered my stomach, oozed through its walls and warmed my blood. In a moment, it surfaced and formed a single word in my brain. And oh, what a word it was! A four letter word! A word I could say! It was a Latin-sounding word with Ms that made it mellow, magical, mesmerizing, poetic. It was a word that belonged to me.

I said it again and again and again. It dangled powerful, irresistible lifelines to me. Until that word popped into my head, I had been one of the malefactors on the cross — a lost soul, condemned to die. But a word from Jesus and all would be well.

Guy on the left: "If thou be Christ, save thyself and us."

Guy on the right: "Dost not thou not fear God, seeing thou art in the same condemnation? And we indeed justly; for we receive the due reward of our deeds: but this man hath done nothing amiss. He only played Bip."

"What's that?"

"It's Marcel Marceau between us."

"Oh, oh! A mime!"

"Rather awkward, isn't it?"

Mime.

"Mime, mime, mime, mime, mime."

Repeating the word over and over and over, I picked an imaginary cherry from an imaginary bowl, tossed it in the air, watched it rise and fall. I caught it in my mouth. It was sweet, delicious and wholesome. I sucked it and chewed it, spit out the pit and swallowed the flesh.

I picked up an imaginary wedge of lemon, tossed it, caught it in my mouth. Oh! How sour it was! My jaws contracted, my shoulders shrugged involuntarily, my mouth distorted, my eyes glossed over.

"Mime."

Sign language? Ha!

"Mime."

Lip reading? Ha!

"Mime!"

Becoming an outfitter? Ha!

"Mime."

I ran from the kitchen and up the stairs, three at a time. I entered the bathroom, threw off my robe and stood naked before the full length mirror.

"Mime."

I looked at my body as if for the first time.

"My palace," I thought.

I ran my fingers through my long, thick, sandy-coloured hair. I stared into my big hazel eyes. I sized up my nose — high bridge, straight, Greek. I needed a shave. I puckered my lips, frowned, smiled — long teeth. Good teeth. I looked tall — six feet, maybe. I flexed my biceps, tightened my chest and stomach muscles. My legs — long, tanned, fuzzy blond hair.

I danced a little jig.

"Mime."

I ate an imaginary apple.

"Mime."

I humped an imaginary woman.

"Mime."

I cradled an imaginary baby in my arms.

"Mime."

An imaginary fly flew every which way about my head. I followed it with my eyes.

"Mime."

Dearest Anne,
   That letter I mailed to you a week ago? So much has changed since then! Let me start from the beginning, with my wanting to be a writer.

Dear Mr. and Ms. Masters,
   I sincerely apologize for the way I acted at your house last week. I should have appreciated your concern, instead of feeling patronized.

Dear Uncle Kid,
   No sense beating around the bush. I owe you so much and have been grateful for so little. You've been blaming yourself for my condition. Well, blame yourself no more. It was I who tongued the spike, not you. And because of you, my condition is not so bad. I am in good condition, as a matter of fact, especially now that I have discovered my destiny.
   Uncle Kid, I want to be a mime.
   Think about it, Uncle Kid. Think about it for days, if you must. Then, tell me truthfully what you think.

My letter to Uncle Kid went on for several pages. I told him I still wanted to be an outfitter, that I would put even more effort into that endeavour but with professional miming the higher goal in mind. I explained that I would probably need to go to a school of acting or some such thing, and that the outfitting business, if successful, would supply the money needed to see things through. Mime schools are apt to be in London, Paris or some place in Italy. "You could go with me," I wrote. "You would finally get to see Florence."
   That evening, when he opened the letter and saw how lengthy it was, he said, "What's this, your last will and testament?"

116

I touched my heart and assumed a pose I hoped suggested the horizon.

"Hmm," he said and went to the living room to read.

I remained in the kitchen, and in a little while he returned.

"Do you still plan to be a writer?" he asked.

I nodded.

"And a guide?"

Nod.

"An outfitter."

Nod.

"A mime."

Nod.

"It would be nice to keep the old farm operating, too, wouldn't it?"

Nod.

"And do a little fishing."

Nod.

"Go to the North Pole Stream and be Denise's assistant?"

Nod.

"Well, you don't need me to confirm your every whim. I think it's a good idea. It'll help you communicate better. There'll be ups and downs, ins and outs, lots of directions. How long have you been thinking about this miming stuff?"

I had my pen poised for answers.

"All day," I jotted. "I did not go to school today."

Uncle Kid smiled, nearly chuckled, thought for a moment, sighed.

"Well, in that case, I do have a little advice for you. When I was a boy I decided I wanted to play the guitar. Around here, there were people who could teach me music, but not a single soul could teach me much about the guitar. Nubert showed me how to apply a few chords, Bill Hall taught me a few more and that was about it. So I had to teach myself.

"I'd been playing for about ten years and living in Fredericton before I found a real guitarist who'd teach me. And you know what? I was the most frustrated, miserable student that fellow ever took on. I was doing everything wrong! I didn't even know how to hold a pick correctly! I was putting the G-chord on wrong! And what was worse, I was set in my ways. The new things, the right way of doing things, felt clumsy to me. I gave up, couldn't be bothered. I had no plans to be a great guitarist anyway, and I was already good enough to back myself at the odd party. So my advice is, before you start into practising and miming everything the wrong way, we'll go to wherever we need to go and get some books on the subject. I don't know if mime books can be found in Fredericton or not. I doubt it. Maybe there's no such thing as a mime book. But, if there is, we'll find one somewhere, Boston maybe, New York.

"Remember we saw that French lad on TV? Marcel Godot?"

I wrote, "Marceau."

"Yeah, Marceau Godot. Well, he must have learned to mime somewhere. I doubt if he invented it."

Miming as a form of communication is as old as the hills. Miming as an art form is ancient but was practically forgotten until guys like Etienne Decroux and Marcel Marceau came along. In reality, miming, the French Classical Mime that we're familiar with today, *was* invented by Marcel Marceau, although he was taught by Decroux. However, Uncle Kid and I didn't know that at the time.

"Do you know what I think? Did I ever tell you what I think?" asked Uncle Kid.

I waited.

"I think that animals are the greatest mimes on earth. For all we know, every time they blink an eye, wag a tail, lift a paw, it might mean something. It would be hilarious if they were the smart ones and we were the stupid ones, wouldn't it?

"Anyway, we've had these hands and these brains for about half a million years, inherited them from old great grandfather Homo Erectus, and the rest is history. I have a feeling miming was in in a big way before then. Ha! The day that history began!

"You know, Corry, you have to ask yourself, Why? Why do people try to do so much? Money? The luxurious state? Fame? Good? Knowledge? Immortality?"

I wrote, "Survival."

"Yeah, well . . . you have to ask yourself if any of us do survive. It seems to me that none of us do. Survive until you die. People work all their lives for material things, then die and leave all the material things behind. Kind of crazy, isn't it?"

I shrugged.

"Well, I think I'll go down to the Legion, have a beer and throw some darts. That OK with you?"

I nodded.

"Oh, by the way. There's a party at Burpee's camps Saturday night. You're invited."

"Me?"

"Yeah! You!"

"Ha!"

I made a bit of a fool of myself at the party. Milly Minor was there. My heart quickened the moment I saw her. She did not see me right away. But when she did? Bang! My penis saluted. When I smiled back at her, she quickly turned away. She glanced at me two more times in the next five minutes but did not smile.

Then she started talking to Kent Holmes. I could not hear what they were talking about, but I could see they were having fun — smiling, laughing.

Uncle Kid was playing the guitar and singing, "Dre-e-e-eam, dream, dream" in harmony with Bill Hall and Nubert Minor. They were in the living room, and I noticed the forty-ouncer of scotch that Uncle Kid had contributed to the party was alone and unattended in the kitchen. I poured myself half a glass and tossed it back.

I went back to the living room.

Uncle Kid, Bill and Nubert were so into the song that they had their eyes closed, and Uncle Kid had stopped playing the guitar so they could hear themselves better.

Milly was still talking with Kent.

I wondered if they'd mind me joining them and participating in the conversation, and the thought made me laugh right out loud.

Milly and Kent looked at me curiously, shrugged and kept on talking.

Back to the kitchen for another double.

"Damn Kent Holmes," I thought. "Damn him! What to do . . . who does he think he is? *I'm* Corry Quinn. I'm intelligent and good looking. *I'm* a mime."

With this thought I had a third drink, toasted myself.

In the living room, Uncle Kid and the boys had picked up the pace a bit and were harmonizing "Old Stewball was a racehorse, And I wish he were mine, He never drank water, He always drank wi-i-i-ine . . ."

About twenty people were talking and laughing at the same time. Alice Hunter came into the kitchen and said, "Hi, Corry. What are you doing out here all by yourself?"

I shrugged, poured some more scotch into my glass and toasted her. Alice Hunter and I were the same age. Alice Hunter was about five feet tall, weighed about a hundred and forty pounds and smiled a lot. When Alice Hunter smiled, she revealed her very long gums and very short teeth. She had blond hair and freckles and wore glasses. Alice Hunter was a very friendly girl. I put my arm around her and sang to her. "O ooah uz a eh hor, A I iss e er iii . . ."

"Ha, ha, ha! That's good, Corry. You should join the men inside. You're better than they are."

I was putting too much of my weight on her. She removed my arm and stepped back, smiling.

"You're going into grade twelve this year, aren't you?"

I nodded.

"Have any idea what you're going to do when you graduate?"

"Mime," I said. God, it felt good to be able to say that!

"Mime? Ha, ha, ha! I hate mimes!"

I pretended to be hurt. "Oooh."

"Ha! I find that incredibly funny! Corry Quinn a mime. It makes so much sense! How does one become a mime, Corry?"

I could think of only one way to answer her question. I picked up an imaginary glass and drank from it.

"Ha, ha, ha! That's wonderful! You're pretty good!" said Alice.

Things started to get a little hazy about then, the scotch was beginning to work its mischief and miracles. Much of the rest of that evening I have no memory of at all. The two things I do remember, however, are that I made a fool of myself trying to get Milly's attention, and, later, I ended up necking with Alice outside on the veranda.

Encouraged by Alice's response to my pretending to drink from the imaginary glass in the kitchen, and emboldened by the scotch that I really did drink, I made my way back to the living room to try my luck with Milly. She and Kent were still talking and smiling and laughing and touching. I didn't like it at all.

I know now how I should have acted; I know now what I should have done. I should have shrugged and walked away, I should have gone home. But alcohol encouraged the fool in me and I revealed him in more ways than I like to remember. I put myself in a conspicuous position, in a place where I knew she could not avoid seeing me. I posed, showed her my best side. When her eyes gave me nothing more than the minutest acknowledgement, nothing more than you'd give to a fly zipping by, I exaggerated my pose, straightened my shoulders, threw my head back, became the arrogant aristocrat. This she ignored completely.

It's funny how you can remember some things and forget others, but I remember thinking, "Milly, Milly, look at me." I would have given a toe or a finger for a mere smile.

I moved closer. I wanted to listen to their conversation, to hear what it was that had them so engaged that they couldn't give me a pleasant look.

Kent was tall, tanned and good-looking, had a brushcut, wore that perpetual smile that some people have even as he talked.

Kid and the boys were singing "Angie," and Kent was commenting on the performance.

"My God, they think they're the Rolling Stones," he said smoothly. "The next thing they'll be doin' 'Jumping Jack Flash.'"

Milly laughed easily at this. I could see her eyes watching his smile, his eyes. It was plain that she liked him.

"I didn't see you at the dance last weekend," she said.

Kent shrugged. "I was in Halifax. Went down to see the McCormicks."

"Any good?"

"Real good. There's three of them. One plays the guitar, one plays the fiddle and the other plays both the accordion and the tin whistle. Irish all the way. Love it. In two or three of the songs, the fiddle player switches to the bagpipes. We went down Friday, caught the show Friday night and went back to see them Saturday night."

"Where were they playing?"

"In a pub, The Stout Kilkennian. Great time."

"You're not old enough to drink in a pub, are you?"

"No, but they thought I was."

Then, like the crack of a whip, Milly looked at me. "Why are you staring at me, Corry? You've been staring at me all evening."

"Has he been staring at you?" asked Kent."

"Yeah. Ever since I stepped into the room."

"He's drunk," said Kent, looking me up and down. "Go home, Corry, you're drunk."

This confrontation caught me off guard and without thinking, I said, "I orry."

"What?"

"I orry."

When they laughed right out loud at my attempt to apologize, I wanted to cry. I reached to my shirt pocket for my pen and pad, wrote "I'm sorry," tore out the page and handed it to Milly.

"It's OK," she said, and she and Kent resumed their conversation as if nothing had happened, ignoring me completely.

"Where were we?" asked Milly.

"Halifax," said Kent. "Ever been to Halifax?"

"No, but I'd like to go sometime. It's big, isn't it?"

"Sort of, I mean, it's not like Toronto or Montreal, but, yeah, it's big."

Too drunk to do the right thing and get the hell out of there, I lingered and stupidly wrote, "I was in Saint John not long ago," and handed it to Kent.

Kent read, chuckled, crumpled the paper and tossed it in an ashtray.

"There must be lots to do down there," said Milly.

"Oh, yeah, there must be hundreds of bars. When I graduate, I think I'd like to go to Dalhousie University."

Kent Holmes was not very bright. Kent Holmes would not get into Dal in a million years. I thought I could do something with this knowledge and wrote, "He might get into Moncton Tech on a bribe." I handed this little joke to Milly.

She read, looked at me angrily, crumpled up the paper and said, "C'mon Kent, let's get a Pepsi."

"What did he write? What did he say to you?" asked Kent.

"Nothing," said Milly. "C'mon, there's Pepsi in the rec room."

I blamed this rude exclusion of me on Kent. I felt that he had somehow manipulated the whole situation to put me at a disadvantage, that he had seen her smiling at me and out of jealousy had made some disparaging remark. I was so angry that I wanted to punch him in the mouth, to turn that perpetual smile into a toothless gape.

"They're assholes," said Alice, startling me, snapping me away from my grimace or whatever it was I was doing.

It was obvious Alice had been watching the whole episode and had ruled in my favour. I realized that to save face I had to pull myself together, and I did it with a simple shrug, as if the whole affair had meant nothing to me. I've learned how to do that very well, to shrug things off, to save the tears for later. It was one of the things I started practising how to do shortly after I met God in the hospital. The only one I could not fool with the act was Uncle Kid. He always knew when I was hurt.

"Let's go and sit on the veranda," suggested Alice, taking my arm.

"Uh-uh," I said, holding back. The last thing I wanted was to be seen leaving with Alice Hunter.

Alice took it that I was reluctant to follow her because I wanted to pursue Kent and Milly. What I really wanted to do was have a drink.

"C'mon, Corry," she urged. "You're better than they are. Let them go."

Alice smiled at me.

"Why would anyone with such long gums and short teeth smile so much?" I asked myself.

She reached up and fixed my hair, allowed her hand to caress and linger for a second on my cheek.

I had a thought, wrote, "Go ahead. I'll get a drink and join you."

"Oh, well. OK." she said. "Don't be long."

I went to the kitchen thinking how easy it had been to get rid of her.

I poured myself a drink, tossed it down and poured myself another. I don't remember much more. I guess I went into another stage of intoxication. I know I necked with Alice Hunter on the veranda, and I recall that, much later, after Alice, Milly, Kent and most of the other people had gone home, I sang "She had pimples on her but she was nice" with Uncle Kid, Burpee Storey and Bill Hall. "She had pimples on her but she was nice" are all the words I know to that song. That's one of the few advantages of not being able to talk, you never have to come up with the right words.

After the queasiness and headaches, after the guilt, self-condemnation and depression, after the hangover, three days later I saw Milly Minor. We were at school and it was during the noon break. I was standing just outside a circle of boys and she was about a hundred feet away, talking with Mary Lynn Thomas and Sheila Hammill.

When I saw her standing there talking easily and smiling often, it suddenly occurred to me that she was not nearly as pretty as I had previously thought. She still looked exactly the same, of course, but after that ugly encounter at the party I was simply not seeing her in the same light. It was the smile that had lost its beauty for me. Where I had previously seen a warm kindness, I was now seeing frivolity, shallowness, an expression filled with mockery. I was contemplating this and staring at the phenomenon more so than the girl when I suddenly realized that she was staring at me. Not wanting her to think that I had been staring at her, I turned away. I was too late. When I heard laughter coming from their direction, I gave them a quick glance and saw that they were all watching me, that I was the source of their humour.

Leaving my friends as quickly as possible, I marched into the school, vowing I would never look at Milly Minor again. "If she ever comes into my line of vision, I'll look over her, or beneath her, but never at her," I thought. "I'll ignore her completely."

But Milly had hurt me deeply and it was difficult to ignore that.

I went to school every day and avoided her the best I could. Looking down, I learned, was the best way to not make eye contact with her.

Although both Milly and I walked to school most days, in bad weather we took the school bus. I lived a little further up the Hemlock Road than she did, which meant that I boarded the bus first. When she got on, I'd pick up a book and read so that I wouldn't have to see her. On one particularly stormy day, the bus was so full of kids that the seat beside me was the only vacant one in the bus. When she got on, she walked past me and all the way to the back of the bus and stood. I heard one of the boys in the back of the bus say to her, "Why don't you sit with Corry, Milly?"

Her reply was, "Go to hell, Mike!" much to the amusement of some of the others back there.

The next thing I knew, which only added to my embarrassment, Alice Hunter came up and sat beside me, giving her seat to Milly.

"How are you, Corry?" she asked.

"OK," I replied, but only because it was easier for me to say than words like terrible, awful, miserable, and I wish I were dead.

"I kept your notes," she said.

"Huh?"

"All the notes you wrote to me on the veranda that night at Burpee's party, I kept them."

"Oh."

Those notes. Yes, I had written her notes. A whole bunch of notes. But I couldn't remember a word. God only knows what I wrote. God and Alice Hunter and hopefully not everyone else in the community.

Feeling a little bit smothered, I nodded.

Alice smiled, short teeth, long gums.

126

Over the next few days, I found myself in a ridiculous situation. On one hand, I was trying not to look at Milly Minor, and on the other hand, I found myself trying to avoid being looked at by Alice Hunter. I was crossing the school's parking lot and heard someone call, "Hi, Corry!" It was Alice. Later that day, I was accompanying a couple of the guys who were stealing a smoke on the windowless end of the school, when all of a sudden Alice joined us and stood close beside me. "How are you today, Corry?" Because of heavy rain, I took the bus on Thursday and Alice sat with me. I went to the school dance on Friday night and Alice Hunter asked me to dance eleven times.

But the Alice predicament I felt I could control. I could allow her into my world or ignore her, depending on how I felt. I was not exactly popular. Everyone needs somebody occasionally. There's an old joke that goes: "Hey Fred, how's your wife?" "Oh, she's better than nothing." To me, having Alice around was better than having nobody at all.

Milly, on the other hand, was becoming downright impossible to manage. The ball was continuously in Milly's end of the court and she served it with a malice that could only have been premeditated. I could not understand why she hated me so much. When I think about it today, I suppose her malice stemmed from a social thing: for some reason, the more she worked me over, the more popular she became; she was playing the role of someone tormented by an admirer. God knows what she was saying behind my back.

She was always in a group, and if for some reason I needed to walk past that group, I always felt their eyes, heard the snorts, comments and laughter.

The next Friday, I was walking up the Hemlock Road from school when I noticed Milly walking ahead of me. She was not a fast walker, so I found myself slowing my pace so as not to close the gap between us. I could usually walk the distance between school and home in fifteen or twenty minutes, but on that day I was sure it would take me twice that long, and I was a little annoyed with the fact that she was interfering with my rhythm. "Why should I feel I·have to slow my pace just because she happens to be in front

127

of me?" I asked myself. "I have a right to walk as fast or as slow as I want. It's a free world. Why shouldn't I catch up with her and walk past her like she didn't exist? Maybe it would put her in her place."

I quickened my pace, closed the gap by half.

Suddenly, she quickened her pace.

"Good," I thought. "That's more like it."

She was nearly home, approaching her driveway, and I was grateful that I would not catch up with her after all. "Thank God for small blessings," I thought. "From here on, I'll have the road to myself, to cover as I please."

When she got to the entrance of her driveway, she did a peculiar thing. She stopped, turned and looked at me. She was still a hundred yards away, but I could see, perhaps from the way she held her head or hands or something, that she was quite angry. The look in her eyes, even from that distance, jarred me, made me feel like a little boy being reprimanded by the mere glare of a parent. Or perhaps it was even worse, like falling under the evil eye of a witch. It made my skin crawl, the hair rise on the back of my neck.

I didn't know how to react. Shit! I'm stupid sometimes! Instead of looking down, or away, or at anything but her, I shrugged and waved.

She responded by stomping her foot and running as fast as she could down the driveway and into the house.

"Hell!" I thought. "I just gave her more material, more ammunition to throw at me."

I couldn't have imagined the arsenal I'd given her until the bomb fell later that evening.

It was after supper, and I was in the living room watching *Cheers* or some such program on TV, when someone knocked at the door.

"I'll get it," said Uncle Kid, who was ironing a shirt in the kitchen, getting ready to go to the Legion.

I heard him open the front door.

"Nubert!" I heard him say. "Come in! Come in!"

Then I heard Nubert say, "I'm not here to be sociable, Kid. I'm very, very pissed off."

"What's the problem, Nubert?"

"Well, it's a difficult matter, Kid. It's your nephew, Corry."

"Corry? Corry's inside. I'll call him."

"No, no. I'm too angry to talk to 'im. I'll not bandy words with you, Kid. You and I've been friends for a long time and have always been straight and to the point with each other. Your nephew . . . Corry has been stalking my daughter."

The bombshell. That miserable, awful girl! How could she do this to me?

I could hear the conversation as plainly as if they were there in the living room with me. I wanted to run, or crawl under the sofa. I did not want to be confronted with this ridiculous accusation. Not, at least, until I had a chance to think. I started to tremble with rage and fear.

"Stalking? What d'ya mean, stalking?" asked Uncle Kid.

"He follows her around, watches her, stares at her. Kid, I'm telling you right now, tell him to lay off or I'll kick the shit out of him!"

"Hold on, now, Nubert! We haven't heard Corry's side of the story yet."

"I don't need to hear Corry's side of the story! My daughter knows what she knows. My daughter has never lied to me. What reason would she have to make up such a story?" Nubert grew more angry at this point, raised his voice. "That asshole Corry has been giving my daughter a hard time and I want it to stop! Do ya hear? I want it to stop!"

"I'll call 'im."

"No! No, I don't want to see 'im. I'm too angry. I'll lose it. You talk to 'im. But just make sure you get the point across. I want him to lay off my daughter!"

"I will, I will, Nubert. I'll tell him. It won't happen again."

"Good. That's all I have to say. See ya later!"

I heard the door slam and Uncle Kid swear. Uncle Kid slowly entered the living room and turned off the TV. He looked at me and I looked at him. He sighed and I sighed.

"Did you hear that?" he asked.

I nodded.

"Is it true?"

I shook my head.

"Then what's it all about, Corry? What the hell's goin' on?"

I shook my head again. I don't know.

"Got your pen and pad?"

I picked up my pad and with an unsteady hand wrote, "We walked home from school. I was on the road behind her. That's all."

Uncle Kid sat on the sofa beside me, sighed.

I waited for him to say something. When he didn't, I wrote "She's playing games."

"Why?" he asked. "Why would she be playing games."

I shrugged.

"How long's this been going on?"

"She hates me," I wrote. "I don't know why."

Another sigh from Uncle Kid told me that he was confused, that he didn't know how to handle the matter. He was finally confronted with a problem that he could not rave on about.

"I think this is a . . . a very serious situation," he said in a moment. "Nubert said you've been staring at her."

I wrote, "I don't think so. Maybe at first. She's pretty. But not now. I try not to look at her now."

"But you did at first?"

"I don't think so."

"It's obvious that she thinks so."

"I have not been stalking her! I don't even like her anymore," I wrote.

Uncle Kid gave this some thought, then said, almost as if to himself, "I suppose you're a mystery to her. You probably play a big role in her imagination. You might even frighten her. You'll have to stay away from her, Corry."

"I've been trying!" I wrote. "She thinks I'm staring! But I'm not! Don't you believe me?"

"I don't know! How am I to know what to believe? You either are or you ain't! Hell! What am I supposed to do?"

"No sense talking to you," I thought, jumped up and ran to my room, feeling very defeated. I didn't even bother to turn on the lights, just sat there in the darkness, listening to the pounding of my heart, trying to grasp onto a single thought that would make sense of all of this. I successfully, stubbornly fought back the tears. I was too angry to cry.

Then Uncle Kid tapped lightly on the door.

"Corry?"

I didn't answer, of course.

He waited a few seconds, then opened the door. He stood and looked at me, a silhouette framed by the light behind him. With his long hair hanging over his shoulders, he could have been a Biblical prophet, Jesus.

"It's Friday night," he said and waited for me to respond. When I didn't, I heard him sigh again.

"Yeah. It's Friday night. Isn't there a school dance tonight?" he asked.

"Yeah." I felt like such a child.

"You going?"

I shook my head. "Uh-uh."

"Because of Milly?"

"Yeah."

"Well, I think you should go."

"Huh?"

"I think you should go. If you don't, it'll look like you have something to hide."

I questioned him with my eyes.

"You have the upper hand, Corry. Whether you know it or not, you have the upper hand. What she's got going against her is her ability to communicate. She's the one doing all the talking. People will notice, people will watch what is going on. You're not saying a word, can't say a word. You will not lie or scheme against her. All the malice will be hers. There's a certain power in saying very little, and that's where you have the advantage. Go to the dance, have a good time. Go clean up and change. I'll wait for you and drive you to the school."

I did as I was told, but as far as I was concerned, it was very shaky advice.

Uncle Kid dropped me off at the school about an hour later.

131

Got enough money?" he asked.

I nodded.

"Want me to pick you up after the dance?"

I shrugged.

"Well, I'll drop around about twelve. If you're here . . ."

I nodded.

"OK. Be good. See ya later."

I had no heart for going to a dance. All I really wanted to do was go home and sulk. I couldn't see how confronting the situation was going to do anything but make matters worse. It seemed to me the best thing to do was to stay as far away from Milly as possible, to never lay eyes on her again. "But how? How can two people exist in such a small community and at the same time completely avoid each other?"

I bought a ticket and entered the school auditorium. There was a pretty good turnout for the dance, about eighty people, ranging from fourteen to seventeen years old. Milly was there, sitting at a table with several other people at the far end of the room, close to the stage. She was talking with Larry Scott and I don't think she noticed me enter. I beelined to the opposite end of the room, back to where the refreshment booth was. I wanted a Pepsi but rather than try to communicate this with the girl and guy working the booth, I decided to do without. Instead, I found myself a wall to lean against and stood there watching the room, the mingling teenagers, the dancers. The music was loud, a mixture of new and old rock and some country. Milly danced with Larry a couple of times and then she abandoned him for Kent Holmes. After only one dance, she went back to Larry. Then she danced with Kent again.

"Larry and Kent are competing," I thought. "That's good. At least she's occupied and I don't have to bother."

It suddenly occurred to me that I was watching her. "Damn!" I thought and quickly turned to watch whatever might be happening at the refreshment booth.

"What's the sense in this?" I asked myself. "How can I avoid seeing her? I'm in the same room, for Christ sake!"

"Hi, Corry!"

Alice Hunter approached me, smiling, looking stupid. Her hair was permed, she wore big earrings, dangling, glittering rhinestones that could only be her mother's. She was wearing a white dress that was probably her mother's, too.

"Better than nothing," I thought. "Better than nothing."

I danced with Alice for the rest of the evening.

Just once, by accident, I made eye contact with Milly Minor. Milly seized the opportunity, threw her head back and laughed theatrically. It was obvious that she was playing a role, making fun of me for dancing with Alice.

I suddenly grew very fond of Alice. The seas were rough and at the time I thought Alice a great old port.

9

Late Sunday afternoon, Mark and Denise Masters dropped in to visit us. They were on their way home from a weekend of hiking in the mountains of central New Brunswick, the North Pole Stream area. They looked tired and in need of a bath, smelled of wood smoke and the forest. Uncle Kid offered them a drink.

"A small one," said Mark. "I still have to drive to Saint John."

"He's driving, make mine a double," said Denise.

We sat around the kitchen table.

"Must've been a bit on the cool side for camping," commented Uncle Kid.

"Not too bad, really," said Mark. "We're well rigged up. But, you know, there's a bit of snow in there already."

"High country. Any signs of the cat?"

"Kid, I tell ya, I could smell him. I *know* he's there. I *know* he is! But no, not a sign. Ya can't do much in a weekend, though."

"We saw a couple of moose crossing the road and a deer drinking from the river," put in Denise. "It's beautiful country in there."

"Many hunters?" asked Kid.

"I think that's the problem. Too many hunters. We didn't have time to hike deep enough into the forest. You gotta get in beyond the range of the hunters. That cat can smell a hunter a mile away." Mark seemed a bit frustrated.

"He can also smell us," added Denise.

"That's what makes it so damned difficult," said Mark. "But one day, we'll luck out, be down wind from him, take the devil by surprise."

"And just hope that he doesn't take you by surprise," said Uncle Kid.

"Bah! They're scared to death of humans. Why do you think they're so elusive? Have you given any thought to what you might be doing next summer, Kid?"

"Not much, really. I think it might be pretty difficult to leave here. There's Izaak Walton's and we'd have to lock up the house. Some of the neighbours around here are pretty shady, would break in the place sure as hell. One of us might be able to go with you, but I don't think it would be wise for us both to leave."

"We could sure use another person or two," sighed Mark. "It would give us so much more time and freedom for the actual search. Someone to look after things, keep the camp fire burning, so to speak."

"Well, I can't think of any reason why Corry here couldn't go," said Uncle Kid.

"How about it, Corry? Want to join us next summer? All you'll have to do is be a happy camper."

I nodded, shrugged. Maybe.

Denise smiled at me warmly. "And what have you been up to, Corry?" she asked. "Writing anything these days?"

"Uh-uh."

Uncle Kid spoke for me. "Corry's been busy enough. Besides this place and school, he's been thinking about getting into miming. Pantomime, if you know what I mean."

"Pantomime! Really!" said Denise, smiling affectionately. "How wonderful!"

"Ha! Makes sense to me!" said Mark as if he had just caught onto a good joke. "Why not, eh, Corry?"

"I think it's a wonderful idea," said Denise. "I love the mime. I had a friend who studied mime. She's an actress, now, and a very good one. She claims learning to mime helped her career a lot."

I perked up when I heard this. Here was a possible contact, someone who could give me some basic information. Denise, the most perceptive person I've ever met, noticed my interest.

As usual, I had my pen and paper handy. I wrote, "Is there such a thing as a book on mime?"

"Well, I suppose there is," answered Denise. "At the library probably. But of course, you're a long way from a library. I could call my friend Tina. She probably has books, or at least she might be able to give you a few titles."

In that otherwise depressing fall, this was a very exciting consideration.

I wrote, "Please and thank you" on my pad.

"I'll do that, Corry," said Denise. "I'll check out the library *and* talk to Tina. You'll have books, I guarantee it."

Smiling, she reached out and touched my hand.

Denise Masters had a pug nose, was short and a bit overweight, and on that day she was not wearing makeup, but I thought she was amazingly beautiful.

"I have this dream, Kid," said Mark. "I dream that I'm in the forest with all my best photography equipment at hand. And all of a sudden, there it is, right there in front of me, standing right out in the open, paying me no more attention than if I were a tree. And don't you know it, I can't get the camera to work. No matter how hard I try, I can't get the damn camera to work. So I call to Denise to come and witness the fact that he's there. At least I'll have a witness, I think. But Denise either can't hear me or chooses to ignore me. It's a nightmare, Kid, because the cat runs off into the woods and I can't even find a track to photograph. And when I tell Denise, she laughs."

"Anxiety, Mark. What will you do when you finally do photograph it? Seems to me there'll be a big void in your life. You'll have nothing to pursue."

"Not a void, Kid. Fulfilment is what you're talking about. I will have proven its existence, resurrected something that's been considered extinct for more than a hundred years. Such a find will leave me so much to write about, talk about, think about."

"You'd be famous, I suppose."

"Bah! Fame's got nothing to do with it. Fulfilled is what I'll be. Fulfilled, sated, content. I will have accomplished something, completed my work. Are you not driven by something, Kid? Do you not have a particular goal that you'd like to reach?"

"I don't know. I guess I have goals. But I'm never driven."

"Well, Denise, we better hit the trail. I'll keep in touch, Kid."

Uncle Kid and I saw them to the door and waited there until they got into their car and drove off. When we were alone again in the kitchen, I noticed that Uncle Kid seemed agitated. He was always that way when he was expected to consider having a goal in life. I'm that way, myself. It's better to ignore the passing of time.

*

The river froze over in late November. A cold snap in early December thickened it enough to walk on. Then a sou'wester brought rain, after which it turned cold again. Nature had created a beautiful skating rink that ran for more than a hundred miles.

Children, teenagers and even some adults skated on the river. You could see their bonfires at night and hear their voices. After I lost the end of my tongue, I never had much of a taste for skating. Every time I stepped onto the ice, it reminded me of that day. Uncle Kid used to go occasionally. Sometimes he'd skate all the way to Silver Rapids and even beyond. He told me he could cut a figure eight. Cutting a figure eight was his idea of figure skating, I suppose.

Me? I stayed home, read, did my homework, studied and occasionally practised pantomime. For exercise, I walked to school in the mornings and home again at night. To make sure Milly didn't think I was following her, I left home ten minutes early and the school as quickly after classes as I could. Ahead like that, I could not be accused of following her.

Alice Hunter lived about a mile up the Hemlock Road and on the other side of the river from Uncle Kid and me, and now that the river was frozen over, she came to visit me just about every other night. That could be a reason why Uncle Kid went skating so often. I guess he felt Alice and I would feel more comfortable if he wasn't around.

Alice was OK. When I think back on it, I guess she was quite wonderful. She crossed that river on the darkest of nights just to be with me. We communicated about many things and she kept every single note I ever wrote to her.

One night she ran her fingers through my hair, looked at me and said, "One day you'll be famous, or rich, or just gone away, and I'll have these notes to remember you by."

"You expect a lot from me," I wrote.

"You can do anything you want, Corry. You're so . . . mature. You know where you're going, I think. God! I wish . . ." She suddenly grew very melancholy. Tears welled in her eyes.

"What do you wish?" I wrote.

She sobbed a little, then pulled herself together. "Don't mind me," she said. "Could I have a drink of water?"

I nodded, started to rise.

"No, no, I'll get it," she said. We were sitting at the table in the kitchen. Alice stood and went to the sink. She was wearing the loose white dress that she so often wore to hide her figure. It was while she poured herself the drink that I noticed the burn mark, the shape of an iron, right on her butt. It looked as if someone had tried to brand her.

I don't know what came over me when I saw that mark, but I found myself rising and going to her. I put my arms around her, hugged her.

"Don't, Corry," she whispered, but made no move to push me away.

It felt so good to hold somebody. I put my face on her head, sniffed her hair. She just stood there, giving me the moment. She was waiting, I suppose, to see what I'd do next. I was in control, saw the situation as potentially dangerous, but I could not let go right away. She was too soft and warm for that.

After several minutes, I went back to the table and sat, quite out of breath. Alice drank, came and sat across from me. She smiled at me, long gums, short teeth.

"Am I your girlfriend?" She asked.

What could I say?

138

I nodded.

Later, I felt guilty about it. I don't know why, other than it just didn't feel right. I guess, down deep, I felt she wasn't popular enough, she had long gums and short teeth, wasn't pretty enough, that I wanted more, that I was only using her as a weapon for combating my own loneliness. I considered her a friend and all that, and she obviously needed me, but, well, it just didn't feel right.

I convinced myself that I would try it out for a few weeks or a month and nip it before it got out of control.

Around the middle of December I received a letter and a cheque for a hundred dollars from my father. He didn't have much to say other than that he was barely making ends meet driving a cab, that he was seeing a nice lady by the name of Gwen Holt and was happy.

The hundred dollars came in handy. I went to Newcastle and shopped, bought a belt for Uncle Kid and a book for Alice. It was a blank-paged book, a sturdy one with quality paper, something she could write her poetry in. Alice gave me a beautiful pen for Christmas. She must have saved her nickels and dimes for weeks to pay for such a pen.

Alice invited me up for Christmas dinner. Usually, I went to Aunt Linda's place with Uncle Kid and yawned through the most boring three hours of the year. "Alice's family could never be so boring," I thought and took her up on the invitation.

Uncle Kid gave me a new shirt, new boots and jeans, all of which I wore to Alice's. The dinner had been scheduled for six. The Hunters lived about a mile up the road and on the other side of the river. I would have to cross on the river ice to get there. I figured it to be about a half hour walk, so I left home at five. I thought it would be appropriate to arrive a bit early.

It took me less than twenty minutes to get there because it was so dark and cold outside and I found myself walking much faster than I normally would. Crossing the river, the wind tried its best to blow me away.

It's a spooky experience crossing a frozen river in the darkness. You have to really know where you're going or you can end up in an air hole or swimming in the frigid waters of some opening along the shore. It's not quite so bad if there's snow and you have a snow-shoe path to follow. However, on a winter like that one, when the river is nothing but glare ice for miles and miles, you have to rely totally on instinct and sense of direction. You have to listen for the sound of open water and, when you hear it, make sure to take a wide girth around it. There was an air hole on the river that night, about a hundred yards long and thirty or forty feet wide, and I nearly walked into it. The only thing that saved me was that my eyes had adjusted to the darkness and I saw it, a huge black hole in front of me. If I had relied on hearing alone, I would certainly have walked into it, for the winds were howling, making it impossible to hear anything else.

If I had been able to talk, to return home and call Alice on the phone and tell her that I would not be able to make it for dinner, I would have. But she was expecting me, it was Christmas. I kept on going, circled the hole, made it safely to the other shore and climbed the hill to Alice's.

Alice greeted me at the door. She was smiling, but I sensed she was a bit nervous. So was I. She was wearing a short, black, tight-fitting polyester skirt, black nylon stockings and a white blouse. Her hair had been permed and she had perfume on. Not only that, but she wore lipstick and eye shadow. "She's trying to look nice for me," I thought. "And she does look nice. Sexy even."

The house was small, clean and tidy. There were many chintzy Christmas decorations around. Alice introduced me to her mother, father and little brother Albert. It was all very awkward. They knew I couldn't talk and for that reason they found them-selves unable to do so. They shrugged, smiled, shook my hand, took my coat. Mrs. Hunter pointed to the living room. I was to go to the living room.

"C'mon, Corry," said Alice, taking my hand. "Come and see the tree."

She led me to the living room and we sat on the sofa. Albert followed us and sat on a chair across from me. He stared at me for the longest time.

"Why don't you go and play," Alice said to him.

"I don't want to!" he said.

Albert looked like Alice in that he had freckles, long gums, short teeth and straight, blond hair, but he was very thin, dangerously thin, I thought.

"He's a brat," said Alice. "Thank you for the beautiful book."

I removed my writing pad and my new pen from my pocket, winked at her.

"I thought you'd like that," she said.

Her father, Jim, came into the room. He was a very fat man with a very red, unshaven face. He smelled of tobacco smoke and cheap sherry.

"What's Kid up to these days?" he asked.

I shrugged.

"Making a living, I suppose," he said. "A man's lucky to make a living these days. Give the man a chocolate, Alice."

There was a box of chocolates on the scratched coffee table in front of me.

"Want a chocolate, Corry?"

I shook my head.

"Ah, c'mon!" said Jim, picking up the box.

He took one himself and held the box in front of me, shaking it impatiently, demanding that I accept his hospitality. "Have a chocolate."

I took one, popped it into my mouth, bit into it. It was the sticky caramel kind. Glup, slurp, gluck, glub . . . trying to eat a sticky chocolate with a tongue like mine is not easy. I sounded for all the world like a pig.

Alice smiled. Albert laughed out loud. When Jim smiled, I had to grin, for there were the gums and the short teeth again.

"Albert!" yelled Alice. "Go and *do* something!"

"I don't want to!"

"Brat."

"Well, I think I'll get myself a drink," said Jim and off to the kitchen he went. I supposed he, too, needed to laugh right out loud, or at least escape.

On an end table by the sofa was a picture of a young man in a graduation gown. I pointed at it, questioning.

Alice picked it up, said, "My older brother Allen. The brain of the family. He's at St. Thomas, getting his BA."

Allen appeared very handsome in his graduation gown, but he was not smiling, and I wondered.

"Not home for Christmas?" I scribbled.

"He's putting himself through. He had to work over the holidays."

"Alice!" Mrs. Hunter called from the kitchen. "Could you come out here and give me a hand for a minute?"

"I'll be right back," said Alice and went to the kitchen, leaving me alone with Albert.

When I noticed that Albert was staring at me as if I was an animal in a zoo, I decided to stare back, to stare him down. For effect, I grinned broadly, foolishly, and froze that way, not blinking an eye, not moving a muscle. I was the mime. Albert was my audience. A moment or two passed. Finally, he looked away. I took on a new pose, frowned, bugged my eyes.

He looked at me, watched this new pose for a minute, then looked away again. I took on my original pose, the foolish grin.

When he looked back at me, he asked, "Are you crazy?"

I kept still.

"You can't talk, can you?"

Still, I did not move.

"I think you're crazy."

I could see he was beginning to feel uncomfortable with my immobility. His eyes began to dart from object to object, seeking a topic for conversation.

"I got a shirt for Christmas," he said. "Did you get that shirt for Christmas? Mine is a red one. I also got a pair of socks and a Mountie jack-knife. Alice got a pair of slippers for Christmas and a book with nothin' in it. Dad got a pair of socks and Mom got a frying pan."

When I did not respond, he glanced about for something else to talk about. I was amazed at how much he needed to communicate. It always amazes me how people can't stand not talking.

"My big brother's gonna be a doctor or a lawyer," said Albert. "Allen's really smart. Alice wants to be a teacher, or maybe a nurse. I wanna be a hockey player when I grow up. Ever play hockey? You're weird, you know that? Alice says you're smart. I think you're stupid. Are you and Alice gonna get married?"

I decided to have some fun with him.

"I on in e ge arry igh a ay. Ow er, e igh. Oo a ery unny ooa oy. Ha, ha, ha!" I said, casually.

Albert grinned. "What did you say?" he asked.

I repeated the whole line in the very same way — I don't think we'll get married right away. However, we might. You're a very funny looking boy. Ha, ha, ha!

"I don't understand a single word you're saying," he said, still grinning.

"O iss up a ump!" Go piss up a stump.

"What *are* you saying?"

Alice returned from the kitchen. "Has he been bothering you?" she asked.

I shook my head.

She reached for my hand. "Come, dinner is on the table."

Jim Hunter was already seated at the table. Mrs. Hunter was bent over, removing a bowl of dressing from the oven. Until then I'd only seen her from the front and she had been wearing an apron. Now I noticed she was wearing a white dress. *The* white dress. The dress with the iron-scorched bum.

It was a good supper — roast turkey, mashed potatoes, gravy, diced carrots, a very sour chow chow, and chocolate cake for dessert. I ate slowly, tried not to smack and slurp. The Hunters ate quickly, as if they were all very hungry, so I finished my meal a good ten minutes later than the rest. They waited patiently.

"Where's Kid having his Christmas dinner?" asked Mrs. Hunter.

"He always goes to his sister's place." Alice answered for me.

"Linda's," said Jim. "I haven't seen Linda for years. Never married, did she?"

"No, she's not married," said Alice.

"But didn't she have a son?"

"Yes, she has a son. You know, Corry's cousin Paul."

"Oh, yes, that's right. Paul. She had that young lad for . . ."

"Dad!"

"So, what will you do after you graduate, Corry?" asked Mrs. Hunter.

"He might go to university, or he might go to a miming school, if he can find one," said Alice.

"Miming school. What do you learn there?" asked Jim.

"You learn how to mime, of course," said Alice. "Corry wants to be a mime. I told you that."

"What's a mime do?"

"Mimics, of course."

"Hmm. Any money in that?"

"There's money in it, if you get work," said Alice.

"I don't quite know what a mime does," said Jim.

"A mime pretends he's doing things when he's not really doing things at all. He's like an actor without props. You know. He drinks a glass of water, but he doesn't have a glass of water?"

"Sounds kind of odd to me. How can you be an actor if ya can't . . . ?"

"A mime doesn't have to talk, Dad! They mime."

"Well . . . pass me another piece of that chocolate cake, will ya, Mary?"

That was the first time I'd heard Mrs. Hunter's name. Mary passed the chocolate cake and once again changed the subject. "What's Kid doing for a living these days?" she asked me.

"Why you asking that, Mom?" asked Alice.

"It's all right to ask, isn't it?"

"Well, you *know* what he does!"

"I *don't* know what he does!"

"A man's gotta do what he's gotta do," said Jim.

"I just don't know how he gets away with it, that's all," said Mary.

"He ain't hurtin' nobody," said Jim. "The cops won't bother a man that ain't hurtin' nobody. It ain't like he's sellin' hard stuff. Ever hear from your father, Corry?"

I nodded.

"Still in Ontario?"

I nodded again.

"What's he working at?"

"He drives taxi, Dad," said Alice.

"Great first impression," I thought. "My uncle sells dope, my father drives a cab and my Aunt Linda has an illegitimate son. And me? I'm a mime. A family on the move."

The highlight of the conversation came several minutes later when Jim asked Alice to pass the sugar. He said, "Pass the sugar, Alice . . . if ya don't mime. Ha, ha, ha!"

Alice and Mary snorted. It was light and all in fun, so I laughed, too. Albert didn't get the joke and circled his ear with his finger, indicating that he thought we were all stupid. That was the high point of the evening. The low point came, as it always does, after the dinner. There's nothing like stuffing yourself with too much turkey to bring Mr. Boredom, Sandman, Ms. Ennui and several other yawn-inducing guests into the room. Uncle Kid always said, "Once you eat, the party's over."

Alice and I volunteered to do the dishes, but Mary would not have it. "You two go to the living room. Corry's a guest here and I won't have a guest washing dishes."

What I really wanted to do was to get some fresh air, to get out and walk, to go home, but I thought it would be rude to just up and leave so soon after dinner. So Alice and I went to the living room and watched TV while Mary and Jim washed the dishes. Albert went to the river to play hockey.

Alice and I were watching an American carpenter build a hundred-dollar box with a hundred thousand dollars' worth of tools, and he was just about to put the finishing touches on it when Jim and Mary joined us.

"I hate that guy," said Jim. "Anyone could build anything if ya had all that stuff to work with." So he changed the channel and settled down to watch a Walt Disney thing. It didn't matter to me what we watched. All I really wanted was to get out of there.

I watched *Snow White* or whatever it was for about fifteen or twenty minutes, then decided to make my move. On my pad I wrote, "Think I'll go home now," and handed it to Alice.

"Oh, you don't need to go home yet," she replied. "Let's play Monopoly or something. Mom? Dad? Want to play Monopoly or cards or something?"

"No, dear," spoke Mary for both of them. "I don't think so. You two go ahead."

"Well, it's no fun playing with just two."

With a sigh, I wrote, "I really do have to go home. I had a great time. Thank your parents for me."

"Well . . . OK. I'll walk you halfway."

Alice and I put on our coats and boots and Alice yelled to her parents from the door that she was walking me home.

"That's nice, dear!" called Mary from the living room. "Don't stay out too late! Come again, Corry!"

Stepping out into the darkness, we were greeted by the cold wind. I had forgotten how dark and cold it was. "Alice is wearing a skirt and nylon stockings and her coat is thin," I thought. "She'll freeze to death out here."

"Brrr, it's cold," she said and headed over the hill to the river before I could do anything to change her mind. She knew the path well, and it was all I could do to keep up with her in the almost total darkness.

"She's not stupid. She'll just walk me to the river and then return home," I thought as I followed her. But when we got to the river, she stepped out on the ice and kept on going.

"I guess you already know that there's an air hole out here," she called back to me over the howling wind. "We'll have to go around it."

She was ahead of me and I reached out and touched her shoulder.

She stopped and turned to face me. "What's the matter, Corry?" she asked.

It was too dark to write and I couldn't talk. How could I make her understand that I wanted her to turn back, that it was much too cold for her to be out, that she was not dressed for it.

I had to try.

"O baa," I said. "Brrrrrr. O ome."

She understood.

146

"It's all right, Corry," she said. "I'm OK. It's not that cold. I'll be all right. You just have to keep walking, that's all. C'mon."

It was futile for me to try and argue, so I followed her over the river and up the hill, thinking all the time that she must be out of her head. "What's she up to? Why is she doing this? It's cold enough out here to freeze mercury. What's she got in mind? Does she plan to walk me all the way home?"

She walked me all the way home.

We entered the house, removed our coats and boots and entered the kitchen. Alice sat at the table and rubbed her hands together. I went to the cupboard and took down some hot chocolate mix, offered it to her.

"Yes, please," she said, trembling. "What time do you expect your uncle to come home?"

I shrugged. You never know with Uncle Kid. He could come straight home from Aunt Linda's, or he could go somewhere and party all night.

I plugged in the kettle and sat across from her to wait for it to come to a boil.

"I like it here," she said, scanning the kitchen. "It's so masculine. Your uncle has good taste, you know."

She stood and walked over to peer into the dining room. "Do you two ever eat in here?" she asked.

I shook my head.

"If I had a dining room like this, I'd eat in here every day. You know what I like about this place the most? No guns. Every house you go into around here has guns in the corner or on the walls. I hate guns. And I hate dead animals, deer and moose heads on the walls, too."

The kettle was starting to simmer. I went to the cupboard and took down a couple of mugs, spooned some chocolate into them.

"Did you like my parents?" she asked. "If they seemed strange, it's only because they're . . . indifferent. Albert's a brat, of course. But, he liked you. I could tell he liked you. How could anyone not like you?"

I poured the water over the chocolate and handed her a mug.

147

A gust of wind shook the house.

We sipped our chocolate.

I removed my pen from my shirt pocket and wrote, "You'll freeze going home."

"Yeah, well. Do you still have a crush on Milly Minor?"

"NO!" I wrote.

"Good. She's a snob and a bitch. I don't like her one little bit! I don't even want to talk about her! Why don't you show me your Christmas tree, Corry?"

I nodded, and, taking our hot chocolate with us, we went to the living room. While I plugged in the tree, Alice put a tape, Handel's *Messiah*, on the stereo. "It's so cozy in here," she said, plopping herself down on the sofa and smiling up at me. "Come and sit beside me."

I looked down at her, swept her body with my eyes. The black polyester skirt had moved up her thighs when she sat. I could see the tops of her black nylons. I find black nylons very sexy. I focused on the tops of her black nylons, could see nothing else. The sight quickened my heart.

I eased myself down beside her. She put her arms around me and kissed me.

We had kissed before, but never like we did then and there in the living room. We were young and healthy, and within a few minutes so excited that nothing short of steel chastity belts could have deterred the natural course of things. Within ten minutes we were in my room with *Messiah* blaring full blast from the living room below.

"Hallelujah! Hallelujah!" It drowned out the sounds of squeaking bed springs.

"Hallelujah! Hallelujah!" It hushed the north wind pounding on the house.

"Hallelujah! Hallelujah!" It muffled our whimpers, moans and cries.

"Hallelujah! Hallelujah!" It covered the sound of Uncle Kid entering the house and climbing the stairs to bed, probably grinning from ear to ear.

And then there was silence and peace and warmth and dreams.

At midnight, I awakened with a jerk.

I was alone.

I leaped out of bed and rushed to the window. The glass was frosted up so far that all I had to peer through was about a half-inch peephole at the very top of the pane. It was snowing, a regular blizzard outside.

"Alice!" I thought. "My God! When did she leave? The fool! Surely she wouldn't . . ."

I dressed as quickly as I could and ran downstairs. There was a light in the kitchen, but no Alice. She was nowhere in the house.

My heart was pounding. "What should I do?" I asked myself. "Should I follow her? Could I find my way over there in such a storm? Maybe she left before the storm and is safe at home. But what if she isn't? Maybe I should call Uncle Kid. The phone! Uncle Kid could call her father on the phone to see if she made it."

I ran back up stairs and tapped on Uncle Kid's door.

"Eh? What? Who? Corry? What is it, Corry?"

I entered his room, turned on the light and threw up my hands in frustration. I did not have my pen with me. "Ouwis!" I tried. "Iss Ouwis!"

"What? What's wrong, Corry?"

I gestured with my head for him to follow me. He climbed out of bed and followed me to my room. There, I wrote, "Alice! She's gone home!"

"Well?"

I wrote "There's a blizzard!" so aggressively that the pen tore the paper.

He had gone to bed an hour or two before, quite drunk, and it took him a moment or two to grasp the situation. When it sank in, he said, "How bad is it?" and rushed to the window to see for himself.

"Holy Jesus! Surely to God you didn't let that girl leave and cross that river on a night like this! Damn you, Corry!"

"Telephone," I wrote. "Call Jim."

Uncle Kid ran downstairs, found the number in the book, punched it in and waited for what seemed like a very long time. The Hunters were obviously in bed.

"Hello? Jim? It's Kid Lauder. Your daughter Alice. Is she home? . . . You'd better check. She left here alone and it's a bad night. . . . Yes, alone. I don't know what's wrong with him. Yes, I know . . ."

Uncle Kid looked at me. "Damn you, Corry! I can't believe you! He's gone to check. You better hope she's there!"

My heart was pounding. I was worried to the point of tears. It wasn't my fault.

"Yes? God! Hell, I don't know!" He turned to me. "How long ago did she leave, Corry?"

I shook my head. I didn't know.

"You don't know? Hell! Where were you?" He spoke back into the receiver. "He doesn't know. Yes, we're leaving right now. OK. Yeah, OK. Good luck." Uncle Kid hung up.

"She's not home," he said as he ran up the stairs.

It was all like a bad dream, a nightmare. With heart pounding and the rest of me trembling, I somehow managed to put on my boots and coat. Uncle Kid came down the stairs fully dressed, put on his coat, toque and gloves, grabbed a flashlight and we were off.

Uncle Kid swore the moment he stepped outside. "God Almighty!" he said. "I can't have been home for more than an hour and not a flake had fallen when I drove in. There's five, six inches of the stuff down already."

We made our way to the Jeep and brushed it off, and Uncle Kid jumped in and started it up while I adjusted the hubs to four-wheel drive.

"Thank God for the four-wheel drive," said Uncle Kid when I climbed in beside him. "She'd be taking the usual path, I hope." This was a combination of a statement, a plea and a question.

I nodded. Surely she would cross in the same place.

We drove up the road to the place where Alice and I had crossed the river earlier. With the high beams on, you could see nothing at all, just a swarm of white like so many darts attacking the windshield. With the dim lights on, you could at least follow the road. I watched carefully for Alice, for her tracks. I could see nothing.

When we got to Alice's crossing-place and jumped out of the Jeep, it was clear that Uncle Kid was not in a mood for communicating, for he just rushed over the hill to the river without looking to see if I was following or not. The wind was so strong that I had to pull my collar over my mouth to keep my breath from escaping. The flashlight illuminated little more than a curtain of driven snowflakes. The temperature was forty below zero and, adding the wind-chill factor, even colder, but I did not feel it. My adrenaline flow looked after that. Uncle Kid walked so fast that I could barely keep up, and we were halfway across the river and he was ten or fifteen feet ahead of me when I remembered the air hole. Alice knew it was there and would look for it, of that I was sure, but Uncle Kid might not know of its existence and walk right into it. I had to warn him.

"Ahhhh!" I screamed. "Op!"

Uncle Kid swung to me angrily and yelled, "What's the matter with you?"

I ran to him and pointed. "Aa o!" I said

"What?"

"Aa o!" I grabbed the light from him and swept the ice in front of us and there it was, just ten feet away.

"Oh, God!" said Uncle Kid. "We could've walked right into it. Does Alice know it's there?"

"Yeah."

Without further delay, we hurried upstream and around the hole. I now carried the light and Uncle Kid was following me. Then, suddenly, I spotted the tracks. Alice's tracks. They were on the far side of the air hole. Alice had made it. What a girl! My heart leaped for joy. I showed them to Uncle Kid. They were barely visible, just little hollows in the snow. Another five minutes of snowing and drifting and they would have disappeared.

"Alice's?"

"Yeah."

A little further along, we came upon another set of even less visible tracks. "Jim Hunter's tracks," I guessed.

Uncle Kid must have guessed the same thing. "Jim!" he yelled. "Alice! Jim! Are you there?"

We waited for an answer, but all we could hear was the howling wind. It makes you feel small and vulnerable, standing in the middle of a river in a snowstorm. "Alice is either crazy or the bravest girl in the world to have attempted crossing this river tonight," I thought. "She doesn't even have a light. And the snow. Her boots are low. There'll be snow in her boots."

In my most intense dreams I find it difficult to envision that young woman alone in that storm, in the vastness of that river, in the darkness of that night.

"Alice! Jim!" called Uncle Kid once more.

We waited for an answer.

"Well, if she made it this far, she'll make it the rest of the way," commented Uncle Kid.

I was equally optimistic, but a new fear had arisen in me. Was Jim Hunter aware of the air hole? Did he meet up with Alice in time for her to warn him?

We kept on going and soon we were clumsily climbing the hill. It would have been easier going had we taken our time and picked our way along. But we were hurrying, puffing and panting, and, even in that cold, perspiring.

Alice's tracks were somewhat more visible on the hill. We could see where she occasionally lost her footing and slid back several inches. It was not a long hill, but it was quite steep, and we, too, found ourselves slipping and sometimes even falling to our knees. We were halfway up the hill when we saw the very dim light of the Hunters' house.

At her doorstep, we stomped the snow from our feet and entered the house without knocking. There in the kitchen stood Alice, looking as if she too had just entered the house — shivering, wet hair, flushed. Seeing her there safe and sound, I thought Uncle Kid would collapse with relief. When she moved to the kitchen door to see who had entered, the kitchen light, the only one that was on in the house, turned her into a silhouette.

"Corry? Mr. Lauder? What are you doing here?" She moved into the hall to greet us. I thought she looked frightened.

"Thank God you're home," said Uncle Kid. "Where's Jim?"

"Dad? I don't know. In bed, I suppose. I just came in. God, it's awful out there!"

"In bed? He's out looking for you!" Uncle Kid did not sound kind.

"I . . . I don't think so. Why would he go looking for me? Is there something wrong?"

"What do you think we're doing here, young lady? We thought you might get lost in the storm! I phoned Jim! He's out there looking for you!" Uncle Kid took a step toward her. He was blinded by the kitchen light, bumped into a chair.

"Well, I'm all right. I'm here. But I don't think Dad's out there. He'd never go out on a night like this."

"Well, I know he's out there! We saw his tracks! C'mon, Corry."

We were turning to leave when a voice called from upstairs. "What's going on down there? That you, Alice?"

"It's me, Dad! I'm home!"

Alice looked embarrassed, ready to cry.

I don't know how Uncle Kid looked, but I know how he felt, for he kicked the chair he'd bumped into so hard that it went flying past Alice, through the kitchen door and hit the ceiling. It broke the light bulb and came down in the darkness on what sounded like the stove.

"What in God's name is going on down there? Did you meet up with Kid? Is that you, Kid?"

"You didn't even go to look for her!" said Uncle Kid, making a feeble attempt to control his anger.

"Well, I didn't see any sense in *all* of us going out on a night like this! What the hell was that noise?"

Cold, wet and exhausted from her recent experiences, embarrassed and frightened, Alice began to cry. She sounded so sad, so alone, so much like a frightened little girl, that it nearly broke my heart. Poor Alice. I wanted to run to her, to take her in my arms and hold her.

"It's all right, Alice," said Uncle Kid. "Let's get out of here, Corry."

"Nigh Ouwis," I said.

The only words he spoke from that moment until we got home were when we first stepped outside. He said, "You got the light, Corry?"

"Yeah."

"Well, turn the fuckin' thing on!"

153

10

When we got home, we were cold, tired, frustrated and down in the dumps. Uncle Kid broke the seal on a bottle of malt whisky Bill Hall had given him for Christmas. He poured us each a double, added a bit of water and we sat at the kitchen table to reflect on our adventure.

"Guess I sort of lost it," said Uncle Kid. "I didn't mean to kick that chair so hard. I didn't realize it was so light. I guess it was wicker or something. Couldn't have weighed any more than a few ounces. Anyway, I suppose it was better to kick the chair than to break that jerk's neck. Can you imagine? His daughter was out there on maybe the worst night of the year and he didn't even care! Damn! I can't believe it!"

"I fell asleep," I wrote.

"Hmm."

"I didn't hear her leave."

"Yeah, well . . ."

"Sorry."

"Well, it's over and done with. A little adventure. Ha! That chair took off. Ha! I couldn't believe it! Sure wakes you up, doesn't it? When that light bulb broke, it sort of shocked me."

He checked his watch. "Here it is two o'clock in the morning and I'm wide awake. You know what Carla Bowes called me tonight? Hippie! She called me an old hippie! A refugee from the sixties! Ha! Oh, well, I guess I am. What can I say? I suppose if I got my hair cut I'd be thought of as something else. But who cares? Do you care, Corry? Do you care what people think?"

I wrote, "Sort of," but shrugged. I wasn't sure.

He sighed and looked me in the eye. I thought I detected laughter in his eyes and wondered if he was about to make fun of me.

"Sowing seeds. Throwing caution to the wind," he said. "I don't know. That's the problem. The Bible says something about that, I think. Better to sow your seeds in fertile soil than in the dust or something like that. But you gotta be careful. Bill Hall always said that dogs attract dogs. Said it was the story of his life. Here! Let me touch that up for ya."

Even though I had only taken a sip or two, he poured some more scotch into my glass and added a splash to his own. Then he read the label on the bottle and grinned as if it reminded him of something, of being a much younger hippie, perhaps.

"What's so funny?" I wrote.

"Ah, nothing. Bill Hall gives me a bottle of this stuff every Christmas. Bill and I go back a long way. Grew up together. Ha! Maybe I should say we *never* grew up together. We haven't changed. We're just the same now as we were when we were ten and twelve and sixteen years old. We'll never grow up! Who in the hell wants to? Carla Bowes would like for a man to grow up! Kyle Drury grew up. There's no artist in this country more famous than Kyle Drury. But that's all he is. Famous! Everybody knows him. You know who I mean, don't ya?"

I nodded.

"He's the lad that painted *The Eye of the Fly* and all that stuff. He's from Silver Rapids, did you know that?"

I nodded again.

"I grew up with him. Hung out with Bill and me for years. Know what he told me last summer? He told me . . . now let me think about what he told me. He told me that it's a long way back to those who doubted you would make it."

"Huh?"

"It's a long way back to those who doubted you would make it. It means he's a stranger in his own home, a stranger in Silver Rapids. He can go anywhere in this country and be known and loved, but in Silver Rapids he's a stranger. Everyone doubted that anyone from such a small place could make it, you see, and now that he has, they don't want him around. He doesn't belong here anymore. It's all about change, Corry. People don't like change. Silver Rapids was thought of as a nothing place and that's the way its people wanted it to remain. Me, now? I belong here. I'll always belong here because I'm a nobody. You saved the life of a nobody tonight, Corry. It wouldn't have mattered one bit if I had walked into that air hole, because I'm a nobody."

When he said that, I wrote, "I think I'll go to bed," yawned and stood.

"No, no, no, sit down. I'm not feeling sorry for myself. Sit down and drink with me. Hell, we haven't had a drink together for a long time. Let's celebrate."

I sat again. It was plain to see that he had something on his mind and needed to talk. On my pad, I wrote, "Get to the point. You don't approve of Alice, do you?"

"Now, why would you be thinking a thing like that?"

"That dogs attract dogs thing," I scribbled. "You think if I hang out with dogs, I'll end up in a pack."

"Very good," said Uncle Kid. "Almost poetic. But you're wrong. I think Alice is the very best of a girl. But just be careful, that's all. The last thing you need is a . . . a young lad. I don't know what I was thinking about when I mentioned the dog stuff. I was thinking about Bill Hall, I guess."

Uncle Kid was backtracking. The dogs attract dogs thing was important and I knew exactly what he meant. He was being suggestive — first the dogs and then Kyle Drury. It was Uncle Kid's way of saying that he thought I was a potential somebody like Kyle Drury, that I shouldn't get into a relationship that might tie me down for the rest of my life. He had completed his whole message by calling himself a nobody. In essence, he had told me not to end up like him. To understand this did not take any extraordinary perception.

I understood it and had picked up the message because I had been thinking along those terms for some time. I knew I had to break it off with Alice.

"I'll be careful," I wrote, raising my glass to him with my other hand. "A toast. To birth control!"

Uncle Kid laughed. He drank deeply and returned his glass to the table with a bang.

"Next summer, I'm going to Europe," he announced. "Want to go?"

"Can't afford it," I wrote.

"Bah! We can do it. We're gonna make a million in the outfitting business."

"Why Europe?" I wrote.

"Europe?" He stopped to think. "Because I want to feel the cobblestones beneath my feet. I want to shop on the Ponte Vecchio in Florence, see the David; I want to get laid in the red light district of Amsterdam and swing drunk from a windmill; I want to see the ruins of Rome and Athens and Delphi. Just once I want to see something that's older than this house. Don't you have ambitions to see the world?"

I nodded.

"We all have our dreams," he said, softly, as if to himself. He stared into his glass, sighed and took a drink. "Mark Masters wants to see the elusive eastern cougar, Bill Hall wants to ride a motorcycle around the world, I want to go to Europe, you want to be a mime and an outfitter and God knows what else. Cam Berkley is the only man I know who has no dreams of his own. Cam Berkley just steps into other people's dreams, uninvited. That's why he'll never cut it. Resolve to be thyself; and know that he who finds himself loses his misery!"

"Huh?"

"Ah, somehow it connects. Matthew Arnold wrote that. There's no more miserable man than a man who doesn't know himself. I know myself. I don't like waves or rapids. I like smooth sailing. I don't like clouds of grey. Ha! Now, *I'm* being poetic."

157

A little later I went to bed. Much later I heard him in the living room, playing his guitar and singing. He was smoking dope. I could smell the sweet scent all the way upstairs. Later still, I heard him screaming "Jumping Jack Flash is a gas, gas, gas!" He was in the living room, dancing and singing along with the stereo.

The next morning I found him asleep on the sofa. The empty scotch bottle was on its side on the floor, there was a fresh cigarette burn in the carpet. On the coffee table there were several stained and toke-burned sheets of paper with some lyrics written on them. Sometime in the night he had tried to write a song or two, or maybe some poetry.

On one sheet, he had written:

> The man in there is a phoney,
> Calling himself a poet.
> It's just a crutch —
> Every time he faces
> His worthless past and cloudy future,
> He picks up his pencil and
> Writes about turtles on fence posts.

On another sheet, obviously much later when he was very drunk, for his hand writing was barely decipherable, he had written:

The Parting

> I hang my head
> With loneliness and despair,
> Knowing separation
> Seems never wise or fair,
> But time continues on
> And we must live our lives,
> Seek out higher levels
> Before we take our dives;
> Step into the midst, display our sex,
> Smile and shout "I'm free! Who's next?"

158

Uncle Kid was very restless, very discontent.

I decided to ease out of my relationship with Alice gradually, and the very next time we were alone together, I started the procedure by writing, "It's dangerous for us to sleep together."

As usual, we were in the kitchen. Uncle Kid was out plowing snow. Uncle Kid is one of those guys who hates the winter but loves the snow. For Uncle Kid, snow means money. For a fee, he plows out all the neighbours' driveways with the Jeep.

Alice read my note and sighed.

"I know," she said. "It was stupid. You'll just have to control yourself."

"Me?"

She smiled and I noticed that she seemed to be controlling it a bit, that she was not exposing so much of her gums. She was working on her smile, trying to look pretty.

"What did Jim say about Uncle Kid kicking the chair?" I wrote.

"Ah, nothing. My father's lost it. He needs a job. He just sits around and gets fatter and fatter. He'll take a heart attack one of these days. He's really not so bad. He's just lost it. He still hasn't replaced the bulb in the ceiling. We don't have a spare bulb, Corry."

I went to the cupboard, found a bulb and offered it to her.

"No, I . . ."

"Pease ake a . . ." I said. I picked up my pen with the intention to write, but she stopped me.

"Don't, Corry. I think you can say a lot more than you think you can. I could understand what you just said. Now, don't write what you have to say, tell me." She had placed her hand on mine to stop me from writing.

I said nothing.

"C'mon, Corry. What were you going to write to me? Tell me."

I shook my head. I knew my capabilities and knew I couldn't say it. I also knew that I didn't want to say it. I didn't need to say it. I was going to write, "Take the bulb. Uncle Kid broke it and should replace it," but my thoughts had wandered to something else. She was touching my hand and I was looking into her eyes. We were alone and I was remembering Christmas night. My heart was pounding and things were happening to my body. She picked up

159

on the vibes and was rising from her chair and allowing me to take her into my arms. And then she was crushing herself against me and we were kissing and grasping for every pleasure our healthy young bodies could provide.

"Just this time and never again," I thought. "Just this time."

I pulled away from her and taking her hand, headed for the stairs.

"I don't know, Corry. We shouldn't." said Alice. She was attempting to hesitate. I suppose she needed a loophole of a sort, that somewhere down the road she wanted to be able to say that she hadn't wanted to, that it was all my idea. But in reality she did not hesitate for a moment. She followed me up the stairs and entered my room. We removed our clothes so hastily that it's a wonder we didn't pop some buttons. We fell into the bed.

"Just this one last time," I thought. "Just this one last time."

It was mid-afternoon and it all seemed very exciting, very naughty, very right.

Sometime during the next two sinful hours, Uncle Kid entered the house, heard our mumblings, the bedsprings. He was gone when we finally came down to the kitchen, and I would not have known he had been there at all if he hadn't acted so irritable that evening.

He showed his irritability by going around in circles, by throwing the dishcloth instead of hanging it up, by slamming the cupboard doors, by swearing when he broke a lace while lacing up his boots, by leaving for the Legion without announcing, as he usually did, that that was his intent.

I watched the Montreal Canadiens defeat the Philadelphia Flyers on TV and went to bed around midnight. I heard Uncle Kid come home shortly after, heard him moving about downstairs. A little while later, I smelled marijuana, heard the guitar, Uncle Kid singing.

I climbed out of bed and went to the top of the stairs to listen. He was singing something I'd never heard before, one line, over and over again. It was a haunting, bluesy melody, played in a diminished minor or some such chord, a knuckle-bender that sounded like raindrops falling into a tin barrel. His voice was a buzz

160

that mingled and flirted with the strange chord, a drone teasing some deadly blossom. I half intended to go down and party with him for a while, but such a melody belonged alone. Uncle Kid was a swamp deity droning out some ancient litany to all that is silent in the world. I could not enter his realm. I went back to bed and went to sleep.

The next morning, I found him in the same way that I found him on Boxing Day, drunk, passed out, asleep on the sofa, a bag of dope, an empty scotch bottle, ashes all over the place. I noticed that at one point he had been so drunk that he butted a cigarette right on the coffee table, a good five inches away from the ashtray. On a sheet of paper he had written:

> He forgot he was an artist,
> That an artist works alone,
> Joined a band for shelter,
> Hid the songs he called his own.
> Now he's singing country music
> In the keys that we all know,
> Left the suffering of the artist
> To Nelson, Cash and Snow.
> Still he wonders what's beyond
> That measured wall,
> If he could touch the heart
> Of anyone at all.

Later, when vacuuming, I found a ball of crumpled paper in the corner. I smoothed it out and read — "Enormous, gigantic, vast, large, huge, astronomical, infinite, massive, jumbo, monstrous, great, elephantine, immense, mammoth, colossal, monumental and mighty are the only big words I know."

*

It might have been the winter that triggered the change in Uncle Kid. Coping with winter can do strange things to the heads of tropical creatures like human beings. But I think it came from more than that. There had been other winters that did not make us so very different. I think the change came from the fact that I had grown, that I had hair on my chest and a mind of my own, that I had changed and he no longer felt responsible for the child he had rescued and nurtured.

Whatever the reason, the change occurred and remained throughout the winter, the spring, the summer. It remains to this day. Before that winter, we had been a father-son act. Ever since, everything has been man-to-man.

At first, I did not like the change, did not understand why Uncle Kid was acting so strangely. He was getting stoned and/or drunk more frequently and at unusual times of the day. Previously, his drinking was a social thing. He'd have one or two before dinner, or a few in the evening with the boys at the Legion. But now, he might start as early as noon or not have a sip until twelve o'clock at night. He also started staying out late, sometimes not coming home until the next day. A tom cat. Sometimes he'd come home smelling like a wino, other times like a French prostitute.

One morning in February, I was having coffee in the kitchen. I had prepared a sandwich for school and was reading something or other, waiting around until it was time to leave. Suddenly, I heard footsteps coming down the stairs that I naturally thought were Uncle Kid's. I was startled when a tall, somewhat beautiful and sleepy-eyed, dark-haired woman entered the kitchen. Never before in my lifetime, or at least to my knowledge, had Uncle Kid played host to a female guest in our house. Her appearance surprised the hell out of me.

"Good morning," she said. "You must be Corry."

I nodded.

She smiled and offered me her hand. "I'm Jane. Jane Lewis."

I shook her hand. She had long fingers, long manicured nails, wore several expensive-looking rings. She was dressed in a long pink nightie. She had beautiful hazel eyes and a smile that revealed perfect teeth.

"Kid has told me so much about you," she said. "Ah! Coffee. Do you mind?"

I jumped up so quickly that my chair tipped over backward and landed with a bang on the floor. I picked the chair up and slid it against the table. Then I went to the cupboard, took down a mug and poured it completely full of coffee. The milk and sugar were on the table. I gave her the coffee and watched her carefully carry the mug to the sink. She had to dump some off to make room for the milk.

"Mind if I sit down?" she asked.

I gestured to the chair at the other end of the table.

She sat, and when I went to sit across from her, I had to pull my chair, the chair that had fallen backward a moment ago, away from the table. It was all very awkward, very noisy, very busy.

"I left Kid sleeping like a baby," she said. "Wish I could sleep in like that. I have to be at the office in . . ." she checked her watch. "Goodness! I'm going to be late. Do you go to school in Silver Rapids?"

I nodded.

"Do you walk or take the bus?"

I pointed at my feet.

"Looks cold out there. I'll be leaving in a minute. You can catch a ride with me, if you like."

That was OK with me. I nodded.

I'll run up and get dressed," she said, rising. "I'll just be a couple of minutes." Taking her coffee with her, she went up to Uncle Kid's room, leaving me alone in the kitchen.

Twenty minutes later she came back down, looking like a million bucks — rouge, eye shadow, lipstick, dangling earrings. She had on a white blouse that revealed a cleavage to die for, a royal blue suit with the jacket belted at her slim waist, black leather boots. She swept me away.

She looked about the room. "I wonder where . . . do you have any idea where Kid might've put my coat?" she asked.

I went into the hall and opened the closet door. There was only one garment in there that could be hers. A mink jacket. I took it back to the kitchen where she waited. Holding it for her to arm into, I noticed she smelled very, very good.

I pulled on my own old jacket and a minute later we were ma-
noeuvring our way down the Hemlock Road in her new red Chrys-
ler convertible.

I put in a day filled with anxiety. Uncle Kid had a beautiful new
woman in his life. "Could this be the reason behind the change in
him?" I asked myself. "Is this why he's staying up all night, smoking and drinking, rambling about, writing poetry and songs? Is this
the wolf coming out in him?"

After school I hurried home, hoping that he'd be in a talkative
mood, that he would tell me all about this beauty.

I found him in the kitchen peeling potatoes. He was putting
together a corned beef stew.

"Did you notice the sun?" he asked.

"Huh?"

"It's coming around. The days are getting longer. Another
month and spring will be in the air. Know what I was thinking?"

I shook my head, went to the refrigerator for a pop.

"I was thinking that we only have a few more weeks of cold
weather and that now's the time to deal with the pool. I got right
on the phone and called Ethan Harris. Then I called Floyd Winslow. They are both available Saturday. Paul Vincent has a pile of
boulders back there about a hundred feet long, some of them as big
as that stove.

"It's the perfect time to do it. The ground's frozen, the river ice
will hold up a truck. Ethan is only charging me a hundred dollars
for him and his loader for the day and Floyd will truck them here
for thirty dollars a load. Paul Vincent doesn't want a cent for the
rocks, wants to get rid of them. I figure we should get about five
loads. There's not that much snow on the ground. I think I can
plow a road to the river with the Jeep. What d'ya think?"

I approved, nodded.

"I changed my mind about how to rig up the shed," he continued. "We'll turn the front end where the junk used to be into a bedroom and a bathroom. My room can remain the way it is, the
lounge, living room or whatever you want to call it."

"What about a kitchen?" I wrote.

"You're in it. We'll cook here and the sports can eat in the dining room. I figure if we hop right around we might even be able to bring in a black salmon fisherman or two. Fifty dollars a day per person for lodging, thirty dollars a day for meals and a hundred a day for guiding. They won't even have to bring their own gear unless they want to. I can rent them all they need from Izaak Walton's. We'll need wood for the fireplace, and I figure we should heat the bedroom and bathroom with electricity, a couple of baseboard heaters."

"Black salmon fishermen?" I questioned. "We'll need boats and motors."

"Well, we have one boat and motor. You can use that. I'll be doing the cooking and running around. If we have more than one sport, we'll hire a guide with his own boat and motor. I got it all figured out. There's only about two good weeks of black salmon fishing. Do you think you'll be able to take some time off from school to guide?"

I nodded. I was doing well in school. Two weeks absence wouldn't lower my grades by much.

I thought of something, wrote, "You could guide, too. We could hire a *good* cook, Mary Hunter or someone. More money in guiding."

"True, but I can't afford to buy another boat and motor."

"You could rent. Charge it to the sport."

"True. I'll think about it."

I wrote, "I met Jane Lewis this morning."

"Ya did, eh? Nice lady, eh?"

I nodded, questioned him with my eyes.

"What?"

I had to write it: "Tell me more."

"Oh! Well, there's not much to tell. She sells real estate. I met her at Andy Porter's place in Newcastle."

"When?"

"Friday night."

Well, Jane Lewis was not the reason why he was acting so strangely. He had changed long before Friday night.

"Gonna see more of her?" I wrote.

"Aren't you the nosy one! I might. She's hot stuff, I can tell ya that much. As a matter of fact, I was thinking that maybe you and me and the girls should get together for dinner some night."

"Ouwis?"

"Yes. You and Alice, Jane and me. We can do it right here. We'll get some wine, a few shrimp, broil some steaks. Do it up fancy, eat in the dining room for a change. What d'ya say? It's time we started acting more like" — he winked — "outfitters."

I didn't like it.

I had to think.

I stared at the floor.

Alice? He wanted to have dinner with that fancy lady and *Alice*? What game was he playing?

"What's the matter?" asked Uncle Kid.

I shrugged.

"Don't you like the idea?"

"Ouwis?" was all I could say.

"Well, who else? You've been dating her, been spending more and more time with her, she's your woman, invite her to dinner!"

Suddenly, what Uncle Kid had in mind was all too clear. There was always reasoning behind his madness and this time he was staging a fiasco with Alice Hunter front and centre. He was planning to compare his silk glove to my sow's ear. He had picked up the silk glove for no other reason.

I didn't know how to feel about it. One side of me knew that I deserved such a performance, that I had promised not to keep Alice around, not to fall in love with her.

The reality of the situation was that Alice was showing up more and more and I was liking it. Alice was kind and good and loving. She touched me.

I don't think Uncle Kid disliked Alice. I think he just felt that if we continued what we were doing, we'd surely get into trouble, that Alice would get pregnant, the consequences of which would be very dramatic. He was right about that.

I could handle that side of things. The side I couldn't handle was how ruthless he was being. He had it in his mind to degrade Alice, to intimidate her, to embarrass me. He wanted me to become an outfitter, a guide, a mime artist, a lawyer, doctor or whatever. He did not want me to get tied down to a poor girl from the back side of the river, from the Hemlock Road, to end up like Jim Hunter, fat, lazy and on welfare. He wanted me to get on with my life.

But to be so ruthless!

I felt totally smothered.

"Gotta go." I wrote, grabbed my coat and left the house.

Outside, I was faced with the confinement of winter. There was three feet of snow on the ground. You just can't walk wherever you feel like going when there's three feet of snow on the ground. If it had been spring, I would have gone to the river to fish or swim or just hang out, perhaps sit on a rock and watch a feeding heron or a soaring eagle. But the winter landscape offers no luxuries. I found myself heading out the lane. When I got to the road, I contemplated going into Izaak Walton's, but it was closed for the winter. It was late afternoon and the sun was low in the northwest. Earlier, it had warmed up enough to melt the ice patches on the road, but now the water there was crystallizing once again. I was crystallizing, myself, I think, spiritually at least. I felt like a zombie, tossed between the weight of the ageing winter, the whims of Uncle Kid, whom I was thinking of as the roué, and the hormones rioting through my veins. I breathed deeply, exhaled little clouds the shape and colour of sorrow, ennui and indecision. What to do, what to do.

For no reason I can think of, I headed down the road toward Silver Rapids. I walked past the pond in the swamp where we used to play hockey, where we played the day I froze my tongue. Covered with snow, with last year's reeds and cattails growing from it, it looked lonesome, abandoned, small. Hard to believe we used to play hockey there.

I kept on going and came within view of Nubert Minor's house, and I suddenly realized how I loathed the place. I got a sick feeling in my solar plexus every time I walked past it. Several months had passed since I'd had any doings with Milly, and she seemed to have forgotten the whole issue, treated me, as of late, with indifference.

It seemed time had erased whatever animosity she once felt for me. Easy for her to forget.

I, on the other hand, would never forget it. Milly Minor had pinned the idiot button on my lapel. Whatever illusions I may have had of being an accepted individual in society had gotten shattered by the mere sound of Milly Minor's laughter. By laughing at me, by showing contempt for me, by labelling me as a weak, inferior person, she had flicked the chip from my shoulder. Stooping to pick it up, at least until that day, there on the road looking at Milly's house, I figured I had met Alice Hunter somewhere while still bending.

Uncle Kid thought that, too. That's why he was being so ruthless.

What Uncle Kid didn't know, however, was how lonely I was. He wasn't putting all the pieces together. When he looked at me, he saw a lad who bent over to pick up a chip and was never quite able to stand up straight again. Other than that, he thought I was all right, able, a fine young man, the complete concoction. What he had failed to add was that I was an adolescent, a teenager who needed friends, love, popularity, acceptance. Like me, until that day there on the road, he did not see that I had found all of that in Alice Hunter.

There on the road, looking at Milly Minor's house, I realized that I had been an impertinent fool who had overlooked some major ingredients that made up the essence and flavour of my life. When I stooped to pick up the chip, I found myself staring at the world from knee-level, from the level that Milly Minor would have me seeing her. She would have every boy bend over so that she'd appear taller. I did not meet Alice Hunter while I was bent. I'd been all wrong about that. Alice Hunter had reached down to rescue me and by taking her hand I had managed to rise up, to stand tall again. To think that I was stooping to her level was the ultimate snobbery on my behalf. Uncle Kid was still thinking that way. Alice Hunter did not have a fur coat or a convertible and she may not have been a sophisticated raving beauty, but she stood just as tall as Jane Lewis, and I had a feeling she could handle herself in just about any situation.

"Uncle Kid hasn't given himself a chance to get to know Alice,"

I told myself. "He won't even hang around when she's around. He doesn't realize how much she means to me."

With this in mind, I turned and walked back to the house.

Uncle Kid was still in the kitchen. He was reading *The Coming of Winter*. The corned beef stew was bubbling on the stove, smelled wonderful.

"You're back," he said.

"Yeah."

"Needed a walk, did ya?"

"Yeah."

"Did ya give the dinner party some thought?"

"Yeah."

"And?"

I shrugged.

"Gonna ask Alice over?"

"Yeah."

"Good." He smiled. "We'll do it Friday night. I'll give Jane a call."

That was the only time I ever hated him.

When I got home from school on Friday, Uncle Kid was in the kitchen. He had driven all the way to Fredericton to shop, and the table was cluttered with bags of groceries.

"You can't buy much of anything any good around here," he said. "Look at these mushrooms. They're like apples, and look, fresh. Surf and turf, I thought we'd have. I got filet mignon, live lobster, a melon, a little caviar to give the hors d'oeuvres some class, and three bottles of wine . . . Mouton Cadet, two white and one red. That should do it, don't you think? I picked out some small potatoes that I'm going to boil, then fry them in a bit of oil and herbs. I got a few shrimp. A little bit of everything. We'll have a feast, Corry! We're going to have a good time tonight! Did you tell Alice to dress for it?"

I nodded. I hadn't, of course. I doubted if Alice had anything fancy to wear. I was sort of hoping that she wouldn't wear the white dress with the burn mark on the behind, but other than that I didn't care.

"Did you tell 'er to be here at six?"

"Yeah."

"Well, just before six, you take the Jeep and pick her up. Maybe you should even leave a little earlier and walk over and get her."

At five o'clock, I took a shower and got dressed. I put on my grey suit pants, a white shirt and blue blazer. Uncle Kid wanted me to wear a tie, but I refused. When he came down from dressing, he was wearing black pants, a white jacket, a black shirt and white tie; he had loosened his ponytail so that his hair hung over his shoulders. He looked like a star.

I pulled on my topcoat and drove up the Hemlock Road. The lingering twilight of late February lit my way across the river and up to the Hunters' little house. I knocked on the door and was greeted by Mary Hunter.

"My goodness!" she said. "Don't you look spiffy! Alice! Corry's here!"

Alice came down the stairs. She had on blue slacks, a snug red jacket and a white blouse. He hair was wavy and shiny and blond . . . my heart quickened at the sight of her. She smiled at me and I smiled and held out my arms in a way that indicated my appreciation for her beauty.

"You look pretty sharp, yourself," she said and kissed me a little peck on the cheek.

Twenty minutes later, we found Uncle Kid and Jane Lewis standing in the living room having a drink. Jane, although she looked like a million bucks, was dressed somewhat casually. She had on pressed blue jeans, a somewhat lighter blue blouse and a tweed jacket.

Uncle Kid introduced the girls and everyone smiled and made small talk and was a bit uptight.

"Get yourself and Alice a drink, Corry. There's scotch, gin and vermouth and wine. Go easy on the martinis, though. They're killers. Would you like a martini, Alice?"

"Well, I guess."

"Corry makes a great martini," said Uncle Kid. "He makes them for me now and then and they're always just the way I like them, very dry. Lots of ice in the tin shaker, gently stirred so as not to bruise the gin, just a single drop of vermouth, eh, Corry?"

I hadn't made a martini more than once or twice in my life, and that was Uncle Kid reminding me of how it was done.

"James Bond always wanted his martini shaken," commented Jane.

"You only shake a cocktail to put air in it," said Uncle Kid. "I can't imagine why anyone would want air in a martini."

"Don't you shake a drink to mix the ingredients?"

"Stirring mixes it, ice chills it and shaking puts air in it," said Uncle Kid the authority.

"Alice, are you still in school?" asked Jane.

"Yes, my last year."

I left for the kitchen and made Alice a martini. I poured myself a scotch and water. When I returned to the living room, Jane and Alice were still talking.

"There's so much opportunity out there nowadays for a woman," Jane was saying. "Men are hiring women and women are hiring women."

"Maybe. Thank you, Corry. Maybe that's because we're smarter," said Alice, smiling.

"No, I think it's blatant sexism, but who cares!" laughed Jane. "Have you given any thought to getting into real estate?"

"I haven't given much thought to anything. I can't afford to go to university. I suppose I'll be looking for a job."

"Well!" said Uncle Kid. "I'd better get the hors d'oeuvres."

Over the hors d'oeuvres, through dinner and during dessert, Jane and Alice chatted like two sisters.

Uncle Kid drank martinis and scotch and wine. While clearing the table, he broke a plate. Later, in the living room, he picked up his guitar and sang several songs. The last one he sang was the one with the haunting melody.

"I never heard that song before," commented Jane.

"I need another drink," said Uncle Kid and went to the kitchen. When he came back with his drink, Jane and Alice were chatting about shoes. Uncle Kid drunkenly interrupted. "You know what's wrong?"

"Oh, is something wrong?" asked Jane.

"No, no, no. Nothing's wrong with us, here and now, tonight! I'm talking about mankind! Do you know what's wrong with mankind?"

"A great deal, I expect," said Jane.

"Well, yes, sweetheart, there is a great deal wrong. But number one is that humans have forgotten all that is poetic in life! How many people do you know who can recite 'The Road Not Taken'?"

"Robert Frost?" said Jane.

"Two roads diverged in a yellow wood, And sorry I could not travel both And be one traveller, long I stood," said Alice, and she and Jane laughed.

"What I have to say about Robert Frost is best kept unsaid," said Jane. "Pour me another drink before I go, will you, darling? A small one. I'm driving."

"Get her a drink, Corry," said Uncle Kid. "Make it a double! Now, what's wrong with Robert Frost?"

"He's got made in the US of A by J.F. Kennedy written all over him."

"He's dead!"

"Yes. I'm really not much into poetry, Kid. I know very little about it, really."

I went to the kitchen, poured Jane a nightcap, a small one. When I returned, Uncle Kid was reciting, "Such heaps of broken glass to sweep away, You'd think the inner dome of heaven had fallen . . ." He was halfway into "Birches," and Alice and Jane were looking at each other and smiling as if they thought he had lost his mind.

He had lost his mind. He was totally drunk.

"You'd better take me home," said Alice.

I nodded.

"And I'd better hit the road, too," said Jane. "I guess I don't need that drink, Corry."

"Home!" said Uncle Kid, coming out of his recitation. "You can't go home yet! The night's young! We've just begun to party! Let's turn on the stereo."

"No! No, Kid, I really must be going. I've a long drive and it's after twelve."

"But I thought you'd be spending the night."

"I'm sorry," said Jane gently. She was handling him with kid gloves. "I must have forgotten to tell you. I have an open house in the morning."

"Well, what can I say? But you and Alice can stick around for a while, eh, Corry?"

"I'm afraid not, Mr. Lauder," said Alice. "I really have to leave, too."

Uncle Kid said nothing, walked over to the sofa and sat.

Jane, Alice and I went into the hall and put on our coats and boots.

"Good night, Mr. Lauder," said Alice.

"Good night, Kid," said Jane.

Uncle Kid did not see us to the door, did not leave his place on the sofa, did not say good night.

Alice and I took the Jeep and Jane sped off in the opposite direction.

I never saw Jane Lewis again.

When I got home an hour later, the stereo was blasting Jethro Tull in the living room and Uncle Kid was passed out on the sofa, still in his white jacket, black shirt, white tie . . . the star.

11

The next day was not an easy one. Ethan Harris and Floyd Winslow were at Paul Vincent's rock pile bright and early. Floyd drove in our lane with a load of rocks at nine-fifteen. I was up and ready to get at it, but Uncle Kid was still in bed. I invited Floyd into the house, poured him a cup of coffee and went up to see if I could shake some life into Uncle Kid. It wasn't easy. Uncle Kid had a hangover and was terribly irritable. It took him a half-hour to get showered and dressed. When he finally joined us in the kitchen, he drank coffee for a half-hour and discussed the game plan with Floyd.

"Do you think the ice will hold up a truckload of rocks?" asked Floyd.

"I don't know. We'll have to chop through and see how thick it is. If we decide it's too thin, then we'll have to dump them on the shore and tote them out a few at a time with a horse or something."

Floyd Winslow was a big man in every sense of the word. Six-foot-six, a pot belly, big hands and feet. He was dirty, his clothes smelled of sweat and tobacco smoke, and he needed a shave. When he talked, he sounded like he had bubbles in his throat.

"Do you think it'll do any good?" asked Floyd.

"Can't hurt. It's a chub hole now. Can't get any worse. If we can get it to hold one salmon, that's better than none."

"Do you have a permit?"

"No permit."

"You ain't scared the wardens might show up?" Floyd sounded like he had so much stuff in his throat that I got the sensation of wanting to cough for him.

"If they show, we'll tell them we didn't know dumping rocks in the river was against the law and quit doin' it."

"It'll be a scrape if we go through the ice."

"Well, we'll take a look at it."

There was something different about Uncle Kid. "What is it?" I asked myself. "He not only acts differently, he *is* different! He's changed."

I took inventory. "His hair is still the same, long, tied in a ponytail, brown with a few grey streaks, no more than usual. His eyes are still green. The beard is gone, but that's been gone for a long time. He hasn't grown or gotten smaller. He still smiles a lot. Good teeth. His voice is still deep and strong." I could not put a finger on his metamorphosis.

"Bart Griffin got fined a pile o' money for dumping rocks in the river," said Floyd.

"He did more than dump rocks. He put a bulldozer out there and changed the channel."

"So long as I'm not getting into trouble."

"If we get caught, I'll tell them you believed I had a permit. It'll be all my fault. You'll not get into trouble."

"Fair enough. I heard you and Bill Hall had quite a spree the other night."

"Yeah. Been doin' that a lot, lately."

"Pole-vaultin' over an air hole is a pretty dangerous game."

"We had a spike on the end of the pole."

"Yeah, but."

"I guess we should get at it, if we're gonna get three loads dumped."

We chopped through and found the ice in the river was a foot thick, blue and solid. Uncle Kid thought it would support the truck. Floyd disagreed.

"I'll take the Jeep out and prove it to you," said Uncle Kid.

"That Jeep ain't no weight at all, compared to that three-ton loaded with rocks. Why don't you tote them to where you want them with the Jeep?"

Uncle Kid gave this some thought and finally agreed. "We'll need a chain and a sled," he said.

"There's not too many there small enough to lift. A man can hurt his back pretty quick, liftin' rocks."

"Well, you dump the rocks right here on the shore and Corry and I'll go borrow a sled."

"Rocks might be a bit heavy for a sled."

"Yeah, well, just dump them. Ethan's back there waiting to re-load you."

"Good, good. I'll just dump them and get out of here. I'll be back in an hour or so."

"This is going to be a pain in the ass," said Uncle Kid after Floyd dumped the rocks and drove away.

I agreed. Some of the rocks were very big. We'd be able to lift a few of them, but it would be hard work. It was going to be a cold task, too, for it was cloudy and there was a cold upriver wind.

"Do you really want to do this?" asked Uncle Kid.

I shook my head.

"Neither do I," he said. "But I suppose we should give it a try."

So, we jumped in the Jeep and drove all over the settlement looking for a sled. We finally borrowed one from Lou O'Hare. It was a big one that Lou used for yarding pulp, would hold about half a cord.

By the time we hauled it up the road and out to the river, two hours had passed and Floyd was back with his second load.

"Tell Ethan to load you with smaller rocks next time," Uncle Kid told Floyd. "There must be smaller rocks in that pile."

"Well, ya see, Paul Vincent is there and it's the big ones he wants to get rid of."

"Yeah, well, we can only lift about half of them, by the looks of it, even if we double up."

Floyd dumped the second load and went for the third. Uncle Kid and I started to work. The first thing we realized we had to do was plow a road out to where we wanted the pool. It was while doing this that we realized that if we wanted piles of rocks all over the place, say in a hundred different locations, we'd have to plow a hundred different roads.

"We'll do nothing but plow all day," said Uncle Kid. "Any ideas?"

I took out my pen and pad and wrote, "Make one big pile upstream from where we want the pool to be."

"Make an abutment, you mean."

I nodded, wrote, "A big pile will alter the current, change the bottom of the river, make bars and holes. We can place the rocks in the summer, or an ice jam might do it for us."

"Well, we got nothing to lose. Any change will be positive and we're just playing it by ear, anyway."

So we plowed one road up to about a hundred yards beyond where we thought the pool should be, went back and loaded the sled with as much as we figured it would hold without collapsing and chained it to the Jeep. The Jeep spun a bit at first, but once it got going it pulled the load with relative ease.

Stopping only for a quick lunch, we hauled load after load until it got too dark to see. I was amazed at how strong the ice was. Our pile of rocks grew to be twice the size of an ordinary sedan and must have weighed many tons, but the ice held. It seemed Uncle Kid had been right, Floyd could have driven his truck out there, dumped them and saved us all that work.

The work didn't end at the end of that blustery Saturday. We were back at it on Sunday. About ten o'clock, Bill Hall joined us. A little later, Alice made me very proud by showing up with a thermos of coffee and some Styrofoam cups.

"Would you like for me to go to your place and fix you all some lunch?" she asked me.

I looked to Uncle Kid to see what he thought of the idea, but he turned away and started talking to Bill.

"Why not?" I asked myself, turned back to Alice and nodded.

By mid-afternoon we had all the rocks small enough to lift hauled out onto the ice and placed on our pile. The bigger ones we chained and toted one at a time. Following the road Uncle Kid had plowed, we placed these big ones in a line, starting at our big pile in the middle of the river and ending about twenty feet from shore, just out from where Floyd had dumped them.

About five o'clock, the job was finished, and although we were tired and sore, I can't remember ever feeling any better about anything else I've ever done. It was something that we had started, persevered with and completed. Bill Hall had been a great help. We could never have handled the bigger boulders without him. And Alice was wonderful, too. She fixed us a nice lunch, vegetable soup and salmon sandwiches, cleaned up the kitchen after we went back to work, then brought us coffee again later that afternoon.

It was during the afternoon, with Bill Hall there, that Uncle Kid became temporarily himself again. If anyone could bring the best of Uncle Kid to the surface, it was Bill Hall. He and Bill were lifting one end of a boulder for me to put the chain under, when I recognized not only that he was himself again but also what the change had been.

He said to Bill, "The German word for child or children is kinder. Their word for garden is garten."

"Where ya coming from, Kid?"

"Well, that's the place where children play. Kindergarten."

"Brilliant, Kid. Now, lift."

Uncle Kid smiled and lifted. "I have given it another layer," he said to Bill. "A garden is also a place where you grow things. Therefore, a kindergarten, or kinder garden, is the place where children grow."

"What's the point, Kid?"

"I just thought that kindergarten might be an all-around good socially accepted word for the female genitalia, that's all."

It was not that brilliant little observation that cleared up the mystery for me. It was immediately after, when he started whistling under his breath, whisper-whistling, that I knew he was himself again.

There are a few traits that are distinctively human. Blushing and smiling and being perpetually sexually active are the ones we most commonly think of. The others are more subtle, like itching at the mere thought of a louse, needing to yawn when you see other people yawn, or wanting to clear your throat when someone talks with bubbles in his larynx, like Floyd Winslow. Another thing that is distinctively human, unless you include birds or howling wolves or roaring lions, is singing. Happy, healthy people have songs in their hearts. You sing through the sleepless nights and the idle afternoons. Even people with *broken* hearts sing, it brings back some of the joy they've lost. The song within you may be synonymous with God. According to Al Jolson, a man ain't got a friend without a song. Mothers can calm a fetus by singing or listening to soft music. Fathers' gardens grow better when they are sung to. In the heart, in the soul, everything from complicated symphonies to whisper-whistled ditties, there's always a song. If you do not have a song in your heart, chances are there's not much happening there.

Drunk, Uncle Kid sometimes sang "Jumping Jack Flash is a gas" all night. It was during the day, when he was sober, that he was without a song. Who would want to carry "Jumping Jack Flash" around in his or her heart?

I really don't know why, but there on the bank of the river, I reached down deep for my best Pavarotti voice and sang as loud as I could. "Some Enchanted Evening" — "Um e yaya e aw, oo a eh a aya!"

Bill Hall looked at me and then at Uncle Kid and said, "OK, OK! Where'd ya get the good pot?"

March tied his lion to February's hitching post and led his lamb into the year and toward the Canadian spring. Carefully, reluctantly, he tiptoed, like a barefooted shepherd in a chicken coop. In one hand, he carried a bag of cold winds and storms, the booty he'd seized from Winter. In his other hand, wrapped and ribboned in a hatbox, so that only the rocks could feel its warmth, he carried the naked sun. The naked sun was a gift for April. One day, at teatime, he unwrapped the gift to show to Ides, his middleman. Exposed, the sun arrogantly bent over and mooned both of them.

Embarrassed by this shameless display, our rocks blushed and fell through the ice.

Uncle Kid wrote that one night while partying with himself and possibly the Muse in the living room. I found it, a crumpled ball, the next morning.

In March, I received a package and a note from Denise Bertrand Masters. The note was a short one.

Dear Corry,
   Hope these books will be helpful. They're all I could find. We'll be seeing you soon and, I hope, a great deal during the summer. Mark has pulled a few strings and either you or Kid can go to work as a guide on the upper reaches (the Crown waters) of the Little Southwest Miramichi.
   Will be talking at you soon.
                                            Love,
                                            Denise

I opened the package and found two books: *Exploring Mime*, by Mark Stolzenberg, and *Mime: A Playbook of Silent Fantasy*, by Kay Hamblin. Finally I had something to work with, something to get me started on the right foot. I went up to my room to read, to get started.

I found both books very informative, but trying to work from the two simultaneously was confusing. They both suggested starting practice with warm-ups, but they had different philosophies on what a warm-up should be. So to avoid confusion I decided to alternate the two, to work with the Kay Hamblin book for a week, then work with the Mark Stolzenberg book for a week.

While Mark Stolzenberg leaned toward somewhat of an athletic and deliberate exercise, Kay Hamblin suggested that the mere observation of everything you might normally do, for instance while taking a shower — turning on the faucet, applying soap, feeling the water tickle your back, drying off — was a warm-up. Mark Stolzenberg got things rolling with "The Statue." Kay Hamblin thought "The Marionette" was a good beginning.

I found the best time to do creative things was early in the morning. At four a.m. my mind was clear and rested and I found it easier to direct my thoughts, to concentrate. You could have entered our house any time after four and you would have found me somewhere, in the kitchen, dining room, living room, up in my bedroom, even in the bathroom, miming. You would have seen me climbing stairs, ladders and ropes that weren't there, walking for miles yet going nowhere on non-existent streets, juggling invisible balls, sitting on make-believe chairs, watching tremendously sad or extremely funny programs on a TV as imperceptible as an atom. Sometimes I'd use that same make-believe chair to tame the many ferocious lions and tigers that frequently visited.

If a passer-by had chanced to peep through the window at me, he would have thought he was seeing a ghost or an extremely insane young man. To see me gracefully playing with my invisible toys, silent as the stars in the sky, would have been a frightening experience.

I guess that's another reason why I did my miming before anyone else was up and about. I didn't want anyone to see me. Ultimately, that was the reason why I eventually quit miming. Not much sense in being an unseen actor. Makes about as much sense as writing a book that no one will ever read. And that could very well be what I'm doing with my life nowadays. Will I do the same with this manuscript as Uncle Kid does with his songs and poems, crumple it up and toss it in the corner? It's not easy for a Canadian artist to have any genuine confidence. People from other places are so much better than we are.

In *Fast Living* (a book published by Fiddlehead Poetry Books, Fredericton, 1982, with the assistance of the University of New Brunswick and the Canada Council), Lesley Choyce (a poet who might have been living in the Kootenays at the time) wrote:

Creative Writing in Canada

There are five published writers
   living in Toronto.
Everything they write becomes a book, becomes famous:
   grocery lists, tax returns, transcribed
   telephone conversations.
They are prolific writers and sell well
   in the provinces.

With the aid of general government grants
All other writers have been silenced, or gathered
   and sent off to camps in Gaspé,
   Baffin Island or the Kootenays.
Canada is proud of her professional writers,
   the rest are criminals
Including the woman from Sackville, N.B. —
   accused of literature and sent to prison
   for a note to the milkman.

Lesley Choyce should have won an award for that.

Uncle Kid and I were busier than usual that spring. In school, I was working toward graduation day. Other than being a mime, I didn't know exactly what I wanted to do after graduation, but I was studying a little harder than usual, thinking that I might want to go to university in the fall and, if so, a scholarship would be a tremendous asset. I could not turn to my father for money, and I doubted very much if Uncle Kid had any. Uncle Kid was too busy spending money to have any. Not only was he spending money on the shed, rigging it up for sports, but he was giving Izaak Walton's a facelift as well. I helped him put drywall on the interior walls and ceiling of the junk room end of the shed, put down a new floor, build a closet and install a bathroom. He purchased a huge window, which we installed on the back side facing the river, and we put in another smaller one on the front side facing the road. The old door with the latch and the huge padlock had to be replaced with a new one with a regular knob. Then we painted inside and out. The shed had borrowed its electricity from the house. To give it independence, Uncle Kid bought a new entrance and hired an electrician to install it. The same electrician wired the place for lighting and heat.

Then there was the furniture — a new bed and mattress, a new dresser, two new lamps, a bedside table, a clock-radio, a couple of tasteful prints for the wall, a bedside rug, curtains. Uncle Kid bought pillows, pillowcases, sheets and blankets, towels, facecloths and soap.

"There's only two things missing," he said to me one day.

"Huh?"

"I won't particularly like the look of it in either room, but we need a fridge. The sports will want to keep some beer and ice, snacks and things."

"An'?"

"Sports."

The renovations to Izaak Walton's were less extensive. All he did out there was add some new shelving and paint. In April, a truck pulled in with a bigger-than-usual selection of rods, reels, lines, leaders, vests and waders. He also bought more flies from his tiers in the community.

Then one day he drove in our driveway in a new green, 4x4 Bronco.

Where all the money came from I didn't know and didn't ask. I don't think he got it by selling dope. He had gotten rid of most of that. I think he must have mortgaged the farm.

One evening I heard Uncle Kid talking on the phone.

"How's she goin', Leonard old boy? . . . Yeah, Kid . . . The very best . . . Well, I might get down sometime, but . . . Yeah, well, maybe, but . . . Yeah . . . Sure . . . I'd like to . . . Sounds like great fun! . . . Well, I'll tell ya. I rigged up a sport camp . . . Yeah, I think it's a wonderful place . . . I also rigged up a pool . . . That's right. Right out front here. Big enough for three or four people . . . Oh, car tires, rocks . . . Ha, ha! . . . Yeah, car tires! Ha, ha! . . . Yeah, well, I need some people . . . One man or maybe a man and wife. I just have one bed, so far . . . Well, I do have a spare room in the house, so I suppose I could handle two men or two couples . . . Two women? Sure. The more women the better! Ha, ha . . . Guides? Well, there's me and Corry . . . Yeah, he's old enough. He'll be graduating in a couple of months . . . One of the best fisherman I know . . . Yeah, he's dating a little lady from over the river. Jim Hunter's daughter . . . Yeah, ha, ha! . . . Like Jim? No, she doesn't look like Jim. Not yet, anyway . . . Yeah, well, I'd appreciate it. Yeah, well, that would be great . . . Oh, I don't think I'll ever give up the scotch . . . Ha, ha! So what kind of a winter did ya have in Albany?"

Uncle Kid talked to Leonard Hoge, his lawyer friend from Albany, for an hour. Uncle Kid had guided, or, more accurately, drunk scotch with Leonard Hoge for a week or two every summer for many years. They were buddies. By the time they finished their conversation, Uncle Kid had Leonard and a friend booked to stay for a week in June. We had customers, sports. We were in business.

"It's too late this year," said Uncle Kid after he hung up, "but Leonard recommends that next year in February we go to Boston, New York, Worcester, wherever a sportsman show is held, and lobby, meet people that might be interested in fishing the Miramichi. He told me that's how other outfitters do it. We're in business, Corry! We're outfitters!"

I gave him the thumbs up sign.

"We need a name," he said. "A good catchy name to put on a sign. Something or other lodge. Any ideas?"

I grabbed my pen and pad, wrote, "The Silver Rapids Lodge?"

"Well, maybe. It would be nice to have something catchy. Now, let me see. There's Wade's Camps, the Old River Lodge. There's Wilson's and Pond's. Lauder's wouldn't sound very good, would it? The Silver Rapids Lodge. I don't know, I don't know."

We were sitting in the living room. Uncle Kid stood and went to the kitchen. When he returned a minute later, he had a marijuana joint with him. "Inspiration," he announced, lighting up the joint. "Sweet inspiration. Want some?"

I shook my head. I would have smoked some of it, but I still had some studying to do.

Uncle Kid smoked it alone. I could actually see him getting high. His voice changed, seemed to come from deeper within; his eyes glazed over, his movements became more premeditated, more deliberate. He was sitting in his big leather chair, had one eye closed as if peeping into something. Carla Bowes was right. He was an old hippie, a forty-six-year-old flower child.

"Stoned," I thought, "it will be hard to keep him focused." He often did that — smoked a joint for inspiration, then forgot why he smoked the joint.

"I had no trouble naming Izaak Walton's," he said. "I actually named Izaak Walton's before I built it. It was the idea of having a pro shop called Izaak Walton's that urged me on. I think if I had called it something like Lauder's Fishing Tackle, or Kid's Kit and Caboodle, or Ye Olde Angler's something or other, it would never have gotten built. The name Izaak Walton's shows imagination, class. I've told you about Izaak Walton, haven't I?"

I nodded.

Uncle Kid sighed, looked at the ceiling. "I'm in transit," he said. "I'll get back to you in a minute."

In transit meant that he was flying on marijuana wings and had not reached a level where he could think long enough to speak or verbalize anything he might think about in passing.

I waited. It usually didn't take long, sometimes no more than a few seconds. It may have seemed longer to him, however, for quite often when he returned his focus to me his mind was in some other state. Apparently flying on marijuana wings was a swift way to travel.

"Clouds," he said.

I grinned and waited. It was always fun to hear him rave.

"Bows and flows of angel's hair, And ice cream castles in the air . . ." he sang. "Joni Mitchell. What a poet! You know, Corry, there's two ways of looking at clouds. Besides being misty, fluffy things that drift about like down on the wind, clouds also represent or prophesy a drop in the barometric pressure, or, in humans, a drop toward disheartenment. A grey day is the day your lover walks away. But it's on the grey days when you meet your real friends."

Uncle Kid was still in transit as far as I was concerned.

"I am a would-be artist," he said with a sigh and fell silent.

"Huh?" I tried to snap him back into my world.

"Oh, I was just thinking . . . a would-be artist, a dilettante has his head in the clouds. You can see very little when you have your head in the clouds. Joni Mitchell was no dilettante. Do you know the difference between the academic and the artist? The true artist is never conventional. The term conventional art is an oxymoron. There is the academic and the artist, two individuals. The academic stands with his feet on the ground, making precise and practical conventional movements toward an understanding. Ha! Understanding, understanding . . . standing under the clouds! Ha! Maybe I should've said standing under the clouds."

"Huh?"

"Never mind. Anyway, the artist soars above the clouds. Both have their place, mind you. We need our academics and we need our artists. What we don't need in this world are the would-bes. Would-bes clutter the world with misinformation. Would-be academics are liars! Would-be artists are plagiarists! Would-bes have their heads *in* the clouds. A would-be writer writes about himself. A would-be painter paints by numbers. A would-be academic is a blind critic.

"Let me fill you in on something, Corry. Denise Masters is a would-be artist. What she really is, is an academic. Fiction is not her forte. That's why she's so frustrated. She has all the skills for developing the perfect syntax, but she doesn't have a creative bone in her body."

I found that a little hard to believe. Denise Bertrand Masters had a list of published novels a mile long.

"Why do you call yourself a would-be?" I scribbled.

"Because I write my poems and songs with my head in the clouds. I do not see clearly. All I can see is myself. I'm egotistical. No matter how it appears, I write in the first person. Everything's about me! And let me tell ya, Corry, there's very few people I know, including myself, that's interesting enough to be a feature character."

He looked at me and opened his arms as if I was an Italian widow and he was my long lost son come home. "And there I go again!" He practically shouted. "Even while I'm talking about it, I'm doing it! Don't you see, Corry, my friend? Here we are, talking, the two of us, and it's all about me! You're here! Why aren't we talking about you? You've got a life! Things are happening to you! Why aren't we talking about you? What's happening in your life, Corry? Tell me! Write it down! There's gotta be something going on with you! I've been busy, I've been working and scheming and planning and writing. . . . Writing. Ha! I haven't written a word worth reading! But who cares? I just jot stuff down for my own enjoyment. It's not like I'm about to send it off to Doubleday or whoever. I'm no Izaak Walton! Actually, I'm glad I'm not Izaak Walton. Izaak Walton often stooped to redundancy for the sake of a rhyme. No, I'm just an ordinary lad trying to carve out a life, and in ten, twenty, thirty years, I'll be dead and gone, forgotten. Eventually, even the gods will vanish. How about the Booze and Snooze Club? Ha! With clients like Leonard Hoge, a name like that would be fitting as anything."

"I've been practising miming," I wrote.

He read my note and laughed. "Well, I won't tell anybody. Mime's the word. Ha! Get it? Mime's the word. Ha, ha, ha . . . ahem! Mime's the word, mime's the word. Maybe mime *is* the word. Why not? The Mime's Inn. We could take our sports down to the Firestone Pool in tights and whiteface and pretend we're fishing. Wouldn't matter then whether the pool held fish or not. All we have to do is pretend, mime. Yahoo! Hooked one! Twenty-pounder I believe! We'd get our limit every day, rain, shine, in the heat of the summer. We'd be the most successful outfitters on the river! We *guarantee* salmon! Ha, ha, ha . . . and if we all dressed like clowns, people would come from all over the world just to see us out there on the river. I'm crazy! I know, I'm crazy."

"And I'll be the mascot," I wrote.

He read and looked at me curiously.

"Ah, now I've offended you."

I shook my head. I wasn't offended. I knew he was stoned.

"I wasn't completely out of 'er right there," he said. "We could call it the Mime's Inn or the Mime's Lodge or something. Couldn't we?"

I nodded.

He stared at me then with so much depth that I was compelled to look away.

"You've been practising?" he asked.

I nodded.

"Do something for me. Mime something."

Suddenly, I felt very nervous. He wanted me to act, to be the centre of attention. I'd spent much of my life in the background. It was not easy to take centre stage, even if Uncle Kid was the only one watching.

"C'mon, Corry. Show me your stuff. Be an individual. Show me that you're an artist. Show me you're not just some would-be. Give me a reason to think that this mime thing is not just a whim already in flight. Remember the song I sang to you and the girls on the night of our dinner party? That was me showing off my stuff. I had to get drunk to do it, of course. But, it was me feeling out my ability. Nobody liked the song."

I looked at him quizzically.

"Oh, it's not the first time I've tried my wares on people. The fools encourage me and the wise ones respond pretty much in the same way that you three did. With indifference. When somebody you respect and love reacts to your work with indifference, you know that they're trying to tell you to get a day job, you know that you're nothing more than a would-be. Oh, I know, I know, I could probably get on some stage and sing my songs, I might even get my poems published. But people would never love or hate me for my work. My poetry would get scanned and placed on the shelf, there forever to collect dust, to be looked upon, if at all, with indifference. The stuff of a would-be artist."

That was heavy-duty persuasion I couldn't ignore, couldn't shrug off. He wanted me to prove myself. I decided what I wanted to do, stood, and, shaking my arms and legs like a rag doll, ran around the room — then suddenly froze. I did not move a muscle, did not bat an eye. I breathed as inconspicuously as I possibly could. I was on the Mark Stolzenberg cycle, had been practising "The Statue" all week.

I don't know how long I held the position, but it seemed like a very long time. I had fixed my eyes on a make-believe Princess Anne, halfway between me and the wall. I felt that watching a fascinating and magnificent creature like Princess Anne would give my eyes, my statue, that twinkle of life, that inside energy that's so important for a statue to have. However, with my eyes fixed on Princess Anne, I could not see Uncle Kid's reaction.

Uncle Kid showed his approval by dropping a quarter at my feet. When I heard it hit the floor, I looked down. The act was over.

"Look for a day job?" I wrote.

"Is it always the same statue?" he asked.

I shook my head. It was always a different statue.

"Ancient Greeks believed that the hand of a statue has no soul because it cannot grasp, and the eye of a blind person has no soul because it cannot see. Aristotle came along and asserted that all eyes have potential seeing."

I sighed and stomped my foot.

"What's the matter?" he asked.

"What has Aristotle got do with my statue?" I wrote.

"I don't know . . . I don't know much about Aristotle, Corry. I just know that little bit. I read it somewhere, I suppose. But it does relate, I think. Aristotle may have seen the statue of Hermes or one of its equals. If he did, he would have seen the life in it. Aristotle was either an artist or an academic, one or the other. He was not a would-be. He could see the energy in the hands and eyes of the statue, he could see it in the faces created by painters. Michelangelo had that gift, too. He breathed life into the David and the Moses. Da Vinci zapped energy into the Mona Lisa. Pavarotti zaps his songs with it, Shakespeare practically overflowed *A Midsummer Night's Dream* with it. And you, Corry, are pretty close. When I saw you as a statue, I forced myself to hold back the tears."

"Bullshit," I said to myself. "Stoned bullshit! He's just trying to back up his rave and sound intelligent."

Stoned or not, he had praised me highly and I showed my gratitude with neither pride nor humility. If I showed anything, it was indifference.

However, the next day, after he'd painted and hung the sign on the side of the shed, I went off by myself and wept.

"Corry's Fishing Camp," it read. I didn't know what the hell was happening to us.

12

About halfway into April, the ice in the river cracked and moved, piled up and jammed a bit, then, with a final groan that we heard all the way up at the house, headed for the bay. The day snorted condescendingly at the calendar, and, in the manner of a fruity prince, arrogantly proclaimed, "*I'm* the first day of spring!"

Crows saluted this day with twenty-one caws. Everything from blades of grass to earthworms, from mosquito proboscises to mammalian penises stood reverently at attention while robins sang "Farewell to Nova Scotia," New Brunswick's provincial anthem. Uncle Kid and I declared it a holiday. That evening we jumped into the new Bronco 4x4, and with me driving, headed for Silver Rapids. I dropped Uncle Kid off at the Legion, then went over to the Pharmasave to do some shopping. I purchased a dozen condoms, and because Easter was just around the corner, I bought Alice a dozen Easter eggs and a card.

That was the first time I ever purchased condoms. Previous to that evening, you couldn't have paid me enough money to walk into that drug store and buy those things in Silver Rapids. Previous to that evening, I would have been embarrassed to even be in the condom section of the store. But that evening? What can I say? It was spring.

The road up the other side of the river is muddy and treacherous in the spring. Very few people drive on it. It's rarely travelled upon any time of the year. If the Bronco hadn't been a four-wheel drive, I wouldn't have made it.

The settlement on the other side of the river is a dying one. There's only three families left over there. No sense fixing a road for three families. That's why Alice crosses the ice in the winter and canoes over in the summer to the Hemlock Road to catch the bus to school. There's about two weeks in the spring, when the ice is still in but is unfit to walk on, that she's completely stranded. With final exams coming up, spring is not a good time to miss out on two weeks of school.

Two weeks before that evening, before the day the ice went out, I wrote to Uncle Kid.

"We must help her."

"How?" he asked.

"I'll pick her up in the mornings and take her home at night in the Bronco," I wrote.

"But that's a brand new vehicle," he reasoned. "You could ruin it driving up that road!"

"The Bronco is made for that kind of terrain!" I wrote. "We just can't ignore Alice! It's very important that she graduate!"

"Ah, hell!"

"She's the only friend I have."

"Ah, hell!"

"She helps *me* with studies all the time."

"But that damned road . . ."

"I can drive on it. It's not that bad for a 4x4."

"Here! Go! Do it!" He threw me the keys.

I was spending a lot of time with Alice, and we were the only kids that drove to school in our very own wheels.

It was a wonderful feeling to be able to drive around with my girl, a feeling that included freedom and adventure. Perhaps the fact that spring was in the air added something. The Bronco was covered with mud from top to bottom, and Uncle Kid walked around frowning every day, but he was patient, knew that it would end when the ice moved out. I guess that's why, when it finally did go, we declared a holiday. I was celebrating the fact that I'd had two wonderful weeks of driving the Bronco, and Uncle Kid was celebrating the fact that he was getting the Bronco back in one piece.

Anyway, I prepared my gift for Alice and drove up that awful road and out the lane to her house. She came running to greet me.

"Corry! What a surprise! What are you doing here in the evening?"

I pointed to the river, then to the sky. I spread my arms as if embracing it all. "Ha, ha!" I said.

Alice smiled.

I pointed at the Bronco.

"You want to take me for a ride?"

I nodded.

"Well, OK. I'll get a jacket."

She went in the house and returned in a minute wearing a red jacket. We jumped into the Bronco. "Where we going?" she asked.

I shrugged. Somewhere, anywhere, I didn't know.

Above Alice's place, the road got even worse, so I headed back in the direction of Silver Rapids. I drove for about two miles, pulled over, stopped and opened the door.

"Where are you going?"

I pointed to the back seat.

"I don't think that's a good idea, Corry."

I sighed and slapped the front seat. It was a bucket seat. You can't make love in a bucket seat.

"Well, I'll go back, but we can't go all the way. You know that. I'm not on the pill. We've talked about that."

So we climbed into the back seat and hugged and kissed, caressed and fondled, steamed up the windows.

"Oh, I love you so much, Corry," she breathed.

I kissed her eyes. Kissing her eyes was my way of saying, "I love you, too."

I pulled away from her and reached under the front seat for the gift. I handed her the bag.

"What's this? Oh! It's a . . . Corry!"

In Silver Rapids, before heading up to Alice's, I had removed the condoms from their box and placed them in the basket with the eggs. Looking at this little treasure, Alice didn't know whether to laugh or cry.

"They're . . . it's . . . very romantic," she said and laughed.

I grabbed my pen and wrote on the bag her gift had been in, "I have something else for you, but I have to wrap it up first."

God, it was great to be responsible.

So Alice and I allowed our bodies to throw a party in the back seat of the Bronco. Even the Bronco danced.

*

On one of those days in April, we deposited a thousand copies of flyers in mailboxes all over the area.

OPENING DAY!
THE NEWLY RENOVATED IZAAK WALTON'S
OPENS ON APRIL 15.
EXPANDED STOCK!
GREAT DEALS!
WE'RE A SKIP AND A JUMP UP THE HEMLOCK
ROAD.
WE SWEAR
YOU'LL FIND A DEAL.
CHECK US OUT.

On opening day, we stayed open until ten o'clock at night and sold over three thousand dollars' worth of merchandise. On the days that followed, business continued to boom. One Saturday we sold over five thousand dollars' worth. Everything was going so right. Life was sweet. If we had kept on selling like that, we would have gotten rich. Being successful and getting rich is not in Uncle Kid's chemical makeup, however.

When you sell twenty-five or thirty thousand dollars worth of goods out of a small store like Izaak Walton's, you leave the shelves virtually bare. What you should do then is curb your domestic spending, pay off your debts and reinvest at least some of the profits in the business.

But Uncle Kid's chemistry leans more toward the party animal than the entrepreneur. Uncle Kid paid off his debts, I think, but he blew the profits on wine, women, Bill Hall and myself. I don't know where he found the stamina. He worked in the store from eight in the morning to ten at night, then partied half the night. I was on the road half the time, buying him booze and clothes and food.

"Go to Newcastle, Corry," he'd say, handing me a hundred dollars. "Pick me up some good porterhouse steaks and a couple of bottles of the old Mouton Cadet. Get you and me a couple of shirts while you're there."

I could buy his shirts and jeans because we were the same size. When it came to buying dress pants and jackets, however, he'd jump in the Bronco and head to Newcastle or Fredericton by himself, leaving me in charge of Izaak Walton's.

It was on those days that I started stealing. If I sold a fishing rod that was worth a couple of hundred dollars, I'd look up the wholesale price and pocket the profit. Sometimes the profit on a quality rod or reel would exceed a hundred dollars. "Better in my pocket than in the hands of some dope dealer or the till of a liquor store," I reasoned.

I had no intentions of keeping the money, of course. It was my plan to reinvest it or give it back to him on a rainy day.

Uncle Kid never caught on because he never knew how much money he was spending on any one particular bash. When he started finding himself short of cash, he simply shrugged and said, "I guess I blew it."

"You gotta slow down," I wrote.

"What d'ya mean, I gotta slow down?"

I scribbled, "Too much spending."

He thought for a moment. We were out in Izaak Walton's and I watched him scan the shelves. He sighed. I could tell he was troubled.

Finally he said, "Yeah, well. I don't know where I'm going, what I'm doing . . . nothing. One time I read my horoscope. You are a Capricorn, it said. You are a late bloomer. I'm pushing fifty. Did you know that? Pushing fifty, and as far as I can see I've never even budded yet. I probably blew five or six thousand dollars in the last little while. But God it was great! You should've seen the blond I picked up in Fredericton last Saturday. Anyway, I blew it. You worried?"

I nodded, wrote. "You could've gone to Florence."

"Ha! Florence. I could have banked the money is what I could've done. You have a prom coming up and a graduation. Did we buy you a new suit?"

I shook my head.

He sighed again, scanned the shelves. "We sold that Orvis? Who bought it?"

"John Flynn," I wrote.

"Dave King bought the eight-footer. Five hundred bucks he paid for it. Bill Hall still owes me for the Sage. At least, I didn't get to spend the profits on that . . . yet. Well, we have our sports in June. The money from that should get you through the graduation. I can go guiding again. I should call Mark Masters and see if he still plans to go cat hunting. It might be good for me to work up there in the woods as a warden. At least I wouldn't be able to spend every cent up there. He'll never find that cat, though. He's chasing a ghost, I think."

He whisper-whistled a few bars of "My Way." He went to the window and watched either his own reflection in the glass or something beyond. When he spoke again, it was as if to himself.

"Providence . . . trailing providence . . . shadowing providence . . . let providence lead the way . . . a late bloomer . . . I hope the frost don't nip me in the bud. Ha! The Dungarvon . . . the Dungarvon Whooper. The ghost of Dungarvon!"

He swung back to me. "Have you heard of the Dungarvon Whooper, Corry?"

I nodded. The Dungarvon Whooper was a ghost that haunted the Dungarvon River country. One man murdered another up

196

there a hundred or more years ago and buried the body in the soft clay of a spring. The ghost of the deceased started screaming and hollering in such a horrible manner that a whole crew of lumberjacks left the woods, afraid for their lives.

"Some claim the Dungarvon Whooper was an eastern cougar, that they can scream like that. The eastern cougar is the cat Mark pursues. Some people think that it's still up there on the Dungarvon. I think Mark is searching in the wrong place, spends most of his time on the Little Southwest Miramichi when he should be on the Dungarvon.

"Weird things happen on the Dungarvon. They claim that Brennen Siding, if you can believe anyone from Brennen Siding, is haunted something damnable. Well, there's still a lot of superstition around. And Mark's the expert. He must know what he's doing."

"I have two thousand dollars of your money," I wrote.

He looked at me with the expression of complete awe on his face. "You have? How?"

"I stashed the profits for you," I scribbled. I was a bit nervous, afraid he might get angry.

"You did? Why?"

"I knew you'd need it and you were sort of out of control," I wrote.

"Two thousand dollars?"

I nodded.

"Where'd you stash it?"

I pointed to the house. "Orry," I said and shrugged.

"Sorry? Don't be sorry. You did the right thing . . . I guess."

"I'll go get it," I wrote and started for the door.

"No! No, don't get it. Not yet. Ha! Some businessman! You know, I didn't miss it. I thought I'd spent it. I must be getting in pretty bad shape. Poets would call a lad like me a roué. A party animal. I wasn't always a party animal. I might have started out as one and I may be heading back into it these days, but for years there I was pretty darn good. Had to be. Couldn't run around like a wild man and be responsible for a young lad. Now you've grown up and can look after yourself, look after me, for that matter. It all happened so fast. One day you're a little kid and the next day you're a man driving around with a little lady, condoms under the seat."

I blushed.

Uncle Kid saw my embarrassment. "Ah, don't worry about it," he said. "That condom I found under the seat was a revelation. It told me more than if you had given me your autobiography. There it was, The Life and Times of Corry Quinn. It told me that you had grown up, that you were a man. It told me that I had done something right, that I had raised you to be a responsible person, a man who can look after himself and his interests. Now you're looking after my interests, too. No, Corry, don't be sorry for anything. I'm an idiot. So, what are you going to do with the money?"

"Give it to you," I wrote.

"You know me! I'll just spend it!"

I shook my head, wrote, "Buy more stock for Izaak Walton's."

"Yeah, well, ya can't buy much with a couple of thousand. Half a dozen fishing rods, a couple of reels."

"Better than nothing. Call Mark."

Uncle Kid eyed me thoughtfully. "Mr. Ambitious. Looking after me. Well, Corry, I don't think it's that easy. We have to think about it carefully. If we go up there in that woods for the whole summer, what will happen to Izaak Walton's? Who will look after the sports when and if they come? I sunk a lot of money into this place and the shed in the last while. We can't just close 'er up."

He was right, of course. We needed a plan.

It was then that he hit me with my handicap. "Do you think you could be a warden?" he asked. "I mean, you could go and I could stay here. Or, you could stay here and I could go on the cat hunt. Could you look after this place on your own?"

Two good questions.

Could I be a warden on the North Pole Stream and the Little Southwest Miramichi? I didn't know, of course. What does a warden do in such a wilderness?

The headwaters of the Little Southwest Miramichi and its tributary the North Pole Stream are what we refer to as Crown reserve waters, special angling waters, waters allotted only to those fishermen who submit applications to the Department of Natural Resources and Energy. Only those persons whose place of residence is within the province of New Brunswick may apply for these special waters. You go to a ranger station or some such place, fill out an application, state what water you desire and when you plan to fish it. All the applications are placed in a hat and a certain number are drawn. It's like a lottery. If you get your name drawn, you get to go. Once there, you might have several miles of river all to yourself. It's all catch and release, however, which means that you go in with nothing and come out with nothing. I could only assume that the duties of a warden in such a place would be to police it, make sure that only the successful applicants were fishing it and that everyone followed the rules and released all their fish. Simple enough job, if you can talk.

Staying home and looking after Izaak Walton's and guiding a few days would be a little easier for me. Most of the people who came to Izaak Walton's were people I knew, people who knew I couldn't talk, people who were patient enough to wait for my written comments and answers. Rig up a rod, perhaps demonstrate how well it worked, collect the money if they wanted it, that's about all there'd be to it. I knew I could do that. I was doing it much of the time, anyway.

Confronting a disgruntled fisherman whom I'd caught killing a salmon up on the North Pole Stream in the middle of nowhere with nobody else around could call for some very carefully chosen words, even some fast talking. The logical thing for me to do was to stay home. Staying home would also mean that I could keep an eye on the business, protect it from Uncle Kid's spending. Plus the Masters were Uncle Kid's friends and he could be spending some time with them. He'd make a better warden and a better cat hunter. Being up there in the woods would be good for his health, he'd be drinking less and spending less.

With all of this in mind, I wrote, "I'll stay home."

It seemed logical to me.

Uncle Kid gave the matter some thought, too, but his flighty perception had perched on a different level.

He read my note, sighed, turned away from me, turned back again, sighed again, went and looked out the window, came back. He seemed at a loss for words.

"Why does everything have to be so complicated?" he said finally.

"Huh?"

"Can you give me a hundred . . . no, two hundred dollars?"

I nodded.

"I gotta go to Saint John."

An hour later he was gone.

That evening, figuring that Uncle Kid would be gone for at least a day, maybe two or three, I locked up Izaak Walton's and canoed up and over to Alice's. I had a note in my pocket and I immediately gave it to her. It read, "Kid's in Saint John. Come and spend the night with me."

She read it and nodded. "I'll have to think of something to tell Mom and Dad."

She thought for a moment then approached her mother. "Well, I suppose Linda will be waiting to get going. I'd better get a move on. Is it all right, Mom, if I go to the movies with Corry's aunt Linda? She's over at Corry's now, waiting. I'll spend the night with her."

"Well, if it's all right with Jim. Have ya got any money?"

"Corry's paying my way in."

That was it. They allowed her to go, just like that. I don't think the Hunters cared what she did. I think if she had told them she was pregnant with twins and was moving in with me, they would have said something like, "Well, you'd better get a move on, dear. Ya don't want to be crossing that river in the dark."

Alice and I went to the river, jumped into the canoe and let the current carry us downstream to our shore. We were in no hurry, we had all night and it was a beautiful spring evening. The sun shone, birds sang and flew about, the river, though still high, was as smooth as glass. I sang "Love Me Tender" to Alice. "Aw e enner, aw e eee, ener ea e o." Alice harmonized. "Oo a ay my eye umpee eah I aw oo o." It was very romantic.

Uncle Kid returned from Saint John the next day about the same time as I got home from school. He looked bedraggled, tired and hung over. The first thing he did was take a shower. A half-hour later, looking refreshed and dressed in a new robin's-egg blue shirt and jeans, he joined me in the kitchen.

"I was talking to Mark and Denise," he said. "We've worked out a new plan. Everything's changed. Their idea was a good one but much too complicated to include you and me. I sort of went down there and played the diplomat.

"Your decision yesterday was a good one, but I needed to think about it. I thought about it all the way to Saint John. I didn't know what to do. On one hand, I knew you had made the right decision, that you could look after this place very well. However, on the other hand, I was not all that keen about spending the summer up there in the woods on a wild goose chase.

"The thing is, Corry, you're graduating and you'll probably want to go to university or to an acting school to learn miming or whatever. I was thinking that maybe the warden's job would help you attain that goal. It would be a job for you, you'd probably learn a lot from Mark and Denise. But then again, I couldn't see you handling a warden's position all that well. Now, if I were to take the job like you said, it might get kind of strange, too. What if Bill Hall or one of the boys went in there to do some poaching and I was the one who had to deal with it? As a matter of fact, if I was a warden in there, they'd sure as hell think they *could* go up there and do all the poaching they wanted and get away with it. I can hear them now. Kid's the warden on the North Pole Stream. Let's go and net a bunch of salmon. Kid'll look the other way. They're a devious bunch, but they're my friends and it would be a very difficult situation. They'd probably take advantage of you, too, because you're my nephew and all that.

"Then there's another aspect of the whole thing that I didn't like, and that is my belief that Mark's looking in the wrong place for the cat. I think he should go looking up on the Dungarvon. Lindon Tucker, Stan Tuney, Bob Nash, every one of those guys from the Dungarvon claim they heard strange noises coming from the forest not more than twenty years ago, and they think it could've been an eastern cougar. Stan Tuney lies all the time, but I don't think Bob Nash would lie about it.

"So, anyway, I brought it up to Mark, told him the situation. I also told him that he and Denise could stay right here with us if they were to search the Dungarvon area. They could make this their base, leave here in the mornings and be on the Dungarvon in less than a half-hour. They could camp, if they wanted to, and you and I could take turns going with them.

"Well, Mark disagrees, still believes the Little Southwest and the North Pole Stream area is where he'll find the cat, but he understands where you and I are coming from, and because he's never found the cat anyway, he's willing to give the Dungarvon a try. They'll be moving in here in June.

"Now, as far as a job for you goes, Mark said he'd be willing to pay one of us for helping him on the hunt, for guiding and whatnot, and I think you're the man for the job. What do you think?"

I shrugged. I didn't like it. I had sort of made other plans. I sort of had it in the back of my head to spend the summer home alone with Alice.

13

Alice and I went to the prom in Uncle Kid's Bronco. Alice was dressed in a pink dress she borrowed from her cousin. I wore the new black suit that Uncle Kid insisted on me buying.

"Take it out of the money you saved for me," he said. "Buy a good one, you'll need it for the graduation and other things, too."

So I bought a $500 suit.

Although it was my last year in high school, it was the first and only prom I ever attended. For one thing, before Alice came into my life, I'd never had the confidence to ask anyone to go with me. I never liked crowds that much, either. I couldn't talk to anyone and it seemed ridiculous to try and pass notes. Standing around saying nothing and trying to look cool seemed pretty ridiculous, too, such a chore.

But with Alice I had fun, didn't need anybody else.

God! What a girl she was! Not all that beautiful to look at, but so tremendously beautiful in every other way I can think of — kind and generous, tactful and considerate, classy and horny. I loved her so much. I just wanted to be with her all the time.

We teamed up for the graduation, too.

The graduation, however, was no fun at all. Even though I was with Alice and should've been happy, I was not. I was carrying around too much reality and responsibility to be happy.

The term had ended like it did every year, but every other year, it simply meant taking the summer off, going fishing and hunting and swimming or just doing nothing at all. But when you graduate, you're expected to do something, get a job, go to university, get married . . . do *something*. This reality is a major confrontation in a person's life. Suddenly, at the age of seventeen or eighteen, you are expected to clear a path and follow it for the rest of your life.

On graduation night, in a room so hot you could hardly breathe, the school principal, an Anglican priest from Newcastle and the mayor of Silver Rapids talked for what seemed like three hours about this very thing. Decide, step out, get a job, be a responsible person.

Alice and I picked up our diplomas and went to the reception, an equally long and boring two hours of speeches, chicken, potatoes, carrots and gravy, washed down with unspiked punch. I think every speaker at both the graduation and the reception said to us graduates, "This is the first day of the rest of your lives."

Uncle Kid told me that they picked it up at AA meetings.

Finally we were outside and all the adults were coming up to us, congratulating us, smiling, shaking hands, speaking loudly to me — "Congratulations, Corry!" — as if I were deaf.

Most of the other graduates rushed to their vehicles, anxious to get into the lemon gin. Alice and I had two bottles of Mumm's Extra Dry on ice behind the seat of the Bronco. Other kids got watches and money from their families; Uncle Kid had given Alice and me champagne.

Most of the other kids went to a picnic site in Upper Blackville to party. Alice and I went to my place and sipped the champagne by the river. It was Alice's idea, she wanted for us to be alone, to talk.

It was one of those evenings that you wait for all year: warm, a rosy sunset, a gentle lilac-scented breeze, nighthawks swooping, birds singing, the peaceful river. We spread a blanket on the grass and sat. I popped the cork and poured some champagne for us. We clinked our glasses and I clucked a toast, "Glyq!" and winked.

"Thank you very much for the ring, Corry. It's not an engagement ring, is it?"

I shook my head. It was only a tiny emerald.

"I have something for you. I would've given it to you earlier, but I didn't want anybody else to see it."

She handed me a beautifully wrapped gift. I could tell it was a book. I opened it. It was the same book that I had given her for Christmas.

"Open it," she said, seeing my puzzlement.

I opened it and found a title page. "My Silent Partner." The book was printed full of poetry, Alice's poetry.

"I'll keep this ring forever," she said with tears in her eyes. "And I want you to keep that book. No matter where you go. No matter where I go. You're my lover, Corry!"

I reached out and pulled her to me, held her, allowed her to cry. She held onto me, allowed me to do the same. She was crying with more conviction than I'd ever seen her cry before, and I knew that these were more than romantic tears, that she was intending to tell me something painful.

I did not have long to wait.

She pulled away from me, pulled herself together, wiped her tears with the back of her hand, kissed my tears away and said, "I'm leaving, Corry."

She saw the disbelief in my eyes.

"Oh, I love you, Corry. There's no mistake about that. I love you with all my heart. You're my Corry! I'll never forget you! You don't know the joy you've given me! It's just that . . ."

Later that night, after I had taken her home and kissed her goodnight for the last time, I went to my room and wrote,

> Dear Princess Anne,
> It's been a while . . .

Alice didn't get a scholarship.

Alice had an Aunt Nora who was the manager of a fast food restaurant in Calgary, Alberta. In a letter from Aunt Nora, Alice learned that she could earn several hundred dollars a week working as a waitress in Aunt Nora's restaurant. A phone call, a bit of financial juggling to come up with a train ticket, a few goodbyes, and Alice was off. She left two days after our graduation.

She didn't want me to see her off, didn't want me to drive her to the station.

"I just want to get it over with," she told me. "Just take me home and kiss me goodbye. It'll be painful for a while, but the sooner we get on with it, the better."

That was it. Alice was gone, and the wave of self-pity and loneliness clouds my spirit to this very day. I felt incompetence, rejection, anger and bewilderment; every humour within me festered, oozed, ached, burned and bled. Her image was before me when I went to bed at night and still there when I arose, after sleepless hours, in the morning. Some nights, especially moonlit ones, I'd go for long walks through the woods or down by the river. I'd go to places where Alice and I had stopped to kiss or laugh or hug or just hang out. And those places became the most beautiful and romantic places in the world. I read her flowery poetry, sipped the nectar from every word as if it flowed from the fountain of Venus.

Every day I took time to write to her. Some days I'd write lengthy letters, sometimes just a poem:

> Day after day I sit and pine,
> Wishing you were here, mine.
> Days whittle down the weeks
> And drop by drop the vessel leaks,
> Seeps away bit by bit . . .

was one I wrote to her. Another went something like:

> You stilled my wandering eye,
> My will to seek, fly.
> Fondly I embrace the past,
> So half the love at least will last.

I sincerely hope that Alice threw those poems away.

It's peculiar how a poem that seemed so funny to me only a few

206

months before now seemed crude and heartless — Uncle Kid's poem about parting, the one that went:

> We must live our lives, seek out higher levels . . .
> Step into the midst, display our sex,
> Smile and shout, I'm free! Who's next?

Uncle Kid recognized heartbreak when he saw it. He tried to help. But there's little you can say in a situation like that. I might not have been graceful or dignified, but I suffered through it. I think it would have taken much longer to rise above it had I not met Sally.

*

Our sports, Leonard Hoge and his friend Wynn Butterfield, from Albany, New York, showed up a few days after Alice left. Uncle Kid guided them. I didn't have the heart for it. I sulked my days away at Izaak Walton's. Leonard and Wynn liked staying at Corry's Fishing Camp, but they didn't catch a thing in our pool. They quit fishing it after three days and started going to other locations, to various open water pools up and down the river. They stayed for a week and caught three salmon and a grilse. Not bad fishing, but not great. Either the Firestone Pool was a failure, or perhaps we hadn't given the rocks enough time to do the necessary eroding.

Though disappointed, we were not totally surprised that the pool wasn't producing, wasn't an instant success. We were dealing with something we knew very little about: nature.

Bill Hall had several theories, or at least aspects to consider in reference to the problem, which he expressed one rainy afternoon at Izaak Walton's.

"I can think of two things that you have to take under consideration that nature never had to deal with," said Bill. "Clear cuts and dirt roads. Nature had time on her side when she was creating her little havens for the salmon. The rocks in the river had years to bury themselves, to get slimy and darkened up; the water, the rocks, the gravel on the river bottom, everything was clean and natural. Nowadays, you have men and heavy equipment going into the woods and cutting down all the trees, dozing up the topsoil, the mulch and the compost, all the components that are required to create growth and prevent erosion. Today, you have thousands of acres of land up there in the woods that is not much more than a desert; vast clear-cuts that you can hardly see across. Then, you have the dirt roads that lead to them, dirt roads constructed from the sandiest shale this side of Doaktown. When it rains, there's nothing to stop it from flowing directly into the river, taking thousands of tons of sand with it.

"Tomorrow, if it keeps raining like this, go down to the river and look at what's happening at the mouths of the brooks. You'll see a sandy streak flowing out into the main stream, depending on how much rain comes down, for as far as fifty yards. All that sand gathers in the little eddies that the current creates behind the rocks. A salmon likes to hold up behind a rock. I'll bet you the tires on my Datsun that no salmon in his right mind will hold up anywhere that has sand churning about."

Bill Hall may have known what he was talking about, or maybe he was just being negative, but his tirade was enough to cause Uncle Kid to frown and sigh.

"Kid, have you ever asked yourself why rocks that held fish twenty years ago are not worth casting over these days?"

"Sand," said Uncle Kid, nodding thoughtfully. "And it wouldn't surprise me if sand plays havoc with spawning as well."

"Well, I don't know about that," said Bill. "There still seem to be quite a few salmon in the river. It's just that they seem to be harder and harder to catch. I believe it's because we don't know where they're holding. Years ago, you'd see a little dent in the water indicating a boulder, make a cast over it, and chances were pretty good you'd catch a fish. Nowadays, in the middle of a big run of fish, you can go out there and come up with absolutely nothing. The dent in the water, the boulder is still there, but no salmon."

"So what you're saying is that the greatest pollutant in the world is sand."

"Clear-cutting and dirt roads."

"Money."

"Exactly."

"But if the salmon are there, they must be holding somewhere," reasoned Uncle Kid.

Bill Hall lit a cigarette and went to the window to watch the rain.

Bill Hall was a tall, slim, handsome man. He was funny, imaginative, adventurous and mischievous. Everyone liked Bill Hall. You couldn't help but like him. He had an aura about him, he was charismatic or something. He and Uncle Kid made a powerful duo that not too many would dare to reckon with. It was always great fun to be with them, to hear them talk, reason things out, philosophize, theorize. They made a great team — Uncle Kid entered his conversations through the back door and Bill through the front. Sometimes they'd be talking about two different things, two separate analogies and go completely through the spiel without meeting, without connecting. It seemed that only *they* knew what they were talking about. But sometimes they'd meet, and when they did, it was like stumbling onto a revelation that made you want to holler, "So *that's* what they're talking about!"

I was sitting there practically in tears, missing Alice. I suppose I was sighing and looking downcast and as gloomy as the day itself. If it hadn't been raining, I probably wouldn't have been there. I probably would've been in some familiar spot trying to sniff out the fading scents of Alice. But there I was with "I just feel like crying" written all over my face, casting shadows on everything in the room, including Bill Hall and Uncle Kid. I was in a trap, and in a way I was asking Bill and Uncle Kid to join me, to share the pain. I was not a good rainy-day companion.

Uncle Kid was standing with his back against the counter, Bill Hall was at the window smoking and watching the rain, and I was seated on the only chair in the place. There was a silence, then suddenly Uncle Kid spoke up. "There's plenty of fish in the sea."

Bill answered, "It's all one great orgasm, all right. Birth, love, joy, ecstasy, pain. Did you know that the human face takes on the same expression, contorts in the same way for severe pain, extreme fear, fury, sexual orgasm and violent death?"

"Of course. Well, no, I didn't know that. But it makes sense. Conception begins with a twinkle in the eye, the other masks of life and death just follow." Uncle Kid turned to me. "What's that song you sing, Corry? You know the one. You sing it in your Pavarotti voice. 'Some Enchanted Evening.' That's it. It's like that, you know. One evening you make eye contact with someone and it starts a whole series of events happening, kind of like that game where you knock one thing down and eventually everything else falls. What's it called? Monopoly. No, not Monopoly. Oh, you know the game . . . what's it called?"

"Follow the leader?" guessed Bill.

"No."

"Fox and geese."

"No, no! You know the one. What's it called?"

"Dominoes!"

"Yes! Yes! That's it! Dominoes! Only instead of everything falling down at first, everything stands up. Then, everything falls down . . . or whatever."

This whole conversation was very painful for me, but I had to laugh at the stupidity of it all. And maybe that was it — maybe they were just trying to cheer me up.

"One block represents conception," continued Uncle Kid. "The next one birth, the next one childhood, and so on, right through life. One block, maybe halfway through, might be very painful, but you can't enjoy the following block that represents joy until the painful block falls and knocks the joyful block over. Follow me?"

"Life is a game of dominoes," said Bill. "That's very good, Kid. You should write that down."

That whole conversation was for me, of course. That was their way of having a heart-to-heart with me. "Cheer up," they were saying. "Tomorrow is another day. You're young and there's plenty of fish in the sea."

"Maybe so," I thought. "But you have to know how to fish for them and where they lay."

On Friday, the twenty-ninth of June, Mark and Denise Masters drove in in a shiny new red Ford pickup with a camper on the back and a canoe on top.

Mark looked just the same — grey hair, dark-rimmed glasses, needing a shave, baggy pants. Denise looked as if she had lost some weight, and she had dyed her hair auburn. The weight loss made her look older.

We made coffee and sat around the kitchen table to discuss the game plan.

"I must tell you, Kid, I cannot feel any confidence in searching the Dungarvon area," said Mark. "It's not hilly enough. The topography map indicates swamps. Essentially, the eastern cougar is a mountain lion. If we're gonna find him, we'll find him forty miles north, maybe in the Christmas Mountain area. That, at least, is what I think. But I know nothing for sure. We're just goofing off, anyway. If we had our act together a little better, we'd be going after the cat in the middle of winter when its tracks are more easily identified and easier to follow in the snow.

"I know some things about the cougar and I'll fill you in on that as we go along — what the tracks look like, how to identify them and not confuse them with dog tracks and bears and whatnot. I've done some reading since you were in Saint John, Kid, and I've learned that the Dungarvon area is not without sightings. Some bird hunters claimed they saw one up there not too many years ago. The Dungarvon Whooper legend has some viability to it, too. I've read that the female cougar in heat will scream."

"When I was a child," said Uncle Kid, "I remember standing out here in the yard one evening and we heard some very eerie screams coming from the woods, from what seemed like a long way off. My grandfather told us that it was an Indian devil. That's the same thing, isn't it?"

211

"The same. They've been called a lot of things, panthers, cougars, Indian or Injun devils, wildcats, mountain lions. The various Indian tribes had different names for them.

"Anyway, their range is pretty much limitless. They've been spotted in just about every part of the province. So we'll give the Dungarvon a try, maybe for a week or two. Then, if we're totally discouraged in the area, we'll move to another location."

"How do you suggest we go about it?" asked Uncle Kid.

"I'm not sure. I do know, however, that they stay as far away as possible from humans and they don't like fire. Another thing I know is that although they'll kill beaver, rabbits, rats and even young moose, their favourite food is deer. Taking that into consideration, I'd be inclined to search the areas where deer are most plentiful."

"How do they get along with the coyotes?"

"Natural enemies, I suspect."

"Well, that's not going to help matters. There's coyotes all over the place these days."

"I know. Let me fill you in on one thing, Kid and Corry. This animal is like looking for a ghost or Bigfoot. I read somewhere that every sasquatch has a cougar purring at his feet. We're not apt to find one. I'm just doing this because . . . because I'm . . . obsessed. I just want to see one. I've been wanting to see one for most of my life."

"We brought some books and papers for you to read, Corry. Mark has written a couple of books on the cat and I have a couple by Bruce Wright. They're in the pickup. I'll get them for you later."

"Have there been any recent sightings?" asked Uncle Kid.

"Nearly two hundred in the last twenty years," said Mark. "Two hundred sightings and not one good photograph. I'll be recording everything we do out there in the woods this summer and we'll all carry cameras. I have a good one for you, Corry, and I'll teach you how to use it. I also brought good, reliable compasses for us."

"What about guns?" asked Uncle Kid.

"No guns," said Mark.

212

"So what happens if you stumble upon one of these things and it decides you might make a nice evening meal?"

"I don't think that will ever happen. They're so skittish, I figure we'll be lucky to get close enough for a good, identifiable photograph. One whiff of a human being and they're off like a bat out of hell. But I must tell you, Corry, more often than not we'll be travelling alone. We'll be following old truck roads, old logging roads, and you must never leave those roads for any reason. If you're lucky enough to see a cougar track crossing a road, mark the spot and come and get Denise and me and we'll follow his trail together. The last thing we need is for someone to get lost out there in the Dungarvon woods."

So we spent the rest of that day talking about the cougar. That evening we moved Mark and Denise into Corry's Fishing Camp. We had planned for them to stay with us in the house, but once they got a look at the newly renovated shed, they insisted on setting up there. "It'll be better for everyone," they said. "We'll be seeing enough of each other as it is."

They were absolutely right, no argument from us.

I went to bed that night with Bruce Wright's book, *The Eastern Cougar: A Question of Survival*, but trying to read it was impossible. I could not clear my head of Alice.

"Tomorrow is going to be a long day," I told myself. "I must get some sleep." But the Sandman kept his distance and I tossed and turned in the dark.

It was after midnight when I turned on the light, opened *My Silent Partner* and read:

> The Aurora Borealis is moonlight
> Reflecting off cliffs of ice;
> The moon, itself,
> Outlining your profile
> Through a midnight window;
> A storm on the sun,
> It's lightning ablaze,

A mockery of morning;
The crack of knowing you,
Cold like frost;
The aura of God peeking o'er the horizon,
Tonguing the sea;
The Autumn dawn, wan
As forgotten passions.
I would not give up
Northern lights for a
Morning in July.

I tried to envision her out there in Alberta, working in a restaurant, my lonesome lover.

Later, I wrote to her.

Dear Alice,

I have a job, sort of. I'm chasing the eastern cougar with Mark and Denise Masters. They're paying me $150 a week. I'm going to save it and, if you want, later in the summer, I'll go to Alberta to be with you.

I miss you very much . . .

14

Searching for the cougar in the Dungarvon woods turned out to be the most boring and difficult job I ever had. It was boring because it was like searching for a needle in a haystack, or even worse, searching in a haystack for a needle that probably didn't exist. What made the job difficult was the terrain. The Dungarvon woods has more swamps, I think, than any other place on earth.

You'd walk back a logging road for a few hundred yards and come to a swamp, three feet of water, bog, barrens, an environment that only a mosquito could appreciate.

After the first night, Mark declared that he would not consider the Dungarvon for more than a few days. I think he based this decision primarily on the mosquitoes. I could have given him a few other reasons for getting out of there — blackflies, horseflies, brassheads and midges.

After the third day of rambling around in the Dungarvon area, we were on our way home in the pickup and I was expecting Mark to announce a move, but instead Denise did most of the talking.

"I came upon a valley today," she said. "There was a very cold spring down in there and hundreds upon hundreds of deer tracks. Then, I began to see the deer. There must be twenty-five or thirty of them hanging out in that valley. If I was a cougar, I'd hang out in that valley, too. I think we should sneak back in there and keep an eye on the deer for a few days."

"Is that what kept you so late?" asked Mark. "I was beginning to think you had gotten lost."

"I had a feeling . . . a strange feeling I was being watched," said Denise. "As sure as I was looking down on the deer, something was looking down on me. Have you ever had that feeling?"

"It all could've been in your head, or it could have been an owl or a fox."

"Or it could have been a cougar. A cougar wondering what the hell I was doing there intruding on his private flock."

"But you saw no tracks, no signs . . . "

"Just a feeling, and food enough to keep a cougar purring for the rest of his life. It's a little valley, so the deer probably spend the nights there and travel abroad during the day in search of food. The cougar hunts at night."

Mark said, "Well, it can't hurt to keep an eye on it for a few days. We'll find a good vantage point, down wind. One of us can pick our way around the perimeter and look for tracks or droppings."

"And if we come up with nothing, then we can move to the North Pole Stream."

My only response was a sigh. I did not want to spend another day in a Dungarvon swamp.

The next morning, Mark spread a map on the hood of the pickup and told us what he had in mind.

"I don't think it's a good idea for all three of us to bother going down to that valley," he said. "Three would be just one more for an animal to smell. Denise and I will go down to the valley, and Corry, I want you to take a walk down this road right here. It comes out, look, at the river. I wouldn't think it's much more than a couple of miles. Hang around the river for a while, if you like. We'll meet back here tonight. I don't want to be going in and out, in and out, so we'll take our lunches with us. OK?"

So Mark and Denise headed down through the woods toward the valley and I drove the pickup back the Dungarvon Road until I came to the trail I was to follow. I parked the truck, locked it up, hung my camera around my neck, threw my pack over my shoulder and headed out. I figured I could make it to the river and back before lunchtime, but I took my pack with me anyway. Mark had insisted that we never go into the woods without our cameras and our packs. The packs contained a can of insect repellent, a hunting knife, a sandwich, a couple of candy bars, a tin cup, a couple of yards of toilet tissue, matches in a plastic container and a compass.

It was an overcast morning, looked like we might get rain. I walked amid a cloud of mosquitoes. I wished I had brought my old yellow raincoat. It would not only keep the rain off me but would also act as a shield against the mosquitoes.

"Oh, well," I said to myself. "I'll keep walking. They don't bother you as much if you keep on moving."

Some people are more attractive to mosquitoes than others. Warmth is the initial attraction, but then your breath and body odours, the chemical qualities of your sweat and other skin glands play their parts in determining just how attractive, how irresistible you really are. When a mosquito, always a female, lands on you, she tastes you with her feet before she drives her sheath home and begins to pump up your blood. She also injects an anticoagulant into you so she doesn't choke on any blood that might happen to clot. I often wonder just what you'd have to smell like to repel a mosquito. And wouldn't it be hilarious to hear an absent-minded mosquito coughing and gagging on your blood just because she forgot to inject her anticoagulant? "Hummmmm . . . Slurp. Cough! Cough, cough! Hack! Spitoo! Slurp. Hummmmm . . ." There were more than a few mosquitoes on that overcast morning that I would like to have choked, I tell you!

Looking down, watching the ground for droppings and tracks, I walked for an hour. There were lots of tracks — moose, deer, dogs or coyotes, bear. There was only one track that drew my attention. It was in the soft mud of a little dip in the path and was the track of what I decided was a very large bobcat. It was very similar to a cougar track, had the four tear-drop shaped toes with no sign of toenails, the heel pad with the three lobes, but it was too small, only about two inches in width, and its stride was not lengthy enough, only about twelve inches. A cougar's stride, according to

Mark Masters, can reach well over two feet. The only thing that gave me any further pause about this track was the possibility of its being the track of an adolescent cougar.

Just to be on the safe side, I placed my lens cover beside it for scale and photographed it. Then I broke a branch from a fir tree and placed it beside the track. The branch would help us find it later.

I kept on going, down through the woods, down into valleys, up and over hills, around bends, over a little brook. Finally, the land began to slope and I figured I was nearing the Dungarvon River.

"Good," I thought. "I'll hang around the river for a while, eat my sandwich, then head back to the pickup." I hoped I could wrap up this hike before it rained.

I was walking along feeling a bit sorry for myself, missing Alice, not expecting to encounter anything other than a relatively small river, when suddenly I came upon not only the river but a fairly large cultivated area, a settlement.

I felt like Christopher Columbus must have felt when he first eyed North America. A surprise! A discovery!

There were several houses on each side of the river, some unpainted, one with a blue bottom and a pink top, another very small one painted the colour of the yellow line, the meridian line on a highway; there was a small church and what looked like, if the Salada Tea sign on the side of it was any indication, a tiny store. The two sides of the small community were connected by a foot bridge.

"Who the hell would be living up here in the middle of the woods?" I asked myself. "Hillbillies?"

I had half a mind to turn and head back to the pickup. But something urged me to take a look around, to investigate. What attracted me the most was the footbridge. I'd heard of them and had seen their abutments, like the one on the Miramichi I had borrowed the rocks from, but never before had I encountered an actual, functional bridge.

I crossed a field that, judging by the moss and the small trees, had been neglected for ten years or more. I came to an abandoned, spooky old house with a rusty tin roof, curtainless windows and a collapsing shed at the back. From here, I could see for a mile in either direction, up and down the river. Downstream, just below the footbridge, was a fairly large cabin. Upstream, on the back side of a little island, sat several other cabins.

"Where the hell am I?" I asked myself. "Those are sporting camps over there. Quite an elaborate set-up, too."

It was a beautiful little settlement, really. There was something mellow and warm about it. There were lots of birds and butterflies around; I saw a salmon leap from the river. Some of the houses were shaded by large crab apple trees, one had a swing beside it. The house that was painted meridian yellow had a number of lawn ornaments in front of it.

And then? "Hello."

It was the soft, mellow voice of a woman, but it startled me so that I nearly jumped out of my Nikes.

I turned to face the voice and there, standing by a weathered old bench with an easel and canvas in front of her, was the strangest looking woman I'd ever seen.

I guessed her age at about twenty-five, maybe thirty. She was about six feet tall. Her hair was a mop of blond that fell haphazardly over her shoulders. Her big green eyes looked out over a long nose. She smiled at whatever expression had fixed itself on my face, and I saw that although her mouth was large, the smile was warm and beautiful. She held a paint brush in her long, slender fingers. She was wearing a white blouse, unbuttoned to reveal a very seductive cleavage. The blouse was tucked into a pair of very close-fitting cut-off jeans. Her legs were long and tanned and her very large feet were bare. She seemed disproportionate in every way, but yet everything seemed to fit. How can I explain how someone with big hands, big feet, big ears, a big nose and a big mouth could at the same time be so extremely beautiful?

I stood there for the longest time, feasting my eyes on her. And she was staring at me. Staring! And everything was so very quiet. A bee flew around her, then around me, making a perfect figure eight.

"Is this all for real?" I asked myself. "Did I lie down in the woods somewhere and fall asleep? Is this all a dream?"

"You . . . you came out of the forest," she said, snapping me out of my trance. "Were you lost?"

I looked down at her feet, her beautiful big feet, and shook my head.

"My name is Sally," she said. "Sally Nutbeam. What's yours?"

"Orry En" I said.

"Orien?"

I nodded. Orien was close enough.

"When I first saw you walking across the field, then standing there . . . I thought perhaps you were someone else." Her voice was something a bit deeper than a whisper. A croon, perhaps. "It's just that . . . you came out of the forest. I'm sorry — are you hungry?"

Hungry? How could I have been hungry with a feast like that in front of me? But then again, maybe I *was* hungry. I'd been walking around, longing for Alice. Maybe I was hungry for love. There had to be some reason for falling madly in love at first sight with a very peculiar woman. Yes, I was hungry. I nodded.

She started to stand. I shook my head and moved toward her. I took out the pen Alice had given me for Christmas and my pad. I wrote "I'm sorry. I can't speak. I have food." I patted my pack.

"You can't speak?"

I shook my head.

"But you said . . ."

"My name is Corry Quinn," I wrote.

"Oh. You read lips?"

I shook my head.

"An impediment?"

I nodded.

I glanced at the canvas she was working on. She was standing in one of the most scenic places on earth — the forest, the winding river, the cabins in the distance, the shabby old house, the footbridge below; I expected to see a landscape. But instead, there on the canvas, was a nearly finished — and what I considered to be a very well-painted — likeness of a plate of spaghetti, topped with meatballs and tomato sauce.

"You like?" she asked, smiling that wonderful big smile.

I nodded.

"You don't find it disturbing?"

I shook my head. Disturbing? I like spaghetti and meatballs.

"I call it Bert Todder," she said.

I raised my eyebrows. Bert Todder?

"The guy who used to live here."

I shrugged. I hadn't heard of him, but I supposed he must have had a love affair with spaghetti and meatballs.

"Can you tell me in twenty-five words or less why you wandered out of the woods like a Greek god just now?" she asked.

I nodded, wrote, "I'm on a safari."

"Safari? What are you hunting?"

"The eastern cougar," I wrote.

"Aha! The elusive cat. The Indian devil. I don't think you'll ever find him."

I shrugged. I didn't care.

"You know what I think? I think that it's not a cat at all. I think it's a real, live devil. You're not him, are you?" She looked at my feet. "Nope. No hooves. Well, it's going to rain soon so I'd better put this masterpiece away. Would you like to see my gallery?"

Gallery? What gallery? I shrugged, nodded. Sure. Why not?

She removed the canvas and dismantled her easel.

"Grab that stuff and follow me," she said, pointing at a box of brushes, pencils, bottles and tubes of paint.

I did as I was told and she led me toward the old house.

"Where are you from, Corry Quinn?" she asked, stepping up on the squeaking boards of the veranda.

I didn't answer, of course, and since I was carrying the box, I couldn't even point.

She pushed the door open, the bottom of which scraped the floor within. The rusty hinges complained.

"It's not the Beaverbrook," she said. "But, then again, Brennen Siding is not the capital."

Brennen Siding. So that's where I was.

When I followed her inside, I was surprised to find that the house was completely furnished. There was a stove and table, chairs and cupboard in the kitchen, a sofa and an armchair in the parlour, a hooked rug on the floor and a great many paintings on the wall. There was an old organ with yellowed pictures on top — one of a girl in a confirmation dress, a young man's graduation picture, one of a man with a big black horse and another of a man in pants that were too long in the legs. The flowered wallpaper was starting to curl and lift in several places, but considering how dumpy the place looked from the outside, everything on the inside was clean and tidy.

Sally set her easel down, scanned the walls and asked, "So what do you think?"

I set the box beside the easel and stepped up for closer inspection.

The first thing I looked at was a painting of a footbridge. It was quite similar to the one on the river, but the cables of this one started at a cracked and weather-beaten old abutment, then reached out into a starry sky. I liked it.

There was another one of a footbridge. This one was exactly like the one outside, crossed the same river in the same location, but the cables in the painting were laden with diamonds and pearls. The river, a slender neck, ran from two hills that could have been the breasts of a woman. The bridge represented a necklace.

Most of the paintings, except for the stars, moons and lighted windows, were done in dark blues, purples, greys and blacks — nightscapes, you might call them. They suggested that Sally Nutbeam was either a very gloomy person or that she spent much of her time wandering around at night.

There were other paintings, paintings of pots and pans with blackened bottoms, a worn broom and a dirty old mop with a broken handle. Further along was a painting of a tired and bedraggled woman. The woman had a peg leg. Upon close inspection, it was plain to see that the peg leg had been made from the broken mop handle in the other painting. There was a painting of a pleasant-looking man with big floppy ears and another one of a younger man who stared from the canvas so intensely that the hairs on the back of my neck stood up.

There were more, but it's enough to say that Sally Nutbeam was a fine artist and that I was very impressed.

The greatest work of art, of course, was Sally herself. She had an aura about her that made me feel warm and relaxed, yet she frightened me. Her eyes were big and green, her ears almost elfin. She was singular, a mystery, an enigma. Just looking at her made me feel high, or drunk. Standing beside her, trying to concentrate on the paintings, I found I could smell her, that she smelled natural, like the summer or the river or gentle rain.

No patchouli oil on Sally Nutbeam.

I was swept away with her presence.

"Weird things happen on the Dungarvon. They claim that Brennen Siding, if you can believe anyone from Brennen Siding, is haunted something damnable," Uncle Kid had told me. Was Sally Nutbeam a ghost? How could a ghost, an apparition, a mere suggestion of existence be so warm and occupy so much of the world about her?

"Owie." I whispered her name.

She looked at me, blessed me with her big green eyes and said, "Nobody will believe me when I tell them about you."

"Huh?"

She smiled. "Adonis from the forest."

And then we just stared at each other for the longest time.

I think to this day that we were entranced, that there was something else at work, some alien force perhaps. It could have been anything from the bee that buzzed a figure eight around us to some kind of energy flow within the old house. It conjured up the same feelings you get when you step into an empty church with stained glass windows and icons. You would get that feeling, I believe, at the alter of Zeus in Delphi, on Calvary Hill or some other holy place. God? Providence? Something was at work.

Whatever it was, I accepted it and liked it. And so did Sally. Today, when I think of us standing in that old house staring into each other's eyes, I envision two very lonely, unique individuals rapt with the joy of finding each other. Never, before or since, have I stared at anyone with such curiosity. Everything — the Firestone Pool, miming, Uncle Kid, the Masters and their cougar, Alice, everything — blended into the (black? blue? purple?) backdrop of my life. I was in one of her paintings. I belonged to her. She had created me.

It was the sound of rain that snapped me out of it.

"Ha!" I said, turned away and went to a window as if the rain was suddenly very important to me.

The spell was broken.

The rain battered the window. I could hear its drone on the tin roof. For several minutes, I watched and listened.

"Maybe one day I could paint you," said Sally. Her voice told me that she hadn't moved.

I found myself debating whether or not to turn back to her.

"Will you be around for a while?" she asked.

I breathed deeply, nodded.

"I'll be here most of the summer. I was raised in this little settlement. I plan to spend all my summers here. You didn't tell me where you were from."

"This is crazy," I thought. "I'm being rude. Why am I afraid to turn and face her? Snap out of it, Corry. Pull yourself together." I took another deep breath, turned.

"I'm fum Ifer Apis," I said.

"Silver Rapids?"

I nodded.

"You can't leave until the rain eases."

I shrugged.

"Did you go to school in Blackville?" she asked.

"Ifer Apis."

"Oh. That's why we haven't met. You're younger than me, too, I suppose."

I signalled eighteen with my fingers.

She smiled, said, "I'm older than that."

"Would you like to sit down? I mean, we could sit in the kitchen. I have cranberry juice . . . would you like some cranberry juice?"

I shook my head. I needed to go. The Masters might have given up on their valley because of the rain. They might be waiting for me. I pointed at the door.

"You'll get wet," she said.

I shrugged, headed for the door, opened it, stepped out on the veranda.

"Bye," I heard her call from inside.

"Bye!" I called back.

I stepped off the veranda and headed across the field toward the woods. I was half way there when I heard her call my name.

"Corry Quinn!"

I stopped, turned. She had followed me outside. She was standing beside the old house, watching me, getting wet.

"Tomorrow?" she called.

I nodded.

"There's an easier way to get here! Take the Gordon Road and cross the footbridge!"

I turned and kept on walking. When I got to the edge of the woods, I turned once again to see if she was still there.

She was. Getting wet, there in the rain, still watching me. I waved and entered the woods.

I walked as fast as I could back to the pickup. Soaked to the skin, I climbed in, made a few notes, then started it up and drove out to where I'd dropped off the Masters that morning. They were waiting for me in the shelter of a pine tree. They climbed into the cab beside me.

"It must have rained an inch already," was how Mark greeted me. "Let's get to hell out of here."

"How was your day, Corry?" asked Denise.

I had my answer already written. I had written it along with my notes. "I think I found a cougar track."

"You're kidding!" said Mark.

I felt like an ass for lying but shook my head.

"Did you mark the place? Will you be able to find it again?"

I could find it with my eyes shut. I nodded.

"Are you sure?"

I lied, nodded.

"Before or after it started to rain?"

"Be'aw."

"Before. Hell! Just the one?"

I nodded.

"Did you get a picture? A scale?"

Again I nodded.

"We should go back to it before it gets washed out too bad."

"No!" said Denise. "I'm soaked to the skin, I'm bitten and itchy, I need a bath! Let's get out of here."

"But . . ."

"If it's around, it's around. There'll be other tracks. They'll be washed out already, anyway."

"When we get home, I want every detail," said Mark.

Sally Nutbeam had burned her likeness on my memory with a branding iron. When we got home and Mark sat with me at our kitchen table to record the details of my track, I was so out of it that I could barely concentrate. I wrote my answers with a shaky hand.

"Big cat. Could have been a large bobcat or small cougar. Three-inch-wide track. No nails. Soft mud. No droppings. Yes, I looked. No hair. Yes, there were deer tracks, too. Did not pursue it very far, maybe a hundred yards. No more tracks. Just the one. Moss covered ground. I marked it with a stick. Photographed it beside lens cap. Yes, it could have been a bobcat. A very large bobcat. Yes, it could have been an adolescent cougar. You would have to decide. Too bad it rained." Some truths, some lies.

Later, we listened to the radio, the weather report. "Rain tomorrow and Friday," said the woman.

Marked sighed deeply.

"We might as well head back to Saint John tomorrow," said Denise. "No sense searching in the rain."

Marked nodded thoughtfully.

226

Things were working out just the way I wanted them to work out. "When it clears, maybe I'll go back and take another look," I wrote.

Tossed between thoughts of Sally Nutbeam and Alice Hunter, I slept very little that night.

I went to bed, turned off the lights and tried to think about Alice — where she was, what she was doing. "Does she know Sally Nutbeam? Sally . . . what a weird girl!"

"Why am I thinking of Sally?" I asked myself. "What has Sally got to do with anything? She's so weird! Big feet, funny ears. She's older than I am. She's too tall for me. Alice is my girl. She's probably thinking of me right this minute. No doubt Sally has forgotten me."

I rolled over, tried to erase Sally from my thoughts, tried to concentrate. "Alice . . . Alice . . ." I could hear the rain, Brennen Siding rain.

I fumbled in the darkness, found the lamp and turned it on. Alice's book of poetry lay beside the lamp. I picked it up, opened it, read her poem called "The Muse."

> Somewhere in the ether world
> Back of time and space she sits
> And to all who aspire to ponder,
> Rhyme and reason she transmits.
> Now, reading from my own few lines,
> I conclude and do believe
> It's not her fault they're not so great,
> But my inability to receive.

"The Muse. My lover, Alice, writing about the Muse. Sitting back there . . . back of time and space, transmitting ideas, inspiration . . . Sally is like that. The rain sounds exactly like it sounded in that old house. Bert Todder's house . . . Sally's gallery . . ."

*

227

The next morning, after Mark and Denise left, Uncle Kid and I hurried through the rain to Izaak Walton's. We had absolutely nothing to do but sit around and wait for a customer.

"In the rain like this, one of us should be fishing," said Uncle Kid.

I supposed he was getting restless.

"You haven't fished at all this season, have you?" he said.

I shook my head. I hadn't. I was too occupied, or preoccupied, with Alice, and now Sally to concentrate on fishing. Sally was foremost in my mind at the time, and I really needed to talk to someone about her. I decided to run her past Uncle Kid.

I wrote: "I met Sally Nutbeam."

Uncle Kid looked puzzled, then he grinned. "Sally Nutbeam. Who's Sally Nutbeam?"

I shrugged. I didn't know much, wrote, "Brennen Siding."

"You were in Brennen Siding? That's where you saw the cat track. Brennen Siding. There might be a few people living in there. It's just a little settlement, dying like every other settlement located on a tributary. Sally Nutbeam. What was she doing up there?"

I wrote "Spends her summers there. She's an artist."

"An artist. A real artist? Did you see her work?"

I nodded.

"Hmm. So she was a pretty little thing, was she?"

"She was very different," I wrote. "Like a witch or a goddess, had big green eyes."

"Ha! Another spook on the Dungarvon! You sure she was real?"

"She did a painting. Called it Bert Todder," I scribbled.

"Ha! Bert Todder! I used to know Bert Todder. Bert shot himself in the face with a twelve gauge shotgun. I guess when they found him, he just looked like a . . . like a . . ."

"Like a plate of spaghetti and meatballs?" I wrote.

"Well, yes, I suppose so."

15

The storm blew in from the southwest, downriver. It rained two inches and the water in the river came up five feet. Uncle Kid and I had to pull our boat and canoe up into the shore hay and tie them, or else they would have gone adrift. It stopped raining on Friday afternoon, but the river didn't start to subside until Sunday.

Big rains and high water have always been kind to Uncle Kid and me. A big raise of water can turn a chub hole into a very productive salmon pool.

New Brunswickers can boast about two things: cold winters and hot summers. We get barely enough rain in the summer to keep our gardens moist. You need a lot more than that to keep the river up. From the middle of June through August and sometimes even through September, the mercury can hover within a degree or two of ninety degrees. The river water can warm up to seventy-five or eighty degrees. Salmon do not like warm water. That's why they are usually found in areas just below a smaller, cooler tributary, a stream or spring brook. If you are lucky enough to own such an area and you also have a bit of a rapids or a strong current, you could be the owner of a valuable salmon pool. Such a pool will produce all summer long, nine out of ten seasons.

If you are the owner of a stretch of water that is slow moving, that has no cool tributaries except for those few days after a big rain, you might as well be fishing in a bathtub. Uncle Kid tells me that 1976 was a very unusual year: it rained every other day all summer long. In 1976, Uncle Kid caught his limit every day, right out front in our very own chub hole.

"If every summer was like 1976, *we'd* be the millionaires," he told me. "We'd have the Million Dollar Pool."

If I could have articulated my thoughts, I would have told him that had Grandfather Lauder owned a million-dollar pool, he would have sold it to a rich American fifty years ago for one per cent of its worth. That's what happened everywhere else. People were poor, needed the money. No one ever thought of water as a private thing. Everyone fished wherever they liked.

When the water rises several feet, the current naturally speeds up. If you happen to have a little point or a gravel bar submerging into the river, and if that point or bar happens to have a few boulders on it, then chances are fairly good that there'll be a salmon or two in the area. If, of course, the salmon are running.

A lot of ifs.

*

Sunday morning, I got up at five, quickly downed a mug of coffee, pulled out my fishing gear and attached my old Medalist to my nine-foot graphite. Then I tied about twelve feet of Maxima leader on the end of my weight-forward Cortland 444, tapering four tippets from twenty pounds to eight. To the end of the leader, I tied a number six Butterfly with a green butt.

I told myself, "I'll catch a fish today or paddle home on a marble slab."

I untied the canoe and poled it up to the Firestone Pool. I anchored about a hundred feet upstream and about sixty degrees west of where we dumped the rocks. The only thing that indicated the rock pile was a little, barely distinguishable dinge on the water. The rocks and tires we had placed were too deep below the surface in these conditions to cause any turbulence.

I moved to the front of the canoe so that it would hang straight on the current and sat facing downstream.

I made a ten-foot cast, straight out toward the eastern bank, and let it swing. With every cast after that, I lengthened a foot until I was casting nearly ninety feet across the water. The Cortland essed through the windless morning like a pink whip. The twelve-foot leader, lighter than the Cortland, transported the Butterfly to the water as if it were a living thing. I had been fly fishing since I was eight years old. Casting ninety or a hundred feet of line was as easy for me as drinking water. I might not have been the best fisherman in the world, but I was a native Miramichier, which meant I was one of the best.

On a poplar across the way sat a murder of crows, cawing their fool heads off. A woodpecker hammered on a stovepipe somewhere downstream. Chickadees and robins entertained me with their songs. A brace of mergansers fished noisily along the shore. The dew-laden fields were as green as Irish mint. The river, rushing past me and beneath me, was as smooth as satin. It sang me a lullaby. It hypnotized me. It made me forget that other things — ambitions, responsibilities, cares, pains, women — existed. A river can be selfish in that way. It's easy for a river to be condescending. Everyone is a child in the eyes of a river.

After my longest cast, I reeled in and pushed the canoe downstream ten or fifteen feet. Then I made a short cast, lengthened out, made a second cast, lengthened, made a third . . . repeated the whole process all over again.

I was out to about eighty feet and the Butterfly was swinging just short of the rock pile when I saw the wake. It was the telltale swell of a salmon rising to the surface. A salmon had risen to inspect my Butterfly.

My heart leaped into my throat.

To see a salmon rise for your fly is the most exciting thing in the world. It's like seeing a flying saucer or a ghost, or seeing a royal flush roll up on a slot machine; it's like hearing Pavarotti sing, or looking into the green eyes of Sally Nutbeam.

The salmon did not even touch the fly. It just took a look and was gone, leaving me with a pounding heart and a feeling of loss.

"Keep calm," I told myself. "Don't panic."

I knew what to do.

I made the exact same cast and let it swing across the exact same location.

Nothing.

There was a second alternative: shorten up and start all over again. I tried this.

Still nothing.

The third alternative is to lengthen out beyond where you rolled the fish and cast straight across. When you cast straight across, the current tends to create a bag in your line, causing the fly to speed up.

I stood up in the canoe to give myself more clearance and made a ninety-five-foot cast, straight toward the far shore. It was a good cast, except for the fact the fly landed a bit heavy, as if it were thrown by something, instead of landing naturally, as if on the wing. The salmon ignored it, of course. No salmon will ever take a fly that lands in an unnatural way.

I made the same cast again, but this time I shot it a bit more into the air, giving it time to reach its destination, stop in mid-air and fall gently to the water.

This time the salmon came for the Butterfly as if it hadn't eaten in weeks. Kersplash! It nearly jerked the rod out of my hands. The battle was on.

Not quite knowing what was happening, the first thing the salmon did was head for the bottom to give the situation some thought. There it stayed, not moving. It could have been a rock. Then it began testing the strength of my leader, bringing little short yelps from my reel as it shook its head. I knew right away it was a very big salmon.

Then, the salmon began to swim almost leisurely away, at an angle toward the far shore. My reel sang softly as it gave up the rest of my casting line and thirty-five or forty feet of the white, thinner backing.

There the fish stopped again and rested, not quite sure what to do next.

My rod arced precariously, to the point where I thought it might break. I tried reeling, but nothing would give. The salmon would do as it pleased for a while yet.

After a few minutes it bumped its way up stream. Bump! Bump bump! Bump! It was trying to spit out the fly. This fish was just beginning to fight!

"I'll have to try to get ashore. I'll never get him into this boat," I said, and I was reaching back for the anchor rope when the salmon turned and took off downstream. It swam so fast that it left a string of bubbles on the surface of the water, as straight as an arrow. I have no idea how fast those things can swim, but only a second passed before it leaped into the air like a silver torpedo a couple of hundred yards away.

Now that I'd seen it, I guessed it weighed in the vicinity of thirty-five to forty pounds. It was not only the biggest salmon I'd ever hooked but also the biggest salmon I'd ever seen.

With the salmon still going, I checked the spindle of my reel. I was running out of line. Now, the options were nil. I had no choice but to go ashore.

I turned and faced the bow of the canoe, freed both my hands by putting the handle of the rod in my teeth, pulled the anchor and paddled as fast as I could to shore, more or less playing the salmon with the paddle.

I paddled hard and the canoe was moving fast. When I reached the shore, it slid half its length up onto the grass and nearly upset. I didn't care. I was out of it in a second and in hot pursuit of my biggest-of-all salmon. "If I manage to land this salmon, I'll have caught the largest one ever taken on the Miramichi," I thought. "Maybe in the world."

It leaped again, and it was so long and deep through that it could only manage to get about two-thirds of its body out of the water. And for an instant, while it was in the air, I'm certain I could see the water drop. I couldn't tell for sure from that distance, but it looked to be about eight to ten inches between the eyes.

It was still heading downstream, and I had very little line left. The only thing I could do was run down along the shore to keep up with it.

Previously I had always beached my salmon. I'd get them coming toward me and pull them out of the water and up on the gravel beach. But that tactic was lost to me that day, for the water was high, the beaches submerged. Also, I knew that even if I did happen upon a high and dry beach, this salmon was much too large for such a method of landing. My leader was only eight-pound test and could break under the strain. I needed help, that was certain. If I really wanted to land this monster, I needed someone to come along with a landing net.

I followed the salmon about two hundred yards before it finally slowed and stopped. Now I could walk and reel, retrieve some of my line. It was not easy going. Sometimes I was walking on slippery stones, and sometimes I was wading through the razor-edged shore hay up to my waist, stirring up midges and blackflies with every step. The sun was rising and the temperature was following it, and I was beginning to perspire. I was beginning to regret I'd ever hooked into such a fish.

I had gained about a hundred yards of my backing line and was parallel with the fish when it decided to go back upstream. Zoom! It went as fast as it could go, taking my precious backing with it. My reel whined and spun so fast that I was afraid the line within would backlash and jam. I could feel the reel beginning to heat up, which worried me, for a hot reel can seize.

Now I was obliged to follow the salmon back upstream, picking my way through the terrain I had just covered. I got a bit of a break, though. The salmon stopped at the same place where I'd hooked it. I walked toward it, reeling as I went, gaining backing once again.

When I got back to where I'd started, the salmon began to play the old waiting game that so many of the big ones resort to. "Wait and rest, wait and rest, sleep for a while . . . the fly will pop or the leader will break eventually." The big ones seem to know this. This is when, more often than not, the novice fishermen lose their trophy fish.

I kept my rod held high, the line singing tight. So sensitive was the lightweight graphite that I could feel the salmon's heart beating, and I'm sure it could feel mine. We were man and salmon, two of Earth's more intelligent beings in battle, using every strategy we knew.

The trick in successfully landing a salmon of this size is to keep it moving, to tire it out. You can play tug-of-war with a sleeping salmon all day. The leader will stretch and wear and eventually break. To snap a salmon out of its inertia, you have to apply a little fish psychology.

All fish are curious. The salmon are no exception. To get a fish to come to you, all you have to do is tap two rocks together under the water. This will work every time if the fish is within hearing range. In my case, the salmon was resting more than a hundred yards from me and in all probability would not hear the tapping of two stones at the water's edge. But with a graphite rod in my hand and a direct line from myself to the salmon's mouth, I had the perfect telegraph system.

I reached down, picked up a stone and tapped the graphite. "Dah dit dah dit   dah dah dah   dah dah   dit   dit dah   dit dit   dit   dit dit dit dit   dah dah   dah   dit dah dit   dit, " I telegraphed. Come ashore.

The salmon stirred.

I repeated the message.

Again it stirred.

I repeated the message a third time, but this time I added, "Dah   dit dit dit dit   dit dah   dah   dit dit dit   dit dah   dah   dit   dah dah dah   dit dah dit   dah dit dit   dit   dit dah dit!" That's an order!

The salmon swung toward me and slowly, cautiously approached. I reeled, kept the rod bent, the line tight.

When it was about halfway in, it stopped and allowed itself to sink to the bottom. There it stayed as if listening for an updated message.

I tapped the graphite once again.

It started to move toward me once again, but this time even more slowly, more cautiously.

"Tick, tick, tick . . ." I reeled as it came.

It was several minutes before the fish was close enough for me to actually see it in the water. It was like a log lying there, five, maybe six feet long — green back, silver belly, the biggest, prettiest salmon I'd ever seen. I could tell by the shape of its head and its hooked lower jaw that it was a male. I could see the white wings of the flyhook, the Butterfly, piercing that jaw. It was even bigger than I'd originally thought. Sixty pounds, I figured. Ten or fifteen pounds heavier than any other salmon ever caught on the Miramichi River. I wished I had a camera.

I looked at it and it looked at me. We were sizing each other up, spying on the foe, so to speak. If we could have communicated, we would have said:

Salmon: "Why are you doing this to me?"

Corry: "If you win the fight, you're free. If I win, I'll set you free."

It's the law on the Miramichi. Based on the assumption that large fish breed large fish and because everyone would like to see large fish in the river, you're legally obligated to release any salmon that is longer than twenty-five inches. This salmon was nearly three times that size.

This twenty-five-inch-or-less law invariably conjures up a question in every successful angler's mind. If you have to release your big salmon anyway, how long should you play the fish? Some say a minute a pound, some say less. If I were to play this salmon for a minute a pound, I'd be into him for an hour or more. An hour-long struggle could very well exhaust the salmon to death. If the salmon is going to die from exhaustion, you might as well land it and kill it, take it home for dinner.

No, no matter how much you might want to get your hands on the salmon, no matter how much you'd like to photograph it and show it off, the thing to do is to snap your leader and set the salmon free before it's too late. Even if the salmon cedes quickly, you should never land it. A salmon is a very delicate creature. One wrong move and you could injure it. Picking a salmon up by the tail, for instance, can hurt its back. You might as well hit it on the head with a hammer as pick it up by the tail, especially if it's a large fish.

The time had come for me to decide what to do. The salmon still had lots of energy, had just begun to fight, really. I was not in a position to land it properly, anyway. I was legally obligated to release it. I asked myself, "Do I release it now or later?"

There was only one logical answer. "Release it."

But, God, you hate to! It's human nature to want to kill.

I looked up and down the shore, hoping that Uncle Kid or someone, anyone, would come over the hill and witness the extraordinary size of this fish. It was too much to ask. There wasn't a person in sight. I would have to release it and write about it, or not write about it. I knew it wouldn't matter either way. Without a witness, no one would ever believe me. It was just too large, too unusual. For me to tell someone I hooked a sixty-pound salmon would be like someone saying he saw an eastern cougar in the backyard.

"A camera is what I need. Well, someday I'll write about it in my autobiography or even in a book of fiction." I snapped the leader.

The salmon, still lying there, felt the release of pressure. With one thrust of its mighty tail, it was gone. The world's largest salmon had vanished forever.

Though a wind came up and made casting a little difficult, I fished until noon, until hunger finally urged me to go home. It's unusual for me to fish that long, but that morning the fishing was good. Including the big one, I hooked three salmon and five grilse. I kept one of the grilse, released all the rest. I hooked every one of those fish on a big number six Butterfly. I keep that fly in a very special place as a reminder of that morning.

"One of the best days fishing I ever had," I wrote.

"Why didn't you come and get me?" asked Uncle Kid.

"I was having too much fun. Sorry. I hooked the biggest salmon in the world."

When Uncle Kid read this, he asked, "How big? Twenty? Thirty?"

I wrote, "60-70."

Uncle Kid laughed. "Ha! OK! Well! Do you know how big a salmon has to be to weigh sixty pounds?"

"I do now," I wrote and spread my arms to indicate about five feet.

"Ha! You sure you didn't hook into a shark?"

"I'm telling you the truth," I wrote.

"Yeah, well, I believe you, but it takes a big fish to weigh sixty pounds. You know, of course, that the biggest salmon ever hooked on the Miramichi didn't weigh that much. It might have weighed fifty."

"60," I wrote.

"Who ever caught a sixty-pounder on this river?"

"Me."

He didn't believe me, changed the subject.

"Where'd you get them?"

"Above the rocks."

"You think there's any more there?"

I nodded.

"In that case, I'm off. What did you get them on?"

"Butterfly. # 6."

"You wouldn't lie about that, would ya?"

I grinned, shrugged. He could believe me or not, I didn't care.

"I want to go for a drive in the Bronco," I wrote.

"Where you off to?"

"A Sunday drive."

He threw me the keys and went fishing.

I went to the bathroom and showered. Then, dressed in a white T-shirt, cut-off jeans and sandals, I jumped into the Bronco and headed out.

Twenty minutes later, I was about ten miles up the Gordon Road near Brennen Siding.

I parked the Bronco beside an old shanty and started down a path I assumed led to the river. I didn't know exactly where I was going or what I would do when I got there. I was letting Providence lead the way. I crossed an old field grown up with poplars and alder bushes, crossed a small brook on a rickety old bridge and, a few minutes later, came to the river about a hundred yards downstream from the footbridge. The rain had affected the Dungarvon even more than the Miramichi. It looked swollen, fast, deep and dark.

"I hope that bridge is safe to cross," I thought.

Crossing a footbridge — a boardwalk on cables — for the first time is not an experience you'll soon forget. It sways and rocks and creaks. The stairs that lead up the abutment looked grey and rotten, the boardwalk looked even worse. If it had not been such a beautiful, sunny, warm day, and if I had not been able to swim, I don't think I would have chanced crossing it. I held onto the cables as tightly as I could, walked fair in the middle of the boardwalk, tested each step before allowing my full weight to come down, and in that way, one step at a time, I made it across. I was so happy to get to the other side that I felt like whooping.

"What now?" I asked myself.

I could see the old house, Sally Nutbeam's gallery, on the hill, but there was nobody standing by the old bench. All the houses looked empty and forsaken. Even the camps behind the island and the big cabin below Bert Todder's seemed unoccupied. The little one, the one painted meridian yellow with the lawn ornaments all around it, was the only one that looked as if it might be lived in.

"Surely Sally doesn't live in the old Bert Todder house," I said. "She must live in the little yellow one."

I had made my mind up and was just about to head in the direction of the little yellow house when I heard creaking and footsteps on the bridge behind me.

It was Sally.

She walked easily, gracefully. She was so familiar with the bridge that she didn't even need to hold on to the cables. She could have been on a city sidewalk.

I was so happy to see her that I nearly cried. I greeted her with a big wave.

"Hi!" she called. She was fifty yards away, but I could see that big, warm smile. I had to take a deep breath to subdue my anxiety or else I would have run toward her, rocking the bridge and making a complete fool of myself by trying to say things.

When she got to the abutment on which I was standing, she looked me up and down with her big green eyes and, in that creamy voice, said "You came back. I thought you wouldn't."

She took my sweating palm in her long, cool fingers. "Come," she said. "Let's get something cold to drink."

I walked with her as if in a dream, down the steps, across the field and up the hill, past the little church and on to the meridian-yellow house. As we walked, she talked, awed me with her honesty.

"I've been wondering about you," she said. "Funny, eh? I even tried to paint you. Hard to paint somebody you only saw once for a short while. But there was more to it than that. I found myself unable to concentrate. I think you spooked me that day. Are you still looking for the cougar?"

I nodded.

"It's not often anyone comes to Brennen Siding. All the inhabitants of Brennen Siding have either moved away or they're sleeping beside that church. Except for me, that is. The way you looked at me that first time, I think you thought I was a ghost. I'm a hard-looking ticket, I know, but I'm alive and well."

She smiled and squeezed my hand ever so slightly.

Hard-looking ticket? Was she blind to her own beauty? To me, she was the most attractive woman on earth!

We entered the kitchen of the little yellow house and while Sally poured us cranberry juice I sat by the kitchen table. The house was very compact. From where I sat, I could see a small living room and a bathroom. If there was a bedroom, it had to be off the living room. I noticed a few more paintings on the wall — one of a salmon in a net with an eel approaching its wide open mouth; another of a mosquito so full of blood that it appeared larger than its host, a baby bird; another of a little boy sitting naked and alone on a rock in the middle of a barren.

Sally set a glass of cranberry juice in front of me, then sat and raised her glass. "To the river's lip on which we lean," she toasted.

I clinked her glass with mine.

"I must say, I'm rather at a loss for words," she said and smiled. "You must understand that I don't see too many people. Don't get me wrong, I like it that way. That's why I'm here. But once in a while I can't help but feel the need for someone to talk to. And what do I get? But never mind. I'm glad you came to visit me. At least I'm not talking to myself."

I removed my pen and pad from my pocket and wrote, "Do you live here all year?"

"Not anymore. When my brother moved to Boston, I moved with him. I live in Marblehead during the winter, but if I can afford it, I'll spend all my summers here."

"You're an artist?" I scribbled.

"A struggling artist," she said. "Do you know how I live while I'm here? I get up in the morning and bathe, swim in the river; then I fish and gather herbs and mushrooms, and I have a little garden with lettuce and Swiss chard. I go to the village once a week on my bike for a few extras like this cranberry juice and chocolate chip cookies. Most afternoons I paint or just lie in the sun, sometimes I go for walks to pick flowers or stalk deer. I'm always up with the sun, though some nights I ramble all night long. I love the night — the stars, the moon, the singing insects, the ghosts."

"Huh?"

"You think I'm weird for believing in ghosts. Well, I don't know . . . once in a while I think they're around. They're very pleasant ghosts. They don't see me as an intrusion. I guess they know me. I belong here, you see. One day, I'll be a ghost here, myself. Why are you hunting the cougar?"

"It's my job," I wrote. "A biologist hired me. Have you ever seen one?"

"A biologist or a cougar?"

I started to write cougar. She stopped me.

"I'm sorry," she said. "I know you mean cougar. What would you do if you saw one?"

I mimed taking a photograph.

"And what would the biologist do?"

I shrugged. I didn't know.

"Shoot a dart into it? Measure it? Weigh it? Show it to the world?"

I nodded. Probably.

"I've never seen one. What else do you do?"

241

"Just finished school. Don't know. Might become a mime."

She smiled when she read this. "You could stand white-faced in a wall cavity in San Gimignano. Collect lire for your poses. I once watched one for the longest time. In San Gimignano, Italy. He was so fascinating. Just standing there like a marble statue, not moving a muscle."

"When were you in Italy?" I wrote.

"A few years ago, the summer of eighty-eight. Come see," she said, reached for my hand and led me into the little living room. She stopped before a small painting of a bare-footed woman in a faded blue dress, sitting on cobblestones with two naked children lying beside her. All three had brown skin and dark hair, but the mother's hair was beginning to turn grey where it was parted in the middle. By the pleading in her dark eyes and the way she was reaching out her arm and extending her slender fingers, she was obviously begging.

"I painted this in Florence," said Sally. "Isn't she beautiful?"

I nodded.

"Uncle Kid will love this girl," I thought. "She's been to Florence."

"I was intrigued by that woman and her children," said Sally. "It seemed as though she had been there, in that same location, just across the street from Ghiberti's doors, forever. I think if you were to go there today she'd still be there. She's a part of the culture, the art of Florence. Begging is her profession. It is the children's job to be innocent in sleep. I think it is no worse to beg than to ask Mother Earth for cherries and grapes, for water, for animals. If I were a beggar, I'd strive to become the very best of all beggars, like the woman in this picture. If God or saints walk among us, they're disguised as beggars. I think everyone encounters God, saints, or angels disguised in one form or another from time to time. Have you?"

"Huh?"

"Have you ever encountered the Divine?"

I remembered meeting the man, God, in the hospital, nodded. Sally smiled.

I found myself enchanted with her. Love, mystery, fear, something crept over me like a warm garment. I found myself looking into those curious, searching green eyes. Was I blushing or turning pale under their inspection, their spell?

"Whew!" she said. "It's warm in here. It's such a nice day. We should be outside enjoying the breeze."

Shifting my eyes from hers, I nodded. Yes, I needed to get cooled off.

We went through the kitchen and stepped out into the glaring sun. "It's cooler inside," I thought. "But at least, out here, I'm not staring at her like an open-mouthed idiot. Not yet."

"Would you like to see the church?" asked Sally.

I nodded. Sure. Why not?

"It's small and crudely constructed, but it's the church I attended growing up. My mother and father are both buried beside it."

When we had crossed the field and stood beside the church, Sally pointed at a flat rock on the ground and said. "That's where my family are buried. When my mother died, my father found that stone on the bank of the river, carved that writing and placed it here. As you can see, he did not last long without her. Just a couple of months. My brother finished the carving."

Carved on the rock were their names, birth dates, death dates and a line that read, *Go placidly amid the noise and haste, and remember what peace there may be in silence.*

"The Desiderata," said Sally. "My father was very fond of the Desiderata. He worked very hard carving that. I think it helped keep his mind off losing my mother. Come, I'll show you the church."

The door of the little church screamed for oil when she pushed it open. When I followed her and beheld the simplicity, the quaintness, the rusticity within, I couldn't help but grin. There were a few benches, a pulpit that resembled a trunk stood on its end, three windows on each side and one tiny stained-glass window on the far end. To the left of the stained-glass window was a cross made from two pieces of two-by-four lumber, and to the right of the cross was a life-sized painting, obviously Sally's, of a man I took to be Jesus. He was not your traditional Jesus, you understand — this Jesus stood naked on a boulder in the centre of a field of goldenrod. There were bees all about — in the air, on the blossoms. When we walked to the front of the church, I noticed there was a bee on the man's shoulder. The eyes of the man looked calmly down on something in his hand, a rock or a coin, a magnet perhaps. On the rock he stood on was the inscription, *Probe the atom; Ponder the echoes of the wise. There lie the secrets of the universe.*

"See this?" asked Sally, pointing to something on the far end of the field in the painting. "That thing. What's it look like to you?"

I moved for closer inspection. What she was pointing at was a shadow, a silhouette with animal ears or horns. I didn't know what it was and shrugged.

"Neither do I," said Sally.

"Huh?"

"I painted the picture. It's my brother Palidin. But that thing, that shadow just appeared there. Somebody else put it there."

"Ha."

"I can't imagine who."

She took my hand and led me out of the church, back into the sunlight.

"Well, Corry Quinn, what would you like to do now?"

I shrugged.

"You know, I bet you could talk if you wanted to."

I shook my head.

"Let me see your tongue."

Again I shook my head.

"C'mon! Let me see it."

I didn't want to gross her out, turned away.

"C'mon, Corry! Show me your tongue!"

With a sigh, I turned back to her and opened my mouth. I studied her eyes for a reaction.

She stepped toward me for what I thought was a closer look, and although she expressed neither disgust nor pity, I felt embarrassed and closed my mouth. And there we were, looking into each other's eyes, so close that I could feel her breath on my face.

"You're one man that won't be telling me any lies, at least," she said with the slightest smile.

I wanted to kiss her, but thought she might think I was being too forward, out of line. I didn't want to offend her. But she moved again and I could feel her breasts against my chest. I made no decisions or moves. Sally Nutbeam was in control. She kissed me, gently at first, cool lips on cool lips, and I felt little more than surprise. Then she put her arms around me and seduced me to respond. That was when my heart took over. Boom! Throb! Boom! My lips got into the act. So intense, so commanding, so entertaining was their performance that the rest of my body applauded, gave them a standing ovation. Sally was soft and smooth and warm; she smelled good and tasted good; she was beautiful and exciting, free and mysterious. And she was absolutely starving for love.

So was I.

16

That afternoon the temperature soared to somewhere around a hundred degrees and Sally's little room became a virtual sweat tank. We slammed, slapped, slipped, slid and squeaked. We soared into space and sank into sweet surrender. We quenched each other's every thirst, every desire, every flame.

At the end of the day, I did not want to leave. It seemed heartless to leave Sally alone in that little haunted settlement, deep in the Dungarvon woods. It was ten o'clock when I reached for my clothes.

Sally stopped me. "Don't," she said. "Don't get dressed."

I gestured that I was leaving.

"I know," she said. "But carry them with you. I'll walk you over the river."

So I bundled up my clothes and put them in a plastic grocery bag. Stark naked, the two of us headed out into the warm, starlit night. Except for the yapping of a distant coyote, the night was as silent as the constellations above.

Sally knew the paths well. I followed her past the church, over the hill and down the shore to the bridge. We climbed the abutment steps and stopped to behold the starlit ribbon, the river.

"I don't know," She said in that milky voice of hers. "I like every hour of the day, but I think I like the night the best. The darkness, the shadows . . . It's more of a challenge to the eye, don't you think?

The stars are brighter in Brennen Siding and there's more of them. Animals know the night. Ha! Talking to you is like thinking out loud. Come."

She took my hand and led me out onto the bridge, onto the boardwalk.

"Lift your feet or you'll pick up splinters," she warned. "And you'll get less rocking if you walk in the centre."

I did as I was told and followed her. I could hear the water rushing beneath me. Had it risen, or did it just seem louder in the quiet night?

On the far abutment, we stopped again, embraced. She felt so warm, so smooth. My heart began to pound. I found her lips, kissed her for the longest time, reluctantly called it quits.

"You'll come back and visit me, won't you," she said, as if she already knew my reply. "I want to paint you. I've already decided what I'm going to do. I'm painting you nude, in white-face."

Before meeting Sally, I would have blushed at the mere thought of anyone painting me nude. But Sally made it so matter-of-fact, so prosaic, the thought actually excited me.

"It's funny," she continued. "Every time I open my mouth, I reveal something about myself. I know nothing about you. I've dreamed about you, I think. Coming out of the forest, young, strong, virile, saying not a word. I think I've created you, Corry Quinn. I think you are just a dream. How else can it be happening, here where I'm in touch, here where my very soul belongs? And now, at this very moment, I'm creating the most vivid, magical memory of my life. I will dream this day on my dying moment.

"Here I am, thinking out loud again. But you can't imagine how mysterious and magical your coming out of the forest, your return, your presence here and now, is. It's the stuff of fantasies."

I understood quite clearly, the magic. And I remember that day as clearly, I think, as she does.

Following the barely distinguishable paths as if they were lit with neon arrows, she guided me all the way back to the Bronco.

"Nice wheels," she commented. "Maybe you could take me for a drive someday."

"Yeah."

She kissed me.

"See you soon?"

"Yeah."

Still naked, still carrying my bag of clothes, I climbed in behind the wheel. I'd left the keys under the seat. I fumbled around a little, found them and started the engine. When I turned on the lights and swung to wave goodbye to Sally, she was gone. Just like that, she was gone.

I backed the Bronco around. The headlights lit up the path, the neglected field, the trees, but Sally was nowhere to be seen. I drove out the Gordon Road with no thought of anything else other than Sally. I suppose there's a law against driving around naked, even in the night, and in retrospect it hits me as a very eccentric thing to do, but on that warm night, with the windows down, caressed by the breeze, it seemed normal.

The Gordon Road was rough, hadn't been graded for years. I drove slowly, keeping a close eye on the road ahead, in case a moose or some other animal should dash into the Bronco's path. Once, ahead in the ditch, I saw the eyes of an animal reflecting my headlights, but when I drew near, it turned out to be nothing more than a porcupine.

"Wouldn't it be wonderful if I saw a cougar," I thought. "That would be incentive enough to keep Mark and Denise searching the Dungarvon area all summer."

Off in the distance, heat lightning swept the sky, betraying the whereabouts of a storm. I felt sated, popular, young, free and alive. Like Pavarotti, I sang "Some Enchanted Evening" all the way home. "Um e yaya e aw, oo a eh a aya . . ."

It was a perfect summer's night.

*

When I pulled in the lane around midnight, I noticed a pickup parked beside the shed. I had to look twice to identify it as Mark's, for he had removed the camper from the back and it looked more streamlined, different.

I got dressed beside the Bronco and went inside to find Uncle Kid pacing the floor with a bottle of Johnny Walker in his hand. He'd had a drink with Mark and Denise and that had got him started. Wanting to get out on the Dungarvon early, Mark and Denise had gone to bed after only one drink. Now, however, the bottle was nearly empty, and Uncle Kid was in the middle of one of his solitary parties. When I entered the house, I surprised him. Either that or his vision was so blurred with drink that he had to give me a second take.

"Corry! My good buddy, Corry!" he slurred.

I half expected him to bawl me out for staying out so late with the Bronco.

"A salmon and three grilse," he announced. "Right in our own pool! I hooked the salmon and two of the grilse just above the pile of rocks. Then I moved down and over toward this side and hooked another one. I think it was behind one of the tires. The Firestone Pool just might be working, Corry! We should've been fishing together. It's almost impossible to land a fish alone in high water like this. I lost a couple of fish trying to get ashore. We might have a good pool there, Corry. I'm celebrating! Have a drink with me."

I faked a yawn, pointed toward the ceiling, the bedroom.

"Ah, hell! It's not late! When I was a young lad like you, I could go day and night. Mark and Denise are no fun anymore. Christ, you might as well have a couple of Baptists in the house as those two. They turned in before ten o'clock! Imagine! C'mon, have a drink!"

I took the bottle from him, sipped.

"That-a-boy! That-a-boy! Drink, enjoy. Fill the cup what boots it to repeat how time is blah blah blah. Why fret if today be sweet, eh Corry?"

I yawned and pointed to the ceiling again.

"Ah, shit! Where were you all day? *C'mon, c'mon, c'mon, c'mon, c'mon, c'mon . . . Please please me oh yeah like I please you!* Now there's a song! God bless the Beatles! Where were you, you young fart? Did I ever tell you about being in the St. Patrick's Concert? Let me tell ya about how I loved and lost. There's lots about me you don't know. Sit down and talk!"

I started for the stairs.

"Corry! Don't leave me. Stay with me, Corry. Just for a while."

I stopped and with a sigh, pointed to the kitchen. Staggering, he followed me and we sat at the table.

"You can sleep all day tomorrow, anyway," he said. "You might as well. You're not gonna find that cat, I can tell you that much! God, it was a hot day! And it's too warm to sleep tonight. Denise and Mark will be getting up soon, eh, Corry? Ha, ha! Kitty, kitty, kitty! Here, kitty, kitty, kitty! Ha, ha! Let me get the guitar! I got a song I wanna sing for you. Wait right here! I'll be right back! Have a drink. Take a commercial break. Johnny Walker is the best in the land! Ha, ha! *Jumping Jack Flash is a gas!*"

He stood, staggered to the living room and returned with his guitar. He sat and strummed a D-chord about ten times.

"Get a pen, Corry. I want you to write this down," he said and hit the D-chord again.

"This is a song about me, Corry," he announced. "It's from my heart. I cried writing it. I've been crying a lot lately, Corry. I don't know what's happening to me. Anyway, it goes like this:

> The chapel bells they tell me that you'll never
>   change your mind;
> That his kindness makes you happy and his
>   wealth will make you kind;
> That you will travel places that I'll not be in my time,
> On a misty summer's morning.
>
> You can't take time to fall in love;
> Your life is meant for better things than me.
> So, turn around and go your way,
> Don't try to lead me on . . .
> On a misty summer's Sunday morning . . .

250

There was more to the song, I think. But that was all he had the heart for singing. He could go no further, began to sob. I reached out and touched him, but he slapped my hand away, stood, set the guitar down on the table and went to bed.

I turned out the lights and climbed the stairs. It had been a very long day. When I got into bed, I felt so tired that I thought I'd immediately doze off. But Alice entered my mind, and I tossed and turned all night.

I remember thinking that it was my turn to write. What could I write? *Dear Alice, it's been a long couple of weeks without you, but I've managed to quell the pain of loneliness by making love to Sally Nutbeam.*

I felt shallow and low. I tried to justify everything with thoughts like, "Alice is away, and I'm young and alone, and Sally is so exciting. I *need* Sally!" But nothing made me feel better. Every picture I conjured up of Alice was a depressing one — a young, naive girl from the New Brunswick woods, alone in a big city, wearing that white dress, the one with the burn mark. There were always tears in her eyes. I felt she needed me more than anything else in the world, that I should be on a plane for Alberta, instead of fooling around with some weird lady from God knows where, an artist who wanted to paint me in the nude, who would probably hang the picture some place where my butt would be on display for the whole world to see.

"No!" I screamed inwardly. "I won't allow it! I'll be a good boy. I'll not revisit Sally. I will write to Alice and tell her I love her and that I'm saving money to go and be with her. I will never tell her about Sally. I will spend my life in the warm, loving arms of someone who knows me and understands me, the girl who loved me when nobody else would, the bravest, kindest, most giving girl in the world — Alice.

"Now, go away, Sally. Leave me to sleep and dream of Alice."

But it was Alice that drifted into the darkness while Sally stood before me, tall, smiling her big smile, green eyes shamelessly scanning my body. "Go away, Sally. Go away."

The night wore on silently except for the sound of Uncle Kid snoring in his room.

"Poor Uncle Kid," I thought. "What a beautiful song you have written. What am I to do with you?"

My thoughts rambled from Alice to Sally to Uncle Kid to Alice to Sally to Uncle Kid all night long.

It wasn't until the darkness of the night made way for the blue twilight of dawn that my thoughts shifted to Princess Anne and I succumbed to a very much needed hour of sleep.

*

A couple of hours later, I was once again in Dungarvon country. This time, however, I was not in Sally Nutbeam's bed. I was wandering around in the mosquito-infested swamps, searching with no enthusiasm whatsoever for the elusive cougar. I dragged my feet, yawned and daydreamed throughout the morning.

Although she never said why, Denise, too, seemed to have little interest in the hunt.

Mark, on the other hand, was more excited about the search than ever before. He had gotten my photographs of the bobcat track developed in Saint John and thought that it could quite possibly be the track of an adolescent cougar.

"If it's the track of a bobcat, it's an unusually large one," he told me.

"Wishful thinking," I said to myself.

We went down through the woods and I showed him where the track had been, the branch of the fir tree I'd left beside it. The track, of course, was washed away with the rain. Mark took a magnifying glass from his pack and began searching the area, scanning branches, twigs, leaves, stones, everything and anything. I supposed he was looking for hair, urine, droppings, some indication that the cat might still be in the area. He reminded me of a greyhaired, slovenly Sherlock Holmes in dark-rimmed glasses.

After fifteen or twenty minutes of this, he said, "OK, guys, get to work."

"What would you have us do?" asked Denise.

252

"Head out, criss-cross, walk in circles, whatever. Look for anything unusual. Cougars love to climb, so remember to look up as well as down. If you find as much as a single hair, I want to know about it. If you *don't* find a single hair, I want to know about it."

"Don't you think we could do this on a cooler day?" said Denise. "It's so damn hot . . . It must be a hundred degrees in this woods!"

"Denise, if you don't want to be here, go back to Saint John! I'm not forcing you to search! You said you wanted to come! Didn't you say you wanted to come?"

"OK! OK! But it's so darn hot, that's all! And the mosquitoes. Ah, hell!" Denise disappeared through the nearest opening in the woods.

"It will be a hell of a lot hotter later in the day!" yelled Mark, then swung to me and said, "Women! The slightest little bit of discomfort and they're all upset. You go that way, Corry. I'll head down this way. We'll meet here every hour. Don't get lost."

I nodded, checked my watch and my compass and started out. I was a little concerned about Denise. She had just stormed off without checking anything, not a good way to enter a forest.

The going was terrible — swamps, shrubs, old broken-down trees, blackflies, mosquitoes, the rising temperature. It was not a fit place for a human. But there was no need to hurry. What mattered more than travelling far was making a careful, thorough search, observing every tiny detail. So I picked my way along.

I can tell you from experience that searching for a needle in a haystack took second place in the cliché department to this particular endeavour. That day, I made up a new cliché, "Searching for cougar shit in the Dungarvon woods."

During the first hour, we found nothing of any interest. We met at the place where I'd seen the track and talked things over.

"I can't believe how many moose are in the area," reported Mark. "Moose tracks everywhere you look, some so fresh they're almost warm, but you know, I haven't seen a single moose."

"That's encouraging," said Denise with obvious sarcasm. "Moose tracks everywhere and we can't see one, not much hope of seeing a cougar when there's not a track to be found."

"Well, all we can do is keep on looking," said Mark.

"We're just wasting our time," said Denise. "It's stupid! We're crazier than three loons!"

"So just what do you think we should be doing?"

"I don't know! How am I supposed to know what we should be doing? You're the expert! All I know is that this is crazy!"

Mark was so frustrated with Denise that he stomped off into the woods.

"He's the most contrary man in the world," said Denise. "What do you think, Corry? Don't you think we're a couple of crazy people?"

I shrugged. I didn't know how crazy they were. All I knew was that she was quite right about the futility of rambling around through the woods. We definitely needed a better plan.

Alone in the woods, Mark had a chance to gather his thoughts. Denise and I were just about to go searching again when he returned. He looked sad, disappointed. With a deep sigh, he confronted us.

"You're right," he said to Denise. "I'm a great big fool. I'm quitting. Let's get out of here."

"Quitting!" yelled Denise incredulously. "We've just begun!"

"You're right! You're absolutely right! This kind of search isn't going to work! We might as well be home."

"We're not going to quit. We've strayed from our plan."

"What plan?"

"You don't remember the plan?"

"Yes, I remember the plan! But there haven't been any sightings!"

"Maybe there have. Maybe that track that Corry found is a cougar track. There's where it was, right there in front of you! That's the first step. What more do you need?"

"Are you saying that it's time for the goat?"

"Why not? It's all we have to work with. We'll tether a goat right here and watch it. We'll take turns watching it. One of us can be here all the time, the other two can be searching for better tracks, more recent tracks. I'm not asking you to quit, my darling. I'm just asking you to get a hold on the situation. I would also like for you to lighten up and have fun with it. You're doing what you always wanted to do, so have fun with it! We'll find a darn cougar, if it's the last thing we do. But don't start talking about quitting."

"I just thought that . . . you seemed like you wanted to . . . I thought you were losing interest."

"I am not interested in rambling around blindly, if that's what you mean."

"OK. We go get a goat."

"Yes," I said to myself. "They are crazy."

*

Goats are not something that very many New Brunswick farmers breed. We spent the whole day looking for one. Mark finally phoned the Department of Agriculture, and after they passed him from phone to phone and put him on hold several times, someone told him that a guy on the Nashwaak River, a Mr. Bill Verne, would probably have one to sell.

"That's sixty miles away," commented Mark after he'd hung up. "An hour's drive. Who wants to come with me?"

"I'll go with you," said Uncle Kid, who was suffering from a hangover. "I need to get out of the house."

"OK. We'll be back in a couple of hours," said Mark to Denise. "You and Corry better get some rest."

I assumed what he meant was that he expected one of us, or perhaps both of us, to spend the night with the goat in the Dungarvon woods. My going immediately up to bed was my way of not volunteering. The thought of spending the night alone in the woods with a frightened goat totally depressed me. But I was so tired and sleepy that going to bed was the only thing I was capable of doing.

Three hours later, I was awakened by the voices of Mark, Denise and Uncle Kid in the kitchen.

When I joined them, they were having a good laugh about the fact that Uncle Kid had to ride on the back of the pickup with Poopbottom, the goat.

255

"You missed a real class act, Corry," said Uncle Kid. "Me coming through Doaktown on the back of a pickup with a goat. I think I managed to get the attention of just about everyone in the village."

"I knew I shouldn't have left the camper in Saint John," said Mark. "There wasn't even any sideboards."

"Oh, don't worry about it. I enjoyed it, actually. The ride helped me get rid of the hangover."

"It made a good picture," said Denise. "I couldn't believe my eyes when I saw you driving in."

"Did you get a picture of it?" asked Mark.

"Several. What did you tell the farmer you wanted the goat for?"

"Nothing much. I just said I wanted a goat. He seemed to think that was perfectly normal. Sold it to me for fifty bucks. I don't know if that was a good deal or not. Anyway, during the drive back, I had a chance to think about what we should do and concluded that until we get used to it, we'll spend the night in the woods together, two at a time. One person can sleep, the other person can watch, but at least we'll be company for each other."

"If you don't mind, I'll let you guys go for it first," said Denise. "I don't think I could handle it just yet. Is that all right with you, Corry?"

What could I say?

Mark and I headed out an hour later. This time, I was the one on the back of the pickup with Poopbottom. Poopbottom was all white, had a little goatee and big dark eyes and a cute little bleat, and he seemed to like me a lot. He wanted to eat my hair, I think.

On the Dungarvon, it took us about two hours to find a suitable location and set up camp. Along with Poopbottom, we took a small tent, a couple of sleeping bags, some snacks and beer, our cameras and packs, a couple of flashlights, two light-weight lawn chairs, lots of insect repellent and a rifle. Mark made it quite clear that he didn't want to shoot anything, that the rifle was only to be used when absolutely necessary. He also made it clear that if a cougar should happen along, Poopbottom was to be, no matter what occurred, a sacrifice.

"We'll scare off bobcats and other predators, but Poopbottom belongs to the cougar," he told me.

The thought would have depressed me, but I reasoned there wasn't a cougar within a hundred miles of the place and that Poopbottom was perfectly safe. We tethered him on a knoll and pitched the tent about fifty yards away. From our tent we could see every move the goat made.

By the time we finished setting up camp and sat on our lawn chairs to watch, it was dusk. We opened a couple of beers and Mark began to talk, easily, softly. Poopbottom seemed a bit nervous at first, tried to get out of his collar, bleated frequently, but after a while he settled down, lay on the mossy knoll and commenced chewing his cud.

"You probably think we'll never see one," said Mark. "And you're probably right. Not too many people do. But there are a few around, I'm sure of it. Every year there are sightings. Of course, New Brunswick is a big woods and chances are small, but, well, we must try.

"The Cherokees called him klandaghi, the Creeks called him katalgar . . . greatest of wild hunters. The Chickasaws named him koe-ishto, the cat of God. According to Bruce Wright, the Indians of California would not let the Jesuits protect their herds from attacks by the cougar. It seems the Indians used to follow the hunting cougar and scavenge its kills when it had eaten its fill. The cat was considered the Lord of Creation and man a mere scavenger.

"They're everywhere, Corry. Or, at least, they were. The wolves are gone in New Brunswick, followed the caribou, got hunted down, trapped, shot. But the cougar? He's more elusive. Travels alone, hunts at night, avoids man."

A coyote howled somewhere in the distance. The forest grew dark. Poopbottom was barely distinguishable on his knoll. The Big Dipper was off to our left, which meant that we were facing east. I thought of Sally Nutbeam, less than a mile away, alone in this great wilderness — alone, but perfectly content, totally capable, perhaps walking on the bridge. What manner of woman was she? The mere thought of her excited me. Alice, I loved. But Alice never stirred me like Sally. Alice was domestic, homely. Sally was an enigma, intoxicating. Both women were brave and wonderful, kind and loving.

I thought, "Humans are not monogamous creatures. Why can't I have both?"

At about eleven o'clock, Mark crawled into the tent and went to sleep. I spent the next six long hours trying to see if anything was stirring near Poopbottom. Once, I was sure I saw something move. I kept my eyes on it for the longest while. Finally I shone the flashlight on it and it was nothing but an old rotten tree stump. My eyes had been playing tricks on me.

"What if there is a cougar in the area?" I thought. "Which of us would it go for, Poopbottom or me?"

The thought was very unsettling and I moved my chair closer to the tent. Later, I got dampened with dew and longed to build a fire. I knew Mark would not allow it, however. At some time he had told me that a cougar would go nowhere near a fire. So I suffered the dampness the best I could and thanked God it was not a cold night. I also vowed that I would not spend another night in the woods without a jacket.

Mark crawled out in the grey dawn.

"Sorry I slept so long," he said. "I guess I was exhausted. Go in the tent and lie down for a while. We're not set up well enough, Corry. Tonight I'm bringing a thermos of coffee with me."

I nodded and crawled into the tent. When I awoke, Poopbottom was bleating, "I'm hungry, you crazy humans! Feed me! Feed me!"

I liked Poopbottom a lot.

17

As all summers do, that summer passed quickly. We spent two weeks on the Dungarvon with no success. Then we moved to the Sevogle, a tributary of the Northwest branch of the Miramichi. We camped there for two more weeks and August was upon us. Then we moved into the woods even farther, to the North Pole Stream. We set up camp at the estuary of the North Pole Stream, where it empties into the Little Sou'west Miramichi, about fifty miles from the nearest telephone, from the nearest human residence. This was far enough away from Uncle Kid's that we did not commute as often, staying in there for four and five days at a time.

I took my fishing gear with me and fished for an hour or two every day. I decided that I could not spend all my time looking for cougars, and fishing became a very pleasant escape. Fishing was good, too. I must have hooked twenty-five or thirty salmon.

Every now and then, Mark and Denise would stay in there by themselves. I spent these days with Sally Nutbeam. Most of the guilt I'd felt about dating Sally in lieu of Alice had dissipated. In July, Alice's letters started coming less frequently. Where at first she had been writing every other day, later I was getting a short note about every ten days. In the last three letters I received from her, she mentioned Harvey. Then the letters stopped coming. I was sad, but I had Sally.

I became good friends with the Masters. They were wonderful people and taught me a lot. Denise gave me one of her unpublished manuscripts to read. I did not like it, but I read it and was honoured that she allowed me to do so. She taught me about writing and the writing business. "It's an addiction," she told me. "Once you start, it seems you can never quit. You communicate everything with a pen, Corry. Maybe you should become a writer."

I nodded. I'd often thought about it. And reading Denise's manuscript encouraged me to think about it even more. Her stories lacked something, seemed dry and uneventful. I didn't care about her characters. I found myself thinking, "Why didn't she give them some idiosyncrasies, breathe some life into them? Maybe Uncle Kid was right about her not being a true artist."

Denise Bertrand Masters had planted the tiny ember, but it was Sally Nutbeam who kindled the writing flame to a burning desire. Sally left me with no alternative but to become a writer.

We were sitting in the shade at the north end of her little yellow house, sipping cranberry juice. Sally was wearing shorts, sandals and a T-shirt that was several sizes too large for her, a T-shirt big enough to fit a very big man. It had "So what!" written on the back.

"The painting's dry," she said. "Want to see it?"

Three days I went to Sally's first to sit for a whiteface application, then to pose for several hours while she did me on canvas. When she finished, she disappointed me by not allowing me to see what she had done. "It's in oils," she told me. "You have to wait until it dries. I might have to do some final touch-ups. It's not finished until it dries."

I had waited for a week, and now she was offering me the opportunity to see it. We left our shady spot and I followed her into the house. Anticipating the showing, she had set it up, covered with a blue silk scarf, on the easel in the living room.

"I hope you like it," she said. "Ready?"

I nodded.

"TA-DA!" She lifted the scarf.

I think that only the subject of a painting could explain how I felt when I first saw it. And I think to do it justice, to explain it properly, you'd have to be an artist, perhaps *the* artist. To me, it was both catharsis and damnation. I did not know whether to slap her, fall on my knees before her, laugh or cry.

She had painted me downstream beside Bert Todder's old house, in the middle of the afternoon. But in the painting, there was no house, no trees, grass, river, fields or anything else that may have surrounded me that day. I think I had expected to see something lewd and impudent, a close-up of a naked man in whiteface.

Well, I *was* naked and in whiteface, but I was quite small, no more than a couple of inches high. I was simply a little naked mime with a very thin blue aura about me. An aura not unlike what the Earth's atmosphere must appear to a passing comet. A foot above my head, at the top of the otherwise dark blue canvas, was a tiny star. At the bottom of the canvas was a barely distinguishable dot. The dot would not have been evident at all but for the fact that its very top reflected, ever so slightly, the light from my body.

"It's you in the centre," said Sally, softly. "Half way between an atom and a star. One's a part of you; you're a part of the other, knowing nothing more or nothing less."

I could think of nothing to do but leave the room, sit at the table in the kitchen and think. She followed me and sat across from me.

"What's the matter? Don't you like it?" she asked.

I shrugged.

"Don't shrug."

I shrugged again.

She sighed. "Write to me," she said. "Tell me how you feel."

I took out my pen and pad, but I could think of nothing to say. How can you explain something as ethereal as perplexity? I looked at my pen, studied it as if it was my only possession in the whole world. The silver pen, the gift from Alice, my voice. "Ouwis," I whispered.

"What?"

Fighting back the tears, I scratched the words, "You made me so small" on the pad.

261

"I put you in the centre," said Sally.

"Small, alone, a nobody in a sea of blue," I wrote.

"What were you expecting, a portrait of the dominant male when you are never dominant? A Dali stud gushing a cloud of sperm like some cocky warlord? Some egotistical beast, when you are as gentle as the Dungarvon summer? We're just little people, Corry, mimes, going through the motions. OK, OK, I know you're a man. Maybe that's why I put your penis at the geographical centre of the canvas, like a little pivot for you to revolve around."

I felt like I needed to bury my head and cry. But Sally upstaged me, began to cry herself. There before me in that little kitchen in that little meridian yellow house, the mysterious and magnificent Sally Nutbeam began to cry! Not knowing what else to do, I knelt before her and looked up into those tearful big green eyes. She reached out and put her hand on my cheek.

"I've been fighting unfairly. I lashed you with my tongue. You know, in Boston and New York, in any big city, a great many people think they are at the centre of the universe. It's a positive thinking thing. You must believe in yourself. If you believe in yourself, all things are possible — wealth, power, popularity. You, Corry, don't seem to care about those things. Your power is silence. You're always on the outside looking in. I painted you all wrong. I should have had you looking up, or down, or in, at both the star and the atom."

She ran her fingers through my hair. "You're such a mystery. Nobody knows anything about you. All I know is that you're gentle. I've hurt you. I've made you cry." She kissed my eyes.

I loved her with all my heart. There was so much I wanted to say to her that I could have written a book.

Sally packed up and went back to Marblehead on the first day of September. I drove her to Silver Rapids, where she caught the bus.

While waiting for the bus, she said, "I'll be back. I can't imagine spending a summer elsewhere. Hope you find the cougar."

The bus pulled in, the door opened, and she mounted the step, turned and said "I think you're going at it all wrong by hunting for it, Corry Quinn. I think you should let the cougar hunt for you."

I watched the bus until it disappeared from sight.

Sally took the painting of me with her. It was the only one she took. "Too much to handle on a bus," she said.

It's funny, she cried when she left the river, but her eyes were dry and she was smiling when she got on the bus. I, on the other hand, wept as the bus was pulling away. I guess she knows something that I don't.

Sally was the only person I ever told about Princess Anne.

"I think about her before I go to sleep," I told her.

She laughed. "There's nothing wrong with that. Everyone has a mantra. I, for instance, have you."

New Brunswick is virtually a mountain, the peak of which is in the north-central part of the province, not far from the North Pole Stream area. The North Pole Stream is fast, rough and rocky, very much like a mountain stream. We tented beside it and could hear the rumble and roar of the water, the boulders rolling and tumbling all night long. The Atlantic salmon learn to leap on the North Pole Stream.

Because of the altitude, the North Pole Stream gets hit with frost a few weeks before the rest of the province. By the middle of August, the nights grew so cold and uncomfortable for goat watching that Mark and Denise decided to accept their failure to find a cougar and head back to balmy old Saint John. They could have stayed at our place and commuted, but I think they had grown tired of the hunt, the woods, and perhaps even me.

Denise was anxious to get started on a new novel and Mark, too, had writing to do.

"It was an experience worth writing about," said Mark. "And it's important to log the failures. The cougar, I'm afraid, could very well be extinct in New Brunswick. But I'll continue to search, of course."

"If you thought for one minute that they're extinct, you'd not waste your valuable time," commented Uncle Kid. "You know they're out there as sure as you know we're standing here."

"Corry, you're now as much of an expert at cougar hunting as anyone," said Mark. "If you come across any tracks or signs or actually see one on your travels, let me know. I'll drop everything to come up and take a look."

I nodded.

"Will you be going to university in the fall, Corry?" asked Denise.

I shook my head.

"Studying mime, maybe?"

I wrote, "I'm going to write a book."

"Really! Well, I must warn you, writing is no picnic. But you can count on one thing, dear, I'll read everything you write."

"You wouldn't consider taking on Poopbottom for a pet, would you?" asked Mark.

I would have taken him.

"No," said Uncle Kid. "I'm afraid Corry and me are too irresponsible to care for a goat."

"Well, I guess we'll drop him off at Bill Verne's place on the way back. Maybe I can use him some other time."

It was time for them to go. We shook hands with Mark, gave Denise a hug and a kiss and off they went. This time, it was Mark who got to ride on the back with Poopbottom.

Later I found I missed Poopbottom more than I missed the Masters. Baa-a-a-a-a! I could speak his language.

In September, Uncle Kid went guiding. I clerked in Izaak Walton's during the days and fished in the Firestone Pool in the evenings. I tagged eight grilse and released six relatively large salmon. At the end of each successful day, when I reported my catch to Uncle Kid, he grew more enthusiastic.

"We're not doing much better fishing than that down at Burpee Storey's, and Burpee's is one of the best pools on the river," he told me one night. "I think we're in business. I'm gonna start booking sports on for next year. We'll operate Izaak Walton's and the outfitting business for six, seven months of the year and you can write your books during the winters.

"I was thinking I might do a bit of writing myself. Oh, don't worry, I haven't got the patience to write books. But I thought I might jot down a few ideas now and again. I'm more of a philosopher than a writer. I'll just jot down lines now and again and leave them on your desk. Would that be all right with you?"

I nodded.

"You have some money saved up, don't you?"

"Yeah."

"Well, you know what I think? I think you should get yourself a computer. Oh, I'll help you pay for it, if you're short. You'll need support, you know. No one can be a writer in this country without support. You just write your books and don't worry about a thing. I'll look after you."

"What if my books are no good?" I scribbled.

"Well, you'll never know until you start. Have you started anything?"

I had written one page that I thought might be the start of something. I nodded.

"Can I read it?" asked Uncle Kid. "That's something I can do. I can read your stuff to you at the end of the day. After hearing it read aloud, you should have more of a handle on what doesn't work, doesn't sound right or whatever. Go get what you've written and I'll read it to you."

The page I had written was up in my room. I went and got it and gave it to Uncle Kid.

He looked at it for several seconds, then went, "Ahem! First person, eh. I don't know about writing in the first person. You might want to reconsider that."

Then, in that wonderful deep voice of his, he began to read.

> I could only feel them. The river seemed mapped and peopled with rain, thousands of little blue dancers in the six a.m. light. Eons of erosion had carved this scene, this stage; the massive boulders rising like curtains twenty feet up, the caves that wormed from their twilight mouths to their ebony bowels, the falls that backed off like a reluctant denizen of the Paleocene, gnashing in fear, roaring a bit. I contrasted the grey of it all — waist deep, the water pressing my rubber waders tight to my legs and buttocks, the yellow raincoat

— alone, front and centre, I could have been a lone mime on some gigantic stage. Even had I turned, I would not have seen those big green eyes watching me, unwavering, curious. I could only feel them. Hoping they would come a little closer, I hadn't made a cast or scratched an itch for what seemed like ten, possibly twenty minutes. I had made the mistake of turning to see before, and always there was the silent forest and nothing more. Would she approach? Could she identify me, the yellow thing on the water? How long would they watch, those eyes? And was that a sound? Did a rock tumble from the falls? Surely she would not be clumsy enough to make a sound . . . the swish of falling rain . . . the pounding of my heart.

I started to cry.